YOU'LL
Never Know

THE HEALTH AND HAPPINESS SOCIETY

YOU'LL *Never Know*

KATIE CROSS

Chick Lit

Text copyright ©2018 by Katie Cross

This is a work of fiction. Any names, characters, places, events, or incidents are either the product of the author's imagination or are used fictitiously. Any similarities or resemblance to actual persons, living or dead, events, or places, is entirely coincidental.

Cover designed by Jenny Zemanek at www.seedlingsonline.com
Paperback interior by Atthis Arts LLC at www.atthisarts.com
Ebook productions E-books Done Right at www.ebooksdoneright.com

All rights reserved. Except as permitted under the US Copyright Act of 1976, no part of this publication may be reproduced, stored in a retrieval system, or transmitted in any form or by any means electronic, mechanical, photocopying, recording, or otherwise, without written permission of the author. For information regarding permission, send a query to the author at kcrosswriting@gmail.com.

Published by THHS Publishing.

ISBN 978-1-946508-19-5

Visit the author at www.kcrosschicklit.com to learn more about *The Health and Happiness Society*.

*For Nancy, Ginger, and Jennifer.
You'll never know what you've given me.*

Shattered Euphoria

The lemony tinge of cleaner embraced me the moment I walked into the gym. Home. My castle. The place where I escaped all my troubles.

The cardio room beckoned like a siren song. *Come*, it said. *Start your day by running all your cares away.* Matt Damon would await me on screen. No, if I was lucky . . . Gerard Butler. My calories burn would skyrocket as I jogged on one of many treadmills sprawled in front of the big-screen TV. Something about losing myself in the pump and burn and flickering lights drew me in.

Ah, euphoria.

Kellie, a girl with bright freckles and gobs of curly auburn hair, smiled when my best friend Lexie and I approached the main desk.

"Hey Rachelle," Kellie called. "How's marathon training?"

"Did my first twelve-miler last night." I held up a fist and shoved through the metallic turnstile. "Nailed it."

"So jealous. Hey Lexie!"

Lexie beamed. "Hey!" Her expression brightened. "It's not free pizza day, is it?"

"Nope."

"Bad idea anyway," Lexie muttered as she pushed into the gym. "Seriously. Who serves pizza at the gym?"

"You love it," I quipped.

Lexie tilted her head back with a sigh. "I know. I *know*."

"Wedding go okay?" Kellie asked.

"Yes," Lexie said. "It was awesome. But I can't lie—it feels good to be back. I'm sad this will be the last time I work out here."

Kellie's lips turned down. "That sucks!"

"I know!"

My throat tightened. "Yeah. Let's go."

After a quick wave, Lexie and I strode past lines of ellipticals and weight-lifting machines, headed for the changing room. "So?" I drawled, nudging her in the ribs with an elbow. "Tell me everything.

We haven't gotten to talk since Bradley whisked you away. How was the honeymoon?"

Her pale cheeks bloomed. "Fine!"

"Fine. Sure."

"I never imagined myself a sit-in-a-cabin-in-the-middle-of-the-forest-for-a-week kind of gal, but it was pretty great. I can see why Megan's obsessed with mountains. I mean, I could never live there. Access to life was severely limited. Still. The quiet was nice."

"Did you even leave the cabin?"

"Yes!" she cried a tad too high. "Just . . . not as much as I would have under . . . you know. Other circumstances. In my defense, it rained. A lot."

"I'm sure Bradley was disappointed."

"Not in the least."

I cast her a sidelong glance, but she had her eyes trained ahead with unusual alacrity. Sweet, innocent Lexie had always been the frosting to my brownies. While I had flaunted my extreme obesity and obsession with food while growing up, she hid hers. In her basement. Away from her perfect sister. To have her even *talk* about sex in public was a miracle. I pushed inside the locker room.

"Aaaand?" I asked.

"And what?"

"Were you as terrified for him to see you naked as you expected?"

The blush on her cheeks deepened. "Oh, *that*. Ha . . . well . . ." She tilted her head with a sly smile. "Let's just say my, ah, *fears* of Bradley not finding me that attractive while naked were deeply unfounded. I may have been insecure about the size of my thighs and boobs, but he sure wasn't."

"I told you!"

"I know. I know. Now that I think about it, I shouldn't have put so much energy into stressing over it. We've been dating for almost two years. You'd think I would have learned that he loves me the way I am. Anyway." Lexie sighed. "In the interest of full disclosure, I ate *way* too many Oreo cupcakes."

A laugh bubbled out of me. "Oreo cupcakes? Seriously? How did you find those out in the middle of nowhere?"

"Bradley made them as a wedding present. They didn't taste the same as the cupcake bakery, but whatever. He tried. You really can't go wrong with sugar, butter, flour, and Oreos, right?"

"Right."

She stopped at the second-to-last locker, where we always hung our bags. She already wore her workout pants and shirt. After all the times we'd worked out together, she still hated changing in a public space. I flung my bag into the locker.

"When do you leave for your in-laws' house?" I asked while peeling off my shirt and tossing it into the locker.

"Tomorrow. After I clean the basement and finish packing. We'll probably drive all day Friday."

Thanks to her recent marriage, Lexie had transferred colleges, sold her car, and started to pack up the basement. Peeling posters of Gerard Butler and glow-in-the-dark stars off the walls had given me physical pain. Still, I couldn't help but be happy for her. She adored Bradley, and he adored her. I pulled on a shirt and rooted around for my running pants.

"I can't believe you're going to live somewhere else," I said. "It's so weird that we won't be in the same town."

"Tell me about it. How am I supposed to leave my little niece behind? My sister is still a hormonal mess, although granted, I think Mom secretly loves it. And Kaylin is three months of perfect chubbiness. She gets it from me."

"She *is* adorable."

"I can't talk about leaving her behind, either. I cry when I think about saying goodbye to either one of you." She blew her bangs out of her face, then tilted her head, her eyes narrowed on me. "Are you going to run for three hours again? I'm fine with working out, but let's not drag this into torture."

My shoulders tightened. "What's wrong with three hours?"

"Chelle, that's *really* intense. Sure. You're the cardio queen. But don't you ever take a break?"

"Of course."

"Have you since my wedding eight days ago?"

I hesitated. Did *not* running on Sunday morning and sometimes only an hour in the evening instead of two count? I jammed my feet into a brand-new pair of shoes and tied them.

"Let's hit the cardio room. The movie is going to start soon. I think it's *Wonder Woman*."

She eyed me. "You just dodged my question."

"I made an observation."

"That turned the conversation away from your exercise obsession."

"It's not an obsession. I'm training for a marathon."

"That you quit your job at an accounting firm to train for!"

"I got new work! I still teach exercise classes four times a week."

"Chelle . . ."

I straightened and acted like I didn't notice the worry in her gaze. The three-hour run with her there had been a one-time thing thanks to a very special movie marathon. Ever since I started teaching Zumba classes a few months ago, I'd had to cut my running time. That day had been an anomaly.

Besides, losing over a hundred pounds in the last eighteen months didn't happen with short walks on the treadmill.

"Just an hour today," I said, straightening. "I promise."

"You sure?" she asked.

"Yes."

"Fine. *One* hour. Although, seriously, I had way too many cupcakes, and maybe I should do three. But I won't. Because that's ridiculous."

We didn't speak as I grabbed a towel and flung it over my shoulder. My water bottle sloshed in my hands as we slipped out of the locker room and through the morning crowd toward the back room. Being amid the quiet whirring of the machines again calmed my suddenly stressed-out heart.

Just an hour.

Well . . . maybe ninety minutes. At most! My Zumba class this evening was canceled for maintenance, so I'd need to fill the cardio time somewhere else.

Lexie could handle an extra half hour. Especially with a good movie going. She'd done it before for me.

Two rows of treadmills filled the cardio room, which boasted sprawling TVs in each corner and mirrors along the far wall. We picked two machines at the far right. Until I dropped from 265 pounds to 175, I'd always hated the mirrors. After that turning point, I didn't mind them so much. Now they were ideal to track my form when I started getting tired.

"Sa-weet!" Lexie cried when the movie started—just as I planned. "Wonder Woman! Teach me your ways, and give me your thighs."

I snorted, and she let out a giggle.

We fell into motion on our separate treadmills without hesitation. Music swelled through the speakers in the corners and rippled through the room. *This* kind of thing was the great part about Lexie. Everything came naturally. She filled the silence when I wasn't in the mood to talk, and when she was too afraid of doing something, I set us in motion. Even though I'd lost more weight than her by far after we started healthier lifestyles, she'd never resented me.

"So," Lexie drawled, one eyebrow lifted. Her blonde hair swayed back and forth in a high ponytail as she walked. "You had a new date after my wedding, didn't you?"

I grimaced and cranked the speed to 4.5 miles per hour for my warm-up jog.

"Yeah."

"That bad?"

"Could have been worse, I guess? He wore suspenders. To a baseball game. Explain *that* logic to me, will you?"

Her forehead wrinkled. "The guy that hit on you at the gym?"

"Yeah."

"Weird."

"I mean, it was fine. But the conversation wasn't great."

"If a first meeting starts with the words, *Hey baby, I think you fell from heaven,* then I'm not surprised. Suspenders? Really?"

Normally I would have laughed, but today I just grimaced. It *had* been a pretty horrendous pick-up line. "He was handsy," I said. "He kept trying to touch me."

"Gross."

I frowned. "Yeah. It's . . ."

When I didn't finish, she lifted an eyebrow. "Yes?"

My thoughts whirled. Although I had frequent dates, and not the glamorous kind, when I weighed 265 pounds, I often dreamed of how dating would be when I was skinny. The beautiful men—that I hadn't hunted down myself—lining up at my door. The gobs of date requests at clubs. Not having to drag the bottom of the barrel for a night out when the loneliness became too overwhelming.

So far, that world had eluded me.

"Let's just say that it's good I won't have to see him again," I said. "I think I might take a dating break. I'm tired of men."

"I took one of those. For twenty-three years."

At that, I did laugh. Then I cranked the speed up to 6.5 miles per hour and enjoyed the rhythmic pattern of my feet smacking the treadmill.

"Right now? That sounds pretty great." I recalled the glassy look in the last date's eyes after one-too-many drinks. Overweight Rachelle would have rejoiced—a chance to score with a muscular guy! Suspenders aside. But now it was annoying. Like a gnat that wouldn't go away.

Maybe that's what Chris felt like, I thought. My stomach twisted, and I cranked the speed to 7.0. Thinking about *him* would get me nowhere at all. Instead, I turned my thoughts to the marathon. Pictured myself crossing the finish line, hands raised. Sweaty. Salty. Euphoric.

Right now? Nothing else mattered.

"Chelle?"

I jerked out of my thoughts to find Lexie peering at me, concern in her bright blue eyes. I shook my head.

"What? Sorry."

"You okay? You seem a bit . . . distracted."

"Yeah. Sorry. I . . ."

"Everything all right?"

"I'm fine. Really. I just—"

A wolf whistle came from the other side of the room. We glanced up to see two men stride inside, shirts torn at the sleeves revealing thick arms and broad shoulders. One of them, a guy with a lip ring, watched me through the mirrors with a lurid gaze. My nose wrinkled. I'd seen him here before.

"Hey pretty lady!" he called. "Always good to see you again in those tight pants."

I turned to snap at him, but a flash of pain jolted up my right leg. I flailed, grabbed for the arm railing, and missed. The quick-moving belt shot out from under my foot. My shoulder slammed into the treadmill, and I tumbled off the moving belt and onto the ground. My right leg slammed into the wall.

In seconds, Lexie was at my side.

"Rachelle!"

I shoved back to my feet but dropped again with a cry. White-hot agony tore up my right leg, like lightning into my hip. Once back on the ground, I grabbed my ankle and bit back a scream.

"Okay," Lexie said. "Oookay. You're not good."

I gritted my teeth and closed my eyes. The *pain*. It magnified through my leg, prickling and flaring in tight spirals. Lexie crouched next to me. The two guys had made themselves scarce, leaving us alone in the room again. When I probed the smarting ankle, heat coiled back through my legs. The muscles throbbed, already swelling.

Lexie stared at my ankle in wide-eyed horror. "That looks awful, Chelle."

"Help me to the car," I gasped. "I think it might be broken."

An hour later, Dr. Martinez stared at my ankle through a pair of tortoiseshell glasses perched at the end of her nose. The skin between her eyebrows wrinkled, and her lips twitched to one side. Slowly, she straightened, causing a waterfall of ebony hair to spill off her shoulders.

"Sprained."

Not broken.

"Grade 3—which is the worst one, by the way." She pulled her glasses off her face. I let out a long breath of relief. *Sprained* I could work with. Broken? That was trouble.

Dr. Martinez sucked in a sharp breath. "I want to cast it."

"Cast it?" I cried. "But it's not broken!"

"It's as close as you can get."

"That can't be right."

She propped a fist on her hip and lifted both eyebrows. "Are you telling me I don't know a sprained ankle when I see one?"

"No! I just . . ." For a long pause, we stared at each other. I blinked. "You're serious. You have to *cast* my sprain?"

"Rachelle, your tendon needs the extra support. As it stands, you're on the border of requiring surgery. Did you hear that? I can repeat it if you need me to."

"Surgery?" I sputtered. "It was a little trip on the treadmill. Nobody has to have surgery because of a treadmill."

Dr. Martinez tapered her gaze. "I don't like this sass. You want me to call your mom? Listen, I know my job, all right?" She jabbed a finger at my ankle. "That's one of the nastiest sprains I've ever seen."

Her sharp rebuke properly chastised me. Dr. Martinez had been my doctor for years now. I swallowed hard. "Right. Sorry."

"Look, we don't *have* to cast it. I just want to stabilize it until the swelling has gone down. There are really awesome boots that are practically armored tanks. We'll do one of those."

"Listen, Dr. Martinez, I'm supposed to run a marathon in four months. Whatever you do, I—"

"Don't count on it."

"What?"

"Do you ever run outside?"

Taken aback by the sudden shift, I leaned back. "Outside? Uh . . . sort of."

"Sort of?"

"*Some* of my runs were outside, but . . . most of them are inside."

"On a treadmill?"

"It's easier to control my environment that way. I don't like running in the heat. Or the rain. Or finding routes. Do you know how hard it is to find fifteen miles of safe roads? Not to mention the boredom of a track."

In other words—movies ensured I didn't cop out early, and having the treadmill control my pace meant I didn't tire out too fast. The mirrors gave me something to look at too. To maintain motivation.

Dr. Martinez rolled her eyes. "In that case, I'm willing to bet that all your treadmill running has weakened your tendons and bones around the ankle. Predisposing you to something like this. So when you stepped wrong . . ."

She didn't need to finish the sentence. One misstep. One idiot that thought he could impress me by acting like a dog. My goal . . . *poof.* Gone. The goal I'd been working toward for the last eighteen months. The one I had lost one hundred and ten pounds for. The one I quit my job and started teaching Zumba classes for. It had to be *this* race. The Crazy Cats Summer Blow Out. Rock and roll music, confetti, and crowds of people lining the streets. This was the only race that would prove I wasn't ever going back.

"There has to be something we can do to speed this up, right?" I asked when the silence stretched too long. A light *tap* came from the door, and Lexie slipped back inside, phone in her hand.

"Sorry," she mouthed, then stood next to the bed, one hand on the crinkly paper. My gaze dropped. The ankle had already bruised a bluish purple. The strange coloring didn't seem to bode well.

"Rest, ice, compression, elevate." Dr. Martinez glanced down at her clipboard. "And time. Ibuprofen, too, but we'll have to regulate that. I'm looking at possibly four months to weight bearing, then physical therapy to full rehabilitation. In an optimistic view, you could probably be running in six months. Realistically? I give it eight. Just to be safe."

Disbelief plummeted to my stomach like a weighted balloon. Almost two years had preceded this. Two *years*. Lexie reached for my shoulder and rested a heavy hand on it.

Dr. Martinez stepped back toward the door. "There's a chance you could impress me. You're young. You have youth juice. With any luck, you'll heal fast, the swelling will go down, and there will be a *very* slim chance you can do it. In the meantime, my nurse will get that boot fitted and get you on your way, all right?"

She left before I could sputter out another denial. I blinked, dazed. How quickly had everything changed? Why was life so transient? Lexie cleared her throat.

"Chelle?"

"This can't be happening."

"It's going to be okay."

"No, it's not! I can't run the marathon. I . . ."

"You can run it next year."

"It's not the same."

"Chelle, maybe this is a good thing. You've been *so* focused on this that it's like . . . it's like you can't see anything else. Maybe this is a good chance to step back and remember how to live your life."

Tears filled my eyes. "I've been working so hard! I . . . I can't just . . . if I can't run, what . . . what am I going to do with my life? With my time? I . . . I can't *not* exercise. I dropped out of college. My job is exercising!"

Another silence descended on us. The devastation, so swift it took my breath away, tripled in my chest. I sank into it, terrified by its power. What would I have to work for? What was the point? Where would I earn money?

Without that marathon, who *was* I?

A cool blast of air conditioning and the smell of stale pizza hit me in the face when I hobbled into our trailer.

Lexie lugged my gym bag in behind her, juggling a handful of paperwork, my keys, and a plethora of pills from the pharmacy. A sitcom blared from the other room, welcoming me home.

"Hey Mom! I'm home," I called. A hand waved over the top of the ratty, mustard-colored couch.

"Go sit at the table." Lexie jerked her head toward the old table with one crooked leg and fold-out chairs ringing the sides. "I'll get your room rearranged a little."

"Thanks."

The boot weighed my leg down as I attempted—very awkwardly—to coordinate the crutches. A challenge almost as frightening as facing a marathon-free future. My armpits already hurt, and my forearms were tired. I had *thought* I was in shape, but managing these deaths traps was proving me wrong. Maybe I should have paid more attention to upper-body work.

I hobbled into the kitchen and sank into a chair, then propped my right leg on the edge of the table. The top of Mom's head glanced over from where she sat on the couch. A bag of potato chips rustled next to her. In front of her sat a movable table that held her laptop, a mouse, and a 72-oz. soda. She brushed crumbs off her chin and took a sip from her straw. Without looking away from the television, she asked, "Everything all right?"

"I hurt my ankle."

She frowned. "That's too bad."

"No kidding," I muttered.

Her hand plunged back into the bag of chips just as Lexie appeared from down the hall.

"I moved your desk off to the side a little," she said. "Then it won't be in the way of your crutches. And I grabbed some extra pillows and blankets to prop your foot up. You'll probably want to rest in bed for a while." Her eyes darted the couch. The corners of her lips turned down, and her voice softened. "Unless you want me to set you up a place out here?"

"No! I mean . . . no. Thanks. My room is just fine."

Something like relief flickered through her eyes. "Great. Then let's get you something to eat. You shouldn't take pain pills on an empty stomach. Trust me. Kenzie tried after her C-section last winter. Wasn't pretty."

She yanked open the fridge and came to a fast stop. Lexie had grown up with me, which meant I shouldn't *still* be embarrassed by the sheer amount of food stuffed in there with unusual precision and cleanliness. The fridge was the only part of our trailer that Mom really cared about—evident by the carefully labeled and stacked containers inside.

Still, the shame burned in the back of my throat. Two gallons of whole milk. A separate chocolate milk. A hidden bag of candy behind mounds of butter. Containers of leftovers stacked high—each labeled with a dry erase marker. Lasagna. Spaghetti and meatballs sweetened with brown sugar. Ravioli. The pasta alone could feed a horde.

"There should be a couple of salads in there," I said, clearing my throat. "Off to the right. Maybe behind the milk?"

Lexie dug around a bag of crescent rolls Mom likely made for breakfast and extracted two ready-made salad containers. We stirred our salads in silence, the tang of vinaigrette filling the air. A couple of ibuprofen at Dr. Martinez's office had taken the edge off the pain, but the swollen, pulsing feeling in my ankle continued. I managed to swallow a few bites, then set the fork down. Before I could protest, Lexie glared at me.

"Eat." Lexie forked a baby tomato into her mouth. "At least finish the salad. Then you can go fall asleep in your room for a little bit, and I won't tell on you."

"Tell on me?"

"To Bitsy."

I opened my mouth to protest, saw the determination that filled her gaze, and decided against it. Wasn't worth fighting Bitsy. She made Lexie seem like a lamb. Something about being home robbed my appetite. Or was it the reality that I might not run the marathon after so much focus on it? Either way, I could force a few more bites down. Needed to, probably.

"Fine."

The sound of a sitcom filled the silence like a second presence. By the time I choked the rest of the salad down, I did feel slightly better. Although I wouldn't have admitted it to Lexie after our conversation this morning, fatigue from the twelve-miler and the two Zumba classes I'd taught in the morning had caught up with me. Lexie popped open a prescription bottle and handed me two pills.

"They'll make you sleepy."

"That's fine."

I washed them down with half a bottle of water. Mom changed the channel in the background, the bag of chips rustling again. Lexie gathered our salad bowls and pointed to each pill bottle.

"Pain medicine. Swelling medicine. I'll write out a schedule."

"I'm not a toddler."

"Bitsy insisted."

Something cold washed over me. "Bitsy?" I hissed. My eyes narrowed in fury. "You already told *Bitsy*? Is that what you were doing in the hall at Dr. Martinez's office?"

Lexie's cheeks flushed. "It just sort of happened! You know how she is. It's like she has a radar for when people need her! Besides, Bradley and I are leaving this weekend. Someone has to take care of you. You have doctor's appointments." Her gaze dropped to my boot, then darted back to me. "Are you going to drive yourself?"

Laughter sounded in the background again. Lexie kept her steady gaze on me, and I wondered how much willpower it required of her *not* to look at Mom.

No. I couldn't get to Dr. Martinez without Bitsy. Mom hadn't driven in years because she hadn't fit inside the car in years.

"Fine," I said. "You're right."

I swallowed the two pills and grabbed the crutches. Bitsy, the self-appointed mom of our support group, the Health and Happiness Society, always planted herself in the middle of our lives even when she wasn't present or wanted. Still, I couldn't deny a modicum of relief. With Bitsy on my side, everything would be fine.

Well, at least not disastrous.

"Thanks, Lex."

She smiled softly. "Anytime."

Lexie grabbed my prescriptions and bustled around the kitchen as I worked my way down the hallway, passing the couch where Mom was sprawled in her subtle gray muumuu that hid most of her body. A logo flashed across her computer screen as she moved the mouse around, her gaze flickering from the TV and back to the computer before opening another graphic design contract. I slipped into my room—there wasn't much space in a single-wide trailer to hide, so the sound of the television followed me—and sank onto the bed.

Lexie set three water bottles and my pills on the bedside table, along with an apple and a couple of granola bars. She pulled my cell phone out of her pocket and laid it next to my pillow. My phone charger dangled in her hand.

"You should probably prop your leg up for a while," she said. "I think it's been down too long."

"Yeah. I can feel the swelling."

"Lay down."

Blankets and pillows already sat at the end of the bed, ready for me. Lexie helped me lift the heavy boot onto the pile. Sinking into the mattress and pillows *did* feel good. By the time Lexie settled me, my leg hovered above my body, an ice pack chilled my skin, and the worst of the pulsing had started to fade. A pile of books and my laptop perched within my reach.

"You set?" she asked, hands on her hips.

"Yeah. Thanks Lex. You're a gem. I can't—"

She waved a hand. "Stop. We're besties. This is what we do. I may not live here anymore, but I take care of you."

Tears filled my eyes at the reminder, but I blinked them away. Of course I would never make her feel guilty about leaving me, but the pain still swelled in my chest. Rotten timing to lose access to my best friend.

"Yeah," I whispered. "Thanks. You do."

She reached to close my closet door and stopped. Her forehead furrowed. She paused, hand halfway to the door, then stepped closer and reached inside. When she stepped back, she held a familiar purple binder in her hand. My stomach flipped.

No.

"Whoa!" She turned to me with bright eyes. "Chelle! Is this what I think it is?"

"Ah . . ."

Magenta pipe cleaners, glitter, and pink construction paper covered the front of a ratty old binder. Lexie and I smiled out from a photograph in the middle of the mess. We'd taken my mom's old Polaroid camera while dressing up when we were eight and snapped our first selfie. Bright smiles illuminated our chubby, freckled faces.

"It is!" she squealed, flipping it open with her wrist. "Our old best-friends diary! I had no idea you still had this. Why didn't you tell me? This thing needs to be photographed or preserved before it falls apart. Like in a museum, sister."

The diary of our small but happy world together. We were the fat girls. The friends who stuck together through everything. Who had sleepovers with epic treats. Mom always baked several types of cookies for us on those nights. We stayed up all night watching cheesy rom-coms.

I'd thought I'd hidden it in the crawlspace below the trailer where it could mold and wither. Where had it come from?

"Where was it?" I asked, my voice raspy.

"Just right there." She pointed into the closet. "Sitting on the shelf. It was about to fall off."

"Oh."

She cracked it open. Panic surged in my chest. That book was filled with memories. Stupid drawings of rainbows and cats. Lists of what our future husbands would look like.

And pictures. Lots and lots of pictures.

"No!" I called as she reached to turn the next page. "Wait."

Lexie paused, forehead ruffled. "What's wrong?"

"Sorry. I'm just . . . I'm really tired. The pain pills must be kicking in. Can we reminisce another time?"

Her shoulders relaxed. "Oh. Right. Sure. You need to get your rest. Bradley and I plan on being back in two months for my mom's birthday in August. We'll do it then."

"Sounds good." I managed a smile. "Thanks."

Lexie set the binder next to my bed, propping it against the nightstand. "Here. You can look through it later. I have no doubt it will cheer you up."

I managed a smile. "Thanks again, Lex. You really are the best."

She grinned and winked. "I know. I'll try to visit before Bradley and I leave tomorrow, but I make no promises. In the meantime, Bitsy just texted me. She's coming over tonight, so be prepared for that."

She left with a teary hug and resounding promise to call at least four times a day. When the door closed behind her, I stared at the ceiling. The muffled sound of the television rang in the background. Mom chortled. A commercial for razors popped up.

After Lexie drove away, the couch groaned as Mom stood up. I pictured her shuffling into the kitchen, barely able to move because of her enormous weight and the apron-like stomach that made it difficult to shuffle her legs. Her searching fingers would reach into the cupboard to find more chips. Maybe those pink-and-white sprinkled animal cookies—her favorite. Something about the crunchiness and burst of sweetness, I imagined. Or maybe that's just what I had loved.

Next to me, the binder seemed to whisper my name. I reached down, shoved it under the bed, closed my eyes, and sank farther into my pillows with a sleepy yawn. Nothing inside of that binder would cheer me up.

Nothing short of defeating that marathon *would*.

The Plan

That evening, I sat at the desk in my room, my leg propped up on a pillow. Getting there had been a good fifteen-minute adventure, but I'd managed. The light from my computer glowed on my face while I perused a website on upper body workouts. A three-hour nap had restored some of my good humor. Not to mention eased the worst of the pain, even in my sore thighs. Although I couldn't see anything but my toes thanks to the boot, even they looked a bit purplish.

A quick *tap-tap-tap* came on my door, and then it opened a crack. Bitsy's hazel eyes peered inside.

"Chelle?"

"Yeah. Come in."

She bustled inside, grocery bags on her arms. She wore a pair of black workout pants and a loose gray t-shirt with *Namaste* written across the front. Her sandy hair was pulled into a low bun. She pursed her lips and gave me an *I'm-on-a-mission* expression, holding the bags higher.

"I come bearing gifts. Groceries, actually."

My eyes widened. "No kidding you brought groceries."

"I have to mom on you for a little bit, if that's all right. Yes," she added, anticipating my question the moment my lips parted. "I *have* to mom on you. It comes with the territory of being a mom to anyone."

"Sounds good to me."

"Just some salads and your favorite foods. Lexie said you were out of natural peanut butter and agave and whole wheat bread."

"Did she inventory the kitchen?"

Bitsy turned around to head for the kitchen. "Yep. I told her to. C'mon. I made you dinner. Need help with the crutches?"

"No. Thanks."

She waited at my door to make sure, one eyebrow raised. I slowly brought my leg down, braced myself against the crutches, and stood. I worked my way out into the hall one peg at a time, moving slowly. Mom had disappeared. She always did when Bitsy came around. Another sitcom played out on the screen. Bitsy grabbed the remote and turned it off with a frown. The ensuing silence rang in my ears until I heard the television from Mom's room seeping under her door. Bitsy headed toward the kitchen with the rustle of grocery bags in her arms.

"I made your favorite for dinner." She motioned to the table with a jerk of her head. "Grilled chicken and mashed potatoes."

"You're a saint. I don't think I've taken in enough protein since my run last night."

"I don't think it's possible for you to take in enough protein *ever* with the amount you've been working out since you started teaching exercise classes."

Bitsy set the grocery bags on the table, nudging them around several half-opened twelve-packs of soda, and studied me.

"Are you still counting calories?"

"Not really."

"Good."

The truth, at least. I worked out enough that I didn't have to worry much about my food intake. Living in the midst of dieting hell—or life with my mom—had taught me control.

Bitsy nodded once and started to unload the groceries while I propped my foot up on a folding chair and glanced at the tinfoil-covered plate.

"Here." She tossed me a plastic fork, produced from somewhere within her plaid mom purse. "Get started on that. I'll grab your pills."

My eyes darted to the clock. "Oh yeah. It's time to take them again."

"I know."

"How?"

"I planned it."

"I'm not surprised."

"There is no limit to my ability to coordinate. Are the pills in your room?"

"Yeah."

Underneath the foil waited a warm plate of lightly grilled chicken with homemade mashed potatoes. A side of quinoa and creamed spinach sat next to them. The smell drifted into my nose. I closed my eyes and inhaled deeply. This house rarely saw freshly made vegetables.

Mom used to warm up frozen veggies, but I couldn't remember the last fresh veggie dish she'd ever made.

"This smells amazing, Bitsy," I said when she returned. She set two pills and a water bottle in front of me. "Thank you."

"Tastes good, too. My girls gobbled it down like I've never fed them before. Start eating."

She bustled around the kitchen, opening and closing cupboards, while I dug into the mashed potatoes, enjoying the way they melted on my tongue.

"So, what now?" she asked over a shoulder, holding a bundle of bananas in one hand. "I'm worried about your marathon obsession."

I rolled my eyes. "It's not an obsession. It's a goal."

"Sure."

"Don't worry, Bitsy. I was depressed about the sprained ankle at first, but I have a plan now."

The rummaging sounds paused. "Oh?"

"I've been doing some research. I think I can still make this happen. Stop. Don't say anything. Just listen. I'll be really careful for the next two weeks, and the swelling might go down. I can use that time for core and upper body strength. Maybe even a few things for my thighs, but I'll evaluate as time goes on. Once the boot comes off, it'll just be a few weeks, I'm sure. Lots of people have reported progress that fast. I could probably be running again by early July. The marathon is at the end of August. I can still do it."

"July is only four or five weeks away."

"But it's possible."

She waved a spatula at me. "For someone with a grade 3 sprain?"

I frowned. "Well, I'm not sure what these other runners had, but . . ."

"Stop." She sliced the spatula through the air. "You're getting ahead of yourself. What if you don't heal that quickly?"

"I will."

She raised her eyebrows, one hand propped on her hips. "You might not. You don't control this process."

"I will! It's all about the swelling and getting the right brace afterward. Trust me. I've been pouring over *Runner's Universe* forums for hours. By the way, could you get me another ice pack?"

Bitsy headed for the freezer and tugged it open. "I'm not deterred, Rachelle. You still have to answer my question. What happens if you don't heal in time to train properly?"

I gritted my teeth. "I *will*. All I need is to take advantage of this time to work a different part of my body. I can see now that I've been irresponsible. I've been really lax on working my core and upper body. Megan would never have approved of my schedule."

"For *many* reasons," she muttered. I ignored it.

"Based on what I've been reading, core work can be just as important for a runner as—"

"What about your job?"

"I'll have to quit."

"Can't you just take a leave of absence?"

"I'll need all that time after I recover to make up for lost runs. Look, it'll work until September. I have a little bit in savings, and Mom's never charged me rent."

"No, but she has you do all the errands and shopping. How are you going to go grocery shopping for her now? Thought of that?"

Her question stopped me in my tracks. Mom and I lived with an unspoken truce. She didn't charge me rent, and I did all the cleaning and shopping with her credit card. It had always been that way.

"Delivery?"

Bitsy opened the cupboard on the far right—my cupboard. A crusty loaf of bread, a few Thai food sauce packets, packages of precooked brown rice, and cans of plain tuna filled the interior. She pulled all of it out, tossed the bread into the garbage, wiped the cupboard down with a wet cloth, and started organizing the new contents by color and size.

"Delivery costs extra," she said.

"Can't be *that* much."

"And your school loans?"

I suppressed a wince. Five years in college and no degree to show for it. I finally dropped out last year, unable to reconcile myself to a particular major. The gym classes and the money I'd made being a caretaker last summer to a rich old man had been slowly dwindling. Less than $300 remained. Surely enough to cover what was needed until I could get a job after the marathon.

Bitsy set the bananas, a fresh loaf of 10-grain wheat bread, and some golden raisins on the bottom shelf and closed it. She eyed the dishes that surrounded the sink in piles. Mom couldn't clean fast enough to keep up with her appetite, nor stand long enough to support washing all the dishes. Bitsy opened the fridge. She tilted her head to the side, then shut it with a shake of her head.

"You need to move out."

I sighed. "I know. I will. After the marathon."

Bitsy cranked the hot water on, plugged the sink, and squirted soap inside. "Mira may have a job opportunity for you. She said a friend is in a bind. I'll put a bug in her ear for you. Maybe it could be temporary?"

Why wasn't Bitsy happy for me? I had new direction. This marathon could still happen in spite of a big upset. She, of all the members of the Health and Happiness Society, should be the most excited.

I leaned forward. "I can do this, Bitsy. I'll throw myself into healing, do everything Dr. Martinez tells me to do, and in two weeks this boot will be off. I'll start physical therapy and get back to exercising. That marathon will not happen without me."

She met my gaze, her eyes filled with concern.

"What are you running from?"

"What?"

"Why are you doing this? Why are you putting everything into this marathon?"

"I-I'm not."

The words almost strangled me.

"You're pivoting your entire life to accommodate an event that you can't control. Do you realize how dangerous that is?"

"I've worked for this for almost two years. I can't just give it up because of a sprained ankle. Bitsy, I am *going* to do this. Losing all that weight, all those nights in the gym? Those weren't for nothing."

Bitsy glanced past me to the couch where Mom usually sat. Then she gazed back at me.

"You *are* running from something, but you don't see it yet. That's what scares me the most."

"Bitsy, I . . ." I trailed off, uncertain what to say.

She pointed to the plate as she flung dirty dishes into the sudsy water.

"Keep eating. I'll do dishes. Your pain pills will be kicking in soon."

The next two days rolled by with frightening stillness.

The sound of sitcoms ran eternally in the background, a horrendous soundtrack that I couldn't block out. My ankle throbbed on and off. My back hurt from lying down so much. The pain pills dulled the edge of the ache but curled my thoughts. Vague dreams whirled through my mind. I woke up twice to Dad's face—a face I hadn't seen in almost two decades—at the front of my mind.

"How's the knee?" Mom asked as I hobbled past her on Sunday morning. She pushed a piece of graying chocolate hair out of her face.

"My ankle, you mean?"

"Oh. Yeah. Your ankle."

"Better."

Sunlight streamed into the kitchen over the sink. She had a few blinds twisted half open, casting blunted light onto the old carpet. A bowl of Apple Jacks sat in her hands. The cereal box waited on the couch next to her, accompanied by a half gallon of milk on the floor. She'd been known to fly through an entire box of cereal in one sitting—mostly when she was stressed over a deadline. A soap opera scrolled across the television, the muted colors and dramatic voices instantly annoying me. Until I'd had to be home constantly, which hadn't happened much in the last year and a half, I hadn't realized just how annoying the TV was.

The usual silence—aside from the television—descended on the house as I struggled around the kitchen, coordinating a piece of whole wheat toast and an egg scrambled in olive oil. The dishes Bitsy had washed had long since disappeared into a new pile of dirty plates. Standing at the sink for more than ten minutes made Mom's hips ache, which led to a lot of paper plates and sticky pots and pans that I usually cleaned. I turned on the hot water and dropped some soap inside to let the dishes soak, then I threw all the cups littering the counter in the dishwasher.

By the time my egg finished and my toast popped, I'd cleared half the counter, tossed the empty fruit snack wrappers, and shoved apple juice cartons in the can for recycling. Despite the pulsing in my ankle, it felt good to do something except sit in bed. I frowned at the overflowing garbage.

"Hey, Mom?"

"Yeah?"

"I can't take the garbage out. Can you do that?"

A pause. I leaned against the counter and scraped the eggs off the pan and onto a plate. My toast, lightly smeared with almond butter, crunched when I bit into it.

"You can't?" she asked.

"No."

"Oh. How long until you can?"

"A few weeks, maybe?"

"Um . . ."

My foot throbbed when I tore through another bite of toast, forked some egg in my mouth, and chewed as fast as I could. By the time I finished, my stomach still growled. The grating sound of a laugh track tore through the room. Mom had switched the channel to another sitcom.

I ground my teeth. The entire day stretching before me looked suddenly bleak. "Crap," I muttered.

No Lexie. Megan was still working at a hospital in the mountains of Wyoming. No immediate Health and Happiness Society meeting. No boyfriend to let me crash at his house—of course. Lexie's mom would take me in, but how awkward would that be?

A knock on the front door grabbed my attention. Mom's head popped up, her eyes wide.

"Hello?" she called.

The front door creaked open, revealing one familiar eye in the slight crack.

"Rachelle?"

My heart swelled. "Hey Mira!" I called. "Come on in."

I swallowed the last of my food and swung my crutches toward the door. Mira shuffled inside the trailer, sporting a familiar grin and a shock of electric-pink eyeshadow under a halo of graying, mousy blonde hair.

Mom reached for the remote and muted the television, straining to see over her shoulder. Mira closed the door behind her with a beaming smile. She had just given up Pepsi for the thirtieth time and had maintained for the last two months, which beat any previous record. She'd lost several pounds. Instead of her usual large dresses, she wore black jeans and a short-sleeve shirt with a potted flower on the front.

"Hello!" she called, waving. "I came to visit the sick and afflicted."

I grinned. "How very Christian of you."

"It *is* Sunday, isn't it? Besides, I just got out of church. Nothing better than visiting a friend after a good sermon about Jesus. Earns points. Plus, I've missed you and was worried about you."

My lips twitched at her deep Southern accent. She glanced at Mom, then away again. The piles of soda boxes and mega packs of ramen noodles on the table seemed wildly out of place now. Mom frantically worked her body off the couch as Mira pulled me into a warm hug.

"How are you?" Mira asked, holding my shoulders. "I imagine you're going stir-crazy here, not being able to run."

"You have no idea. I'm so happy to see you, Mira."

She smiled, then wrapped me in another hug. I sank into it, eyes closed, enjoying the comfort and the heady scent of potpourri. When she pulled away, Mom was trundling toward her room as fast as she could, using the wall to stabilize herself. Her bedroom door closed with a *thud*, followed by the muffled sound of the television starting up.

"She still scared of us?" Mira whispered, staring over her shoulder.

"Not scared," I said. "At least, not of *you*. Just . . . nervous, I guess."

"Does she know that she and I are the same age?"

I shrugged. "Maybe? I told her once, but . . ."

"She wasn't listening?"

"Yeah."

"I understand. It's Bitsy who scares the bejesus out of her, isn't it?"

"Definitely."

Mira nodded. "Don't blame her. That woman terrifies me sometimes. It's like she has ESP or something."

"It's really not you, Mira. Mom has been like this for . . . forever. The only person she doesn't run from anymore is Lexie."

In fact, I couldn't remember a time when Mom didn't shy away from *anyone* except Lexie. At least since I got my driver's license at sixteen. Mira waved me into a chair, clucking like a mother hen. "Well, bless her heart. I'll pray for her too. I've got my entire prayer circle working on your ankle."

"Aw, thank you."

"It'll help. Those women could channel the angel Gabriel if they wanted. Sit down, sit down! Prop that leg up. My goodness, it looks sore!"

"It's a boot, Mira."

"A big one! Are you in pain? Do you need some meds?"

Just then, I noticed that two brown grocery bags hung from her arms. She set them aside and grabbed a pillow from the couch when I lifted my ankle onto another chair.

"Here." She patted the pillow into place. "Use that. Keep that swelling down so you can get to that race. I brought us some brunch. Have you already eaten?"

"Only a little."

"Good. Nothing exciting. Just some warm scones I made this morning before the service—reduced fat. I used applesauce instead of butter! They're soft as velvet. You're just going to die. It's hard to make a moist scone."

I smiled. It wouldn't have mattered *what* she brought. Just having her here brightened the house considerably—and it wasn't just her electric makeup or the sunshine that spilled into the trailer as she yanked open drapes and zipped the blinds all the way to the top.

"Thanks, Mira."

"My pleasure, honey."

After laying out napkins—ignoring the stacks of regular soda and fruit snacks—and setting out a plate of fresh scones, she settled down across from me. Her kind, wrinkled eyes met mine. She leaned forward and grabbed my hand, peering intently into my eyes.

"Now," she said. "How *are* you, really? No lies. No bluffs. Don't act brave. Tell me just like it is. I won't nag you like Bitsy."

My body relaxed into a sigh. Mira really wouldn't. She wouldn't even report to Bitsy.

"Stir-crazy. Sad. Determined. I'm going to go insane here."

"I can't imagine."

I sat back. "I guess I never realized how busy I was until I couldn't leave the house. I never really was home much."

Mira patted my hand and reached for her scone. "I love being at home, but even I need to get out sometimes. That's when I go haunt Bitsy's place and play with those adorable girls."

I'd missed the last Health and Happiness Society meeting because I was filling in for a last-minute Zumba class, but longed for the next one, which wouldn't be for another week or two. A veritable eternity, at this rate. Mira reached into her sprawling, floral purse that was almost as loud as her eyeshadow. She pushed a stack of Redbox movies at me.

"I brought these. Thought it might help." An assortment of action, romance, and new Disney movies sat in the mix. "Wasn't sure what you'd want to see, so I grabbed a bunch."

"I haven't seen any of these, thanks. This will definitely help."

She patted my hand again and took a bite of scone. Her eyes darted to the couch, the television still droning in the background.

"Your mom okay?" she asked quietly. "I worry about her."

Hesitation stopped me short. *Was* Mom okay? I couldn't remember the last time I'd asked her. In a world that never changed, how could she be anything *but* okay?

"Fine."

Mira's brow furrowed, but she didn't pursue the topic. What did *fine* mean, anyway? Instead, she leaned forward, eyes bright. "I can see you're just about to go insane, so I came with a proposal. How about a temporary job?"

My back straightened. "Really?"

"Mmm-hmm. Good pay, too. Great boss."

"How temporary?"

"Ten days at most. Two or three of training, then you work for a week. My friend needs some help with her business. It's busy season, and she just needs someone to help her with a few . . . errant things. Doesn't even require you to stand."

"Where will you be?"

"My brother is having open heart surgery in Chicago, so I promised I'd be there for the first week after discharge to help take care of him at home. My brother doesn't know his head from a hole in the ground sometimes and his wife has severe anxiety."

"What's the job?"

"She's paying fifteen dollars an hour."

"Doing what?"

"And it's up to eight hours a day. More if you want it."

"Right, but what will I be doing?"

"Fantastic location, too. Air conditioned."

"Mira, what *is* it?"

Mira hesitated, mouth half open, then shrugged. "Oh . . . you know."

I blinked, waiting. "Uh, no. I don't."

"Little things, I guess?" She shifted in her chair. "Paperwork, maybe. Sorting. Organization. A bit of . . . creative design? That . . . that kind of thing."

I frowned. "I'm not good at office work."

"Oh, none of that." Mira fidgeted with her napkin. "It's kind of hard to describe. But anyway, I'm heading there tomorrow afternoon for four hours and could start training you then. You interested in freedom?"

She picked at her scone and didn't quite meet my eyes. What could she possibly be hiding? My mouth opened, then closed. What did it really matter? Money was money. Escape was . . . escape. At this rate, I'd pay someone to let me work for them. Mira could throw me into the burning depths of hell to mop up errant ash and I'd throw myself into the work with gratitude.

"Okay."

She perked up. "Really?"

"Sure. Can't be worse than sitting here for another day."

"I agree! I'll pick you up at 8:30. I told her I'd be there around 9:00. We'll probably end up staying until early afternoon. You can sit the whole time, and we'll bring pillows to prop your leg up. Do you need any help in the morning?"

"No. I think I've figured it out so far. I just take a long time to do everything. Took me almost an hour to bathe the other day."

"Keeps you busy."

"Good point."

Mira broke off another piece of scone with a grin. "Thanks, Rachelle. I'll owe you one. I can't wait for you to meet Sophia. You're going to love her. Now, tell me more about this upper body workout plan. I have some serious old-lady arms I want to get rid of."

The quaint shops that characterized the historic downtown space barely stirred this early, though a couple people were walking down the sidewalk, when Mira pulled to a stop in lower downtown the next morning. Wrought iron trellises, empty bike racks, and flower boxes filled the street. Two- and three-story brick buildings lined the road. No doubt the new studio apartments above the shops cost more than our food budget every month.

Which was prodigious.

Sticky heat swept over me when I opened the car door. Tar squished beneath my flip flop when I slid my good leg out and drew in a deep breath. I climbed out of the car on one foot and reached back for the crutches. The sun hit my face with a delicious tang.

Mira bustled around her pearlescent Cadillac and shut the passenger door behind me. The moment I smelled buttercream frosting in the air, my blood froze.

Frosting?

"Ah, Mira?"

"Yes?"

"What's that smell?"

"Frosting!"

Frosting. My archnemesis. The dessert topping that could have been an entire food group in my childhood. The saccharine scent lay thick as humidity and twice as sweet. Was that cream cheese frosting? My nose was like a bloodhound when it came to sugar. Scratch that.

A *frosting* hound.

"I've got the pillows!" Mira said, her voice a bit high. "Let's head inside."

"Head inside where?"

"What?"

"Mira . . ."

A two-story brick building stretched in front of us, complete with a wooden sign painted with bright white letters. *The Frosting Cottage.* Without being told, I knew that's where I'd be working. Felt it deep in my frosting-loving bones.

"This. This is your friend's business? The Frosting Cottage?"

She gulped, forcing a smile. "Yes! Isn't it adorable?"

Visions of 265 pounds of unhappiness floated through my mind. *Adorable,* I thought. *Hardly.* Sugar and I could not be friends. I couldn't trust myself around any temptations. Months had passed since my last sugar splurge, but I still dreamed of cupcakes at night. Whenever Mom dove into a pint of Ben and Jerry's, which was almost every night, I had to lock myself in my room.

I definitely shouldn't be here.

"Why didn't you tell me?" I screeched.

She sucked her bottom lip through her teeth. "Ah . . . because Bitsy told me that you'd say no, and I really needed you to help."

I scowled. Bitsy's habit of being right really got on my nerves. "I thought you weren't in her pocket like everyone else."

Mira rolled her eyes. "*All* of us are in Bitsy's pocket, and none of us really want to get out of it. You know it."

"But—"

"You can't eat the food, Rachelle. We have to sell it. Does that help?"

"You said *organizing* and *paperwork.* You said this would be a desk job!"

Her finger twitched back and forth. "No, no, honey. I said that we'd help organizing and sorting. That's what we'll be doing! I mean, you'll be *organizing* cupcakes and *sorting* the right color of frosting onto them. It's the same thing!"

"No, it's not!"

"The cupcakes aren't going to eat you."

That wasn't my worry.

"Mira, I—"

"You'll mostly just be frosting and decorating cupcakes. Sometimes I help her with the macarons, but they're more delicate than dew on a hot petal. Have you ever piped frosting before? Never mind. I'll teach you all that. Come on now. Stop standing out here with your mouth open catching flies, all right?"

A pit opened up in my stomach. Cupcakes. Macarons. Frosting. Bakery.

The inner fat girl who always screamed at me woke up at the first sniff of sugar. I tried to stuff her back with visions of long runs and working out, but she wouldn't be controlled. If I lost control, I couldn't run this off. There was no *Plan B* here. Except for staying at home with Mom, which seemed far worse.

"Fine," I snapped. "But only because I'm desperate and so are you."

Mira beamed. "C'mon, sugar. It's adorable inside, and it's only ten days. Temporary help, that's it. I'll introduce you to my friend, Sophia. She owns the place."

A glass-paned wooden door groaned when Mira shoved through it. Open, sparkling windows soared all the way to the second floor, spilling beams of sunlight onto a small collection of tables that lined the wall. Maybe *Sophia* lived on the third floor above the bakery. Wouldn't that be a nightmare? To live above the source of the ways I'd been fat my whole life?

I shuddered and pressed inside after Mira.

The tinkle of a bell rang on the door as it wheezed shut. As expected, the delicate scent of spun sugar and warm yeast hit me like a wall. Or, perhaps, my past. My mouth watered for a cinnamon roll. I envisioned myself crossing the marathon finish line. Cinnamon rolls wouldn't get me there. Well, not having them now, anyway.

"Hello?" a voice called. "Mira, is that you?"

"Just me, honey!"

A middle-aged woman popped into view, cheeks dusted with flour. Her eyes smiled from beneath the brim of a black hat that perfectly matched her locks of ebony hair.

"Are you Rachelle?" she asked.

"Yes."

"Welcome!" She waved flour-coated hands. "I'm Sophia. Can't tell you what it means to have your help while Mira's gone for the week." She beckoned me through a door next to the main display. "Come on back. I have everything set up for Mira to start teaching you."

Mira shot me a glance that I ignored, then motioned me ahead of her. We passed a sprawling wooden counter with a glass display. Eclairs, puffy cinnamon rolls, hot cross buns, and petit fours lined the inside.

My stomach growled.

Above the counter, a blackboard menu decorated with colored chalk displayed the prices and names of different soups. I tried to breathe through my nose but swore I could still taste the sweetness. My crutches thudded on the worn wooden floor. Behind the counter, the prep area was visible. Gleaming metallic counters, tub-sized sinks with hanging spigots, and barrels of flour, sugar, and colored frosting awaited. Naked cupcakes filled three racks at least five feet tall. I passed through a doorway next to the display and into the prep room.

"Here it is," Sophia said, hands spread. "This is where the magic happens. Sorry I can't show you around right now, but I'm meeting with a bride in ten minutes. Can you teach Rachelle how to frost the cupcakes, Mira?"

"Of course."

"Four containers of frosting on the counter. I've frosted a plate just to show you the designs that I want. Tips are in the drawer! Mira, if you'll teach her how to ring a customer up, that would be great too. Thanks."

Sophia smiled again and tucked a strand of hair behind her ears. Her smile was warm, the kind that expanded into the laugh lines around her eyes. She was lithe and thin, with lean arms and thin shoulders, like a runner. Definitely a runner. I relaxed. Proof that one could work in a place like this without weighing 265 pounds. Besides, it was just for ten days, anyway. The money could buy my final pair of running shoes. Or cover next month's student-loan payment.

Mira motioned to two chairs near one of the tables in the middle of the prep room.

"That's where you'll sit."

"Thanks."

While I settled into the chair and lifted my ankle—which had already started to ache after riding in the car—Mira fluffed the pillows underneath my foot. She passed me a bottle of hand sanitizer.

"Keep this close. We'll wash our hands a lot."

"Do I have to wear gloves?"

Mira shrugged and tossed me a black hat with the words *Frosting is in my Blood* written in a bold white font. "Don't think so, but you do have to wear a hat."

"Oh. Am I supposed to have a food handler's permit?"

"Nah. Sophia does. That counts, doesn't it? I'll grab the piping tips and bags."

While Mira pulled a huge bowl of frosting from the fridge and gathered white bags with small, metallic tips, I finished my study of the bakery. The smell of cake lingered in the air, along with an occasional wave of heat from the ovens lining the wall on the other side. Two massive fridges gleamed like they'd been recently cleaned. The wooden floor was well cared for, glossy even. A gentle tang of cleaner drifted through the air.

Impressive.

Mira passed me a chubby bag filled with bright purple frosting. She pointed to the plate of decorated cupcakes a few feet away. "See the spiral one?"

"Yep."

A cupcake with a jagged frosting pattern, swirled into a mountain-like pitch, sat at the edge of the plate. On the top stood an electric pink star flanked by a spray of sprinkles. Definitely would have been the first one I went for with a mound of frosting that high.

"That's what you'll do with this bag. Here, I'll show you. It's all in the wrist, honey. Take it from a Southerner."

For not doing this every day, Mira had surprising dexterity. She taught me how to hold the bag, control the speed of frosting with my hand, and swirl it around from the top with my wrist.

"How often do you help?" I asked, accepting the frosting bag. "You're really good at this."

"Every day recently. I'm getting the hang of it. It's actually not so hard after a while."

"Maybe *you* should work for her."

"Can't. I still have to run the sewing shop!"

"Oh. Right."

"Besides." She shifted on her feet, her nose wrinkled. "All this work is killing my feet. I can hardly sleep at night. Not to mention the five pounds I've already gained!"

I frowned, and she paled.

"B-but that's just me and my Pepsi, you know. Nothing to do with working here, of course!"

My gaze tapered. "You're off Pepsi."

"New bag!" She snatched the purple one from my hand. "Here, I'll fill it back up while you grab a cupcake."

Thanks to the high chair, the table sat at my elbow, making it easy to reach over and grab a cupcake. I stared at it in apprehension.

You, I wanted to say. *You are the reason I was 265 pounds. Your villainous butter and sugar are the reason I hated myself but acted like I loved who I was. I didn't. I hated being fat. I hated taking up space. I hated not being perfect. You are the reason I was unhappy.*

"It isn't going to bite you, you know." Mira stared at me, eyebrows high on her forehead.

"Right. Of course. Just, ah, planning my course of attack."

The frosting raced out when I first squeezed the tube, resulting in an awkward blob on top of the cupcake. I tilted my head to the side.

Mira laughed. "Don't worry. Set that aside and try another one."

The second came out painfully slowly, which made it easier, even though the design still ended up wildly lopsided. Mira chortled and slid a small box of candy stars my way, followed by a shaker of glitter.

"Push the weird top over and put the star on. It'll be fine."

Although it still looked lopsided, I obeyed and set it back on the tray. My third attempt resulted in a too-wide circle that eventually collapsed in the middle. Once I finished, I leaned back with a heavy sigh. Who knew food art could be so difficult?

The fourth came out almost normal looking, except for a straight line on one side instead of a curve. Once I set the star on top and dribbled some sprinkles, I nodded. Not too bad.

"Well done," Mira said. "Now do it 142 more times."

I stifled a groan.

"What are all these for?"

"Not sure. A wedding, maybe?"

"Huh."

"Sophia had more cupcake orders than she could handle alone.

Then her assistant Kate ended up going into labor three months early. She's hospitalized for the rest of her pregnancy, with no plans to return. Sophia can't afford to turn down the cupcake orders, which is when I stepped in to help."

"Ah."

"These bulk orders keep the business running." Mira lowered her voice, her eyes darting to the front of the store. "I don't think she's earning enough on bakery goods to cover rent. Her cinnamon rolls do okay, but it's her wedding cakes that most people buy. She's only one woman. If she doesn't pick up more foot traffic, she may have to close."

My eyes flitted around. "It's a cute place."

"I know. But that doesn't sell eclairs."

We fell into an easy silence. Mira hummed as she worked. Easy music trilled in the background. All things considered, it was a nice place. Or perhaps I was just ecstatic to get out of the house.

By lunchtime, my wrists ached, and the bones in my butt hurt from sitting in the hard chair. One at a time–sometimes painstakingly slowly when I had to learn a new design—Mira and I worked through hundreds of cupcakes. Sophia bustled in and out, talking to herself under her breath, darting from the fridge to the sink to the freezer and back. Brides shuffled past us in the background every now and then. All in all, this wouldn't be the worst temporary job.

If I could just keep the old Rachelle in check.

Too Far

"**The swelling is looking better** than I expected," Dr. Martinez said the next day. "Especially for less than a week out."

She tilted her head to the side, regarding the black-and-blue skin that swelled along the ankle. Just looking at it, so swollen and discolored, made me sick. How could it ever heal in time?

No, I thought. *I will do this marathon. It will heal in time.*

"I've been keeping it elevated like a religion."

She straightened up. "Good. It shows. We can cut back on some of the pain pills if you can handle it."

"Sure."

Bitsy stood near the door, her hands folded in front of her, wearing a pair of jeans and a plain black t-shirt. Dr. Martinez probed around my toes.

"I'd like you to stay on the anti-inflammatories for now. Keep that swelling moving down the right direction."

"Since it's doing so well, does that mean I'll be able to start running soon?"

Bitsy tilted her head back and rolled her eyes. Dr. Martinez peered at me over the top of her glasses and blinked once. The awkward silence that followed answered my question. I bit my bottom lip.

"You're kidding, right?" Dr. Martinez asked.

"Er . . . no?"

"You're not even ready for weight bearing."

"Right, but give it a few days?"

"No."

My heart sank. "How long will this take?"

"Impossible to say, but keep all weight off it for the next week at least. Keep it elevated and iced too. We'll start working on toe-touch weight bearing once I feel you're ready to handle it, but we're probably weeks away from that."

"Toe-touch weight bearing?"

"That means you only touch your big toe to the ground."

"That's nothing!"

"Exactly."

"But—"

She held up a hand, her lips pinched. "Trust me, Rachelle. The more conservative we are right now, the better for you. Do you want a long-term injury?"

"No."

"Then listen to my medical expertise." She jabbed a finger toward my ankle. "That's an intense Grade 3 sprain that I don't want to exacerbate. If you stick with this, you'll heal faster. If you don't, you may never run a marathon at all."

My mouth snapped closed again. Of course she was right. I nodded once. Although I was determined to run the marathon, I wasn't about to sabotage *any* chance I had. Across the room, Bitsy peered at me with a lowered brow and intent gaze. I acted like I hadn't noticed. My reckoning with her would come in the car. I could already feel it building.

"All right," I said with a heavy sigh. "I'll keep doing what I'm doing."

Dr. Martinez headed toward the door, a finger held straight up. "I'll see you in one week, Rachelle."

The door closed behind her with a resounding *thud*. For some reason, I felt as if she'd taken me with it.

Bitsy's voice broke the strained silence that pervaded the car once we left the doctor's office.

"You're lucky it's healing so well."

I sighed, ready to get this over with.

"I know."

Houses flashed by us, her Honda's engine whirring with an obnoxiously loud purr. She tapped the steering wheel with her thumb—the radio didn't work—and pursed her lips. I sank deeper into my seat.

The steady silence continued for several minutes before I couldn't stand it anymore. I licked my lips and said, "Thanks for taking me. I know this isn't convenient for you. I appreciate your help. All of it."

"Don't thank me yet."

I swallowed. "Why not?"

She moved into the left lane instead of the right. My eyes narrowed as she drove through the green light rather than taking the turn toward the trailer park.

"Uh . . . where are we going?"

"I'm taking you to Janine."

"Janine?"

"My therapist."

My body stiffened. "What?"

"You need to talk to a professional."

"You're crazy."

"No, I'm not."

"I don't need to talk to a therapist."

"We all need a therapist, Rachelle. You have unresolved issues."

"Bitsy, I sprained my ankle. I'm not *crazy*."

"Are you saying I'm crazy because I had counseling?"

"No."

"Then what are you saying?"

"I-I'm just saying I don't need it. I'm fine. Nothing's wrong with me."

The words came out like bad fruitcake. Even as I said them, I knew they weren't true. The hair on the back of my neck stood up. What could be wrong with me pursuing my goals related to health and happiness? Nothing.

At least, I didn't think so.

"*Nothing* is wrong?" she asked. "Let's talk about your abandonment issues because of your father."

"Whoa!"

"Or the fact that you lost the weight of a whole person and still aren't happy."

"Hey, I—"

"You can say that everything at home, in your life, and at your job is just peachy, Rachelle?"

"I don't have a job anymore," I snapped.

"Exactly!"

I'd expected a confrontation, but this had gotten out of control too quickly. I dug my fingertips into the thinning seat beneath me and let out a long breath. "That's not fair. You've pushed me too far."

Bitsy met my glare without fear. "No," she said quietly. "I'm the one that's finally pushing you at *all*. You have issues, Rachelle. Your exercise and search for love in the wrong places has gotten out of control. I'm the only one saying what needs to be said. Finally. Probably about twenty years too late."

My mouth opened and shut.

"Janine is an outside person with no connection to your life. She can give you a different perspective on what you're experiencing. She can even help you understand why you always date losers and why you're obsessed with working out. Losing weight is one thing, Rachelle. This has gone too far."

"It hasn't gone far enough," I mumbled.

"You're not even happy! We're part of the Health and *Happiness* Society, Rachelle. I didn't formulate the group to push you into an early grave. Happiness. That's what we want to find. Not marathon trophies."

"Marathon trophies make me happy!"

"You don't know that."

"It will," I growled.

"The way losing over a hundred pounds has made you so *happy*? You're not just chasing one more ghost?"

"I'm happy!" I snapped.

Bitsy rolled her eyes.

Sharp pain shot through my bottom lip as I chewed on it. Analysis of my dating habits? Fine. They were decidedly sucky. Talking about exercise? Sure. Maybe I'd even concede that I exercised a lot. But I would *not* broach the topic of my life before my weight loss. Certainly not my father. Bitsy pulled to a stop at a curb and put her car into park. Her gaze bored into mine.

"No way. I won't do it. I will *not* go in there."

"We're here."

"I'm not doing it."

"I'm not leaving until you do. I dare you to test my willpower, Rachelle." Her expression hardened. "Because you will never win."

Twenty minutes of steely silence later, I trailed Bitsy up the sidewalk with a bitter scowl. I knew I didn't have a chance of winning, but at least I'd put up a good fight. Lexie would be proud of me. I could hear her now. *You lasted twenty minutes against Bitsy? Well done!*

My crutches *thunk-thunked* along with me, a painful staccato that matched my pounding heart. A therapist?

Seriously?

Janine's office was in a nondescript brick building. A dove-gray sign planted in the grass near the sidewalk said *Wings of Hope Counseling Services*.

"Wings of Hope?" I asked.

"No judgments," Bitsy said. "It's a great place."

"I don't want religion."

"It has nothing to do with God. That's a *dove* on the sign. Let's go. You don't scare me with your acerbic comments, Rachelle. It'll take a lot more than that for me to give you what you want instead of what you need."

I followed her inside the office. A silver-haired receptionist behind a glass front desk greeted Bitsy with a smile.

"Welcome back, Bitsy."

"Sorry we're late."

"No problem. Janine anticipated it after your warning."

"You knew I'd stall?" I asked.

Bitsy scoffed. "Of course I knew. I paid for two hours just in case."

I shot her a scathing look. Did she really think of everything? As if she'd read my mind, she smiled. The muted, warm walls had a soothing effect, but I snorted at the tinkle of a waterfall in the corner. As if a zen atmosphere *really* helped. Everything about this felt wrong.

"Before you see Janine today, would you mind filling out a few papers?" The receptionist smiled at me with bright-white teeth as she slid a clipboard across the counter. "Should only be a few minutes."

"Ah . . . that's not necessary. I won't be coming back."

Bitsy grabbed the clipboard. "Sure." She pointed me to a chair. "Sit."

With a hot glare, I hobbled over to the plastic chair. Pen in hand, I skimmed a questionnaire. Rows of boxes with tiny text lined the page, each column alternating between shades of gray. Statements like *I have thoughts of ending my life* and *I like myself* ran down the left column, with the options of *Never, Rarely, Sometimes, Frequently,* and *Almost Always* on the right.

Did I like myself? I quickly checked *Rarely* and then crossed it out for *Never*.

Might as well be honest.

After ten questions, my attention waned. I buzzed through the rest without caring. What did it matter? It's not like I'd be back, anyway. The receptionist came around the desk and reached for the papers as I struggled to stand.

"I'll take that. Thank you."

A woman in a knee-length skirt and slate blazer stepped out of a room at the back with a warm smile. "Rachelle, it's good to meet you. I'm Janine." Streaks of blonde ran through her bobbed brown hair. She held out a hand. I reluctantly shifted my weight onto my left foot and accepted.

"Hi."

Bitsy remained in her chair, magazine in hand. "Thanks Janine! I'll be waiting when you come out, Rachelle."

"Wait. What? You aren't coming in with me?"

"Why would I?"

"Because you control everything?"

"You're a big girl, Rachelle. You don't *need* me in there. You just needed me to nudge you."

"This was your idea! You should have to suffer through it too."

She flipped another page of her magazine without looking up. "Ooh, quinoa with veggies!"

Bubbling panic welled up inside me. Go in without Bitsy? Didn't she know I needed her? Janine smiled when I turned back to her. I'd never felt so lost or confused in my life.

And I hadn't even started yet.

"It's going to be all right, Rachelle. My office is back here." Janine motioned with a sweep of her arm. "If you want to follow,

I'll take you there. If you're not comfortable, Bitsy can come in. And she will."

Bitsy's gaze flickered up, but she said nothing.

"Fine," I muttered. "I can do this without her."

The idea of talking about anything made me want to vomit, but I followed the gentle tap of Janine's heels into a room with a mahogany desk, an iMac, and several paintings of women. One caught my eye. A willowy mother bending over a young child, painted with broad lines of pearl and ebony. I turned away with a heavy swallow.

Janine waved a hand toward a padded leather couch fifteen feet from her chair. "Have a seat." The distance reassured me. I slumped into the seat and set the crutches aside, my hands as cold as ice. Her gaze dropped to my boot.

"Bitsy told me about your ankle." She grimaced. "I'm very sorry. Sounds quite painful."

"Thanks."

The sincerity in her tone couldn't be denied; I made a mental note to stay wary. This woman had a confident air and the plaques on the wall to prove herself. She knew what she was doing.

"I understand that you came because Bitsy made the appointment for you. I don't usually take clients under these circumstances but decided to try it. Your situation sounds unique."

"I don't want to be here."

"I can understand that. Therapy is good for anyone, really, regardless of past issues. Everyone could use some help achieving their goals."

Uncertain what to say, I just leaned back against the couch. My *goal* was taking a little nap right now.

"Would you like to tell me about your upcoming marathon?" Janine asked. She rested her hands in her lap with an open expression. Could they train someone to look receptive and attentive? She said *upcoming*. Did she think it was still possible? Was this a trick to get me to talk? I cleared my throat.

"It's in August."

"Twenty-six miles is a lot to run. How far are you into your training?"

"I've run a twelve-miler so far."

"With two months left, you're well on your way."

How did she know that? My brow furrowed. "Do you run?"

"Not that much anymore, but I have done a few marathons in the past. I still do a few half marathons and 10ks here and there. Six miles is a good base to maintain, I've found."

"Oh."

"Why do you want to run a marathon?"

Something in the easy question struck a nerve. I sucked in a sharp breath, realizing what had happened. Whoa. She *was* good. I'd been funneled right into talking to her without realizing it. I frowned.

"Oh. Uh . . ."

She blinked as if she didn't notice the sudden chill in the air. Surely *I* wasn't imagining it.

"Look," I said, "I'm not really interested in being friends or chatting about marathons so you can get me to spill my childhood secrets. I don't really want this to continue."

A bemused expression flitted across her face. "Do you always think people have an angle when they interact with you?"

"Don't they?"

"I believe people are genuinely interested in learning more about others without getting something from it."

"You would get more business if I talked to you."

"And you would get clarity."

"Clarity?"

"Who are you, Rachelle?"

The straightforward way she asked caught me by surprise. Any other time, I would have brushed the question aside, but something about being in that room with her stopped me.

"What?"

"Who are you?"

"I . . ."

Words failed me. How was I even supposed to answer that? "I'm a twenty-five-year old that dropped out of college and still lives at home."

The bitterness in my own voice caught me by surprise.

"But is that who you are?"

Hadn't I once been morbidly obese? Hadn't I lost over a hundred pounds and still felt hollow inside? Hadn't I once been a cosplayer that dressed up—sometimes daily—without regard to what people said about it? But I wasn't those things all the time.

Who *was* I?

Janine waited without a change of expression. The air weighed heavy on my shoulders.

"I don't know."

She nodded once, her lips pursed, and said nothing else for what felt like an eternity. My chest tightened. Was this some kind of trap? Would every session feel like this? How could anyone tolerate something so . . . naked?

"Clarity," she said again. "Through our meetings, I can give you clarity. On a different note, Bitsy mentioned that you've lost a lot of weight. Congratulations."

"Yeah."

"How much did you lose?"

"One hundred and ten pounds."

"That's a big change. Losing that much weight can usher you into a new life. Some women grieve the loss of their old life. Some still believe they're overweight."

My chest tightened. We could focus on my love of exercise or the marathon but not on my life before losing the weight. I shook my head.

"Next topic."

"Would you like to tell me about your family?"

"Nope."

"Your job?"

"Dropped out of college. Next topic."

Janine folded her hands in her lap. "What would *you* like to talk about? How about we start there?"

"Nothing. I'd like to talk about nothing."

She leaned forward. "Is there something you're afraid of?"

Skeletons rattled in my closets. Skeletons best left in the dark. I shoved off the couch and scrambled for my crutches.

"I'm done."

Janine calmly stood. "Of course. You control this meeting. But I want you to know that there is no judgment. Just guidance and . . . clarity. Clarity into what's bothering you. Clarity beyond that stretch of darkness that you can't seem to find your way through."

"I'm not interested."

"Do you mind if I ask what you *do* want?"

My heart ached. How was I supposed to know? I'd *never* known what I wanted. Every time I chased it, it disappeared, a gossamer wisp in a barren landscape.

"Honestly?"

"Yes."

At a total loss, I said the first thing that came to my mind. "I want to be fat again."

I swung my crutches and hobbled out with as much dignity as I could muster.

That's It?

The meeting with Janine simmered inside of me with fiery agitation long after I left her office.

I kept seeing her open expression. Her amused smiles when I said something that *should* have been off-putting. Not that she was making fun of me, or anything. Just that she seemed like she knew something I didn't and, like Bitsy, didn't care if I gave her attitude.

With a growl under my breath, I yanked the fridge open and pulled out a water bottle. The fridge door trembled after I slammed it, not realizing the strength of my own vengeance. I closed my eyes, sucked in a breath, and let it back out again. The smell of simmering onions and oregano filled the air, distracting me from my rage.

"Pass me the ground beef, will you?" Mom asked.

My eyes opened, and I saw Mom standing at the stove. I'd been so wrapped up in my thoughts, I hadn't even seen her there. Several seconds passed before I registered the fact that she was actually standing. Cooking. Doing something *off* the couch. She wore a gray robe today. It stretched across her wide shoulders, hinting at a dingy white house dress underneath. A fan stood in the window, pointed out to remove the heat from the stove, no doubt. Mom had set a chair against the far counter so she could rest in between stirs. I held onto the counter and hopped on my left leg toward the package of ground beef.

"Sure."

I slid the unopened package toward her. She grabbed a pair of scissors from the drawer without looking and cut into it. Was I imagining it, or was Mom *humming*?

I leaned against the counter and cracked the lid off my water bottle before taking a swig of water.

"What are you making?" I asked.

"Spaghetti."

"Ah."

Her favorite. No green beans or salad accompanied spaghetti here. Just a bowl large enough to be a serving bowl filled with buttery pasta, thick meat sauce, and the fresh tang of parmesan. My lips twitched. A small wedge of parmesan cheese sat on the counter near the grater, right next to the bulk-sized bag of brown sugar she always used to sweeten the sauce. Mom could be a total food snob sometimes. She'd buy frozen chicken nuggets and tater tots—and finish off an entire cookie sheet by herself in one sitting—but wouldn't buy pre-shredded parmesan. Nor would dry herbs suit, either. When it came to Italian food, she went all fresh.

"Smells good," I said.

She sprinkled a little salt into the simmering meat sauce but didn't say anything. Next to it, a pot of water frothed. She tipped over a package of pasta into her hand, then cast the dry noodles into the pot. With strained breath, she backed up and carefully sat in the chair. It groaned beneath her weight. For several seconds, she was out of breath.

My thoughts spun.

"Hey Mom, who taught you how to cook?"

Her brow furrowed into a heavy line over her eyes. She scratched at her cheek with stubby fingernails.

"Just learned it."

"From Grandma?"

Her expression darkened. "No."

I opened my mouth to ask something else but stopped. I'd never actually met my grandparents. It felt unnatural to even bring them up because Mom never spoke about them. Before I could say another word, she broke the silence.

"It was my Aunt Bell."

Her words startled me; I almost forgot to respond. Instead, I took another drink and pushed myself back to sit on the counter, then propped my foot up onto it. If Mom was willing to talk, I was ready to listen. I'd never heard of anyone named Aunt Bell; I didn't even know she *had* an aunt.

"Bell was her name?" I asked.

"Bella." Mom stared at the stove top with a deadpan expression. "But I always called her Bell."

"You've never mentioned her before."

Mom reached out and, using the edge of the sink as a handhold, slowly stood up. She shuffled over to the stove in tattered slippers.

Today, her hair fell down her back in a braid. Rare. She normally just left it stringy on her shoulders. Although I noticed her lack of response, I didn't point it out. Maybe she just didn't want to talk about Bell.

Whoever Bell was.

"Well, you are an amazing cook," I murmured. "Bell must have been too."

I felt a little pang in my stomach. I *did* miss Mom's Italian food, especially when she attempted to mimic recipes from popular local restaurants. Lately, that had died down. Her body didn't have the stamina to stand for too long. I wondered if it was coincidence that her fading work in the kitchen coincided with when I started to lose weight.

Mom stirred the pasta, which had started to curl in the water, with her head tilted to the side. "I always have enjoyed being in the kitchen."

"Yeah." My nose wrinkled. "Except for the dishes."

A wheezy sound came out of her. Was it a chuckle? A laugh? The strange noise made me realize I hadn't heard her *really* laugh in a long time.

"Found a new recipe book," Mom said just as I was about to leave. I paused, even though her back was to me. We hadn't talked about food—or maybe really talked at all—in months. Maybe even a year. A brief moment of hesitation rippled through me, and I stuffed it away. Instead, I planted my hands back on the counter and stayed put.

"Oh?"

"There's a carrot cake that looks good. You eat healthy now. Maybe we could try it out."

There was a hint of yearning in her voice, almost a gentle pleading. Although carrot cake was far from healthy, there was something in her childlike words that I just couldn't turn down. I didn't usually like to mix my vegetables with pleasure. Preferred them straight. Roasted, with olive oil. But this?

"Yeah," I said. "Of course. I can add the ingredients to our next food delivery."

Her shoulders slumped a little. "I mean, maybe it's not even good."

"*Sounds* good, Mom."

For her sake, I'd risk the cream cheese frosting.

"I'll look it over again, see if I even want it. I might be remembering it wrong."

"Okay. Well, whenever you decide to, I'd love to make it."

Mom didn't say another word, and I could tell by the slope of her body and the way her head hung downward that she likely wouldn't speak again. With a flick of her wrist, she turned off the boiling pasta and used a spatula to break up the simmering meat. For half a breath, I stared at the image, thinking of Bitsy.

What are you running away from, Rachelle?

I shook my head to dismiss the thought.

"Night, Mom."

She lifted a hand in farewell.

I fell asleep staring at the ceiling, listening to the rolling laugh track of a comedian in the background, wondering why my mom always looked so sad.

Later that week, I stood beneath the anemic lights of my bathroom and stared into my own eyes.

Sometimes I still caught myself doing a double take every time I passed a mirror. Surely the overweight, loud, obnoxious Rachelle would come screaming back any minute now. After losing all that weight, I'd grown out my bangs. My hair fell to my shoulders, straight and chocolate and silky. When I was twelve, I used to dream of what it would be like to see my cheekbones. The day I realized they had emerged—the same day I realized I had lost seventy-five pounds—replayed through my mind.

That's it? I remember thinking.

I forced air out of my mouth with pursed lips and splashed cold water on my face, banishing the thought. Cheekbones or not, I had to hobble outside. Mira would arrive at any moment to take me to the Frosting Cottage. A gray cloud hovered above me, placed there by Janine, even though the appointment had been days ago.

After a dash of lip gloss and a quick tug of a comb through my hair, I left the bathroom. I hadn't dressed up in any of my old cosplay outfits in months, which made getting ready really fast compared to what it used to be. No more braiding, curling, or coiffing my hair. No more elaborate makeup, long nails, or complicated boots. All my old cosplay clothes were stuffed in my closet, gathering dust, too large to wear now.

I missed the gold glitter.

Just as I opened the door, Mira pulled up to the curb. She honked once and waved, her teal eyeshadow visible even from this distance. I turned to call over my shoulder.

"Bye Mom."

"Where are you going?"

"My new job."

The stymied silence that followed made me sigh. I'd told her twice that I'd gotten a new job. My crutches moved easily beneath me when I headed out the front door, letting it slam shut behind me. My palms had started to harden, even. Mira leaned across the seat and opened my door.

"Ready for today?" she called.

"Sure."

"It's your last day of training. We just have one more frosting tip to learn and two more designs." A wide grin crossed her face. "Isn't it exciting?"

"Thrilling."

My crutches clattered when I pulled them inside. She peeled away from the curb, tires squealing, before I could buckle my seatbelt. I gripped the seat, thrown back against it by the force of her speed.

"Geez, Mira!"

"Sorry." She grimaced as we took a corner too fast, throwing my shoulder into the door. "I forget that I need to drive more responsibly when other people are with me. Are you all prepared for today? I'm glad I taught you the register before now. You're going to get lots of opportunity to practice it today."

My brow furrowed. Today? She skidded to a stop at a red light just a few moments before sliding into the intersection, and I let out the breath I'd been holding. As long as we were stopped, I'd be relatively safe.

"What's going on today that will give me so much practice?" I asked.

"SummerFest at the college."

My eyes widened. SummerFest. Right. The four biggest fraternities in town hosted a party to kick off summer. They invited other college students from all over the state. The sheer number of football players that streamed in from two states over were enough to cause a surge in the local economy. This wasn't an event to miss. Last year, I'd gotten drunk with a guy named Nigel and woken up in his dorm room the next morning.

"Are cupcake sales supposed to be high?" I asked.

"Anything with sugar." Mira's tires squealed as she soared through a fresh green light. "Sophia said she sells cookies, lemonade, brownies, and small pastries pretty well. Says the college students get really munchy for some reason."

I suppressed a snort. Munchy. Right. Smoking too much pot had a way of causing that.

First, however, I had to stay alive. With Mira driving, there was no guarantee. I braced myself as she slowed down just a few inches from another car and prayed I'd make it to work.

After today, just a week left until I didn't have to face another scrumptious-looking cupcake again.

When we entered the Frosting Cottage, Sophia stood behind the counter, a vat of dough in front of her. She glanced up—her ever-present baseball cap still perched high on her head—and grinned.

"Hello, ladies!"

I dropped my backpack in her office, picked up my hat off a sprinkled marshmallow peg on the wall, and went back into the preparation area. A quiet, yoga-like track trilled in the background. Sophia was a new-age goddess. Megan would adore her.

Sophia plucked a fistful of dough out of the mass, grabbed a metallic square with her other hand, and cut the dough piece free. Then she rolled it into a circle, tossed it around, and slapped it onto a waiting cookie sheet. Poufs of flour billowed into the air. I could already feel the gritty tinge of it. It made me think of wintry nights at home, when Mom used to make her own pasta.

"Need some help?" Mira asked.

"Just finishing the last hot cross buns. Cupcakes for you again, Mira, if that's all right with you."

"Sure."

"Rachelle, I have something else for you to do."

I paused. "Me?"

Sophia tilted her head to another pile of dough in a different vat. "I need to get three batches of cinnamon rolls going. I had a sorority call and ask for two dozen for SummerFest, and I'll want extras for the munchies that walk in."

"I don't—"

"I'll walk you through it."

I hesitated for half a breath. Why couldn't I just do cupcakes? Mira had done the cinnamon rolls before, so why wasn't she doing them now? I stuffed it aside. Getting my hands into some dough actually sounded . . . not so bad. Maybe I could punch them into submission, unlike my life.

"Um . . . okay."

Sophia glanced up with a smile. "If your ankle is bothering you, you can try to do it sitting."

"Actually, it's okay right now. It's been up all morning. It's been less sensitive to that lately. I'll just kneel on a chair."

Which, now that I thought about it, seemed like excellent progress.

"Good. Wash your hands at the sink. Be sure to use the scrub brush underneath your nails. Scrub at least sixty seconds. Are your nails short? Good."

Ten minutes later, my fingers were knuckle deep in sticky, gooey dough that wasn't, actually, as fun as I'd hoped. The bogginess clung to me like tentacles whenever I touched it. So much for getting my hands into dough; it had practically absorbed them. Sophia grinned.

"The rolls stay more moist when it's that wet."

"I can't even form it."

"Try a little bit more flour, but not too much!"

Once I beat the dough into a *form* of submission—and had gobs of it clinging to my knuckles and fingers—Sophia walked me through each step until I had a doughy roll stuffed with melted butter and packed thick with cinnamon and sugar. She slid the square, metallic tool toward me.

"Now, slice it with this. Two-inch strips."

While I cut, Mira puttered in the background, moving cupcakes, stirring frosting, and singing an old Frank Sinatra song. The air conditioning blew a cold breath against the back of my neck. All told, it wasn't entirely unpleasant working here, even if the smells did make me want to melt *into* the rolls. My frustration with the dough made me want to punch it, not eat it. Who needed Janine? Apparently cooking was the only form of rage control I needed. Once I finished slicing each roll, Sophie strolled over, a hand on her hip.

"Nice. The perfect thickness."

"They're good? I did them pretty thick, but that creates better middles."

She nodded toward the far wall. "Agreed. I'll stick these suckers in the oven. Then I'll walk you through the cream cheese frosting. I layer it nice and heavy. Excuse me for a minute. I'll be right back."

Sophia slipped into the back while I rubbed flour off my fingers with a satisfied slap of my hands. Something about finishing that first batch felt *good*.

The door chimed before I could pitch in to help Mira with frosting the cupcakes, so I grabbed my crutches and made my way over to the register instead. The light from outside illuminated a familiar, muscular silhouette. It took a moment for my eyes to adjust. Even longer for my brain to comprehend what—no, *who*—I saw. A man advanced further into the shop, a beam of sunshine from the tall window casting light on his face. My heart dropped into my stomach.

Chris.

Handsome, attractive, linebacker Chris. The man who once had my heart. The only man I'd ever run away from. The only one I still thought about.

No, I thought. *No way. Not today.*

His blond hair, buzzed short, seemed to glow in the bright summer light. Cornflower blue eyes peered back at me in befuddlement. He blinked and tilted his head to the side.

"Rachelle?"

"Hi," I squeaked.

His expression drooped. For a long moment, neither of us spoke. I cleared my throat.

"Yeah. Hi. Uh . . . h-how are you?"

"You look—"

"Yeah. I know," I said quickly. "I, uh . . . I lost a lot of weight after . . ."

That horrible, awful night.

He tucked a hand into his pocket. The other reached back to rub his neck. "You look . . . ah . . . great. It's . . . good to see you again."

"You here for SummerFest?"

He glanced over his shoulder, as if hoping someone would be there to save him from this awkward encounter.

"Yeah. Yeah. My friends are in a frat here." He motioned to the chalkboard. "I'm here for desserts for tonight. Not sure what . . ."

"Good. Yeah. Uh, just let me know what you want when you figure it out." I turned around and screwed my eyes shut, grateful for his intent study of the chalkboard. The moment to compose myself turned into three. Then five. My throat felt as parched as a fire.

"Hey Mira?" I called. "Can you get me a drink of water?"

She glanced up, concern on her face. Frosting dotted her apron. She opened her mouth, then with a sharp *no* from me, closed it again. "Sure, honey."

She disappeared long enough for me to wonder if I'd ignored Chris for too long. He had to be feeling even more awkward now that I'd kept my back to him, but I couldn't force myself to turn around. I couldn't. Because then I'd remember it all again.

That horrible, horrible night.

When Mira returned, ice cubes clanked against each other in a fresh, sweating glass. I tossed the water back like a shot. The ice-cold liquid burned my throat, reminding me of vodka. Just like the last time I'd seen Chris. I gulped three more times. The water slid down my throat like a shock but didn't banish any memories.

"You all right?" she whispered.

"Fine." I set the glass down. "Thanks."

Mira returned to the cupcakes but kept a wary eye on me. I put a hand to my flushed face and willed my body to calm down. Like that fateful night happening all over again, I felt a crack. My body falling. Heard the sound of my own awful singing. After making such a fool of myself, there was no doubt about it. Chris and I were ancient history.

He cleared his throat, drawing my attention back.

"Uh, yeah. I think I know what I want."

I spun around.

"Sure."

While I bagged four cinnamon rolls, a dozen cookies, and six brownies, shame burned hot at the back of my throat. Should I apologize to him now? Maybe he'd forgotten about it, but the way he fidgeted banished that idea. Nope, he hadn't forgotten.

This was intolerable.

I set the box down and pressed my hands against the counter. "Can we clear the air?"

Chris shifted his weight. "Uh . . ."

"Look, I'm sorry about what happened a year and a half ago. It was all my fault. I made an ass of myself, and—trust me—it wasn't the first time. Hopefully it was the last. I'm . . . sorry for embarrassing you and putting you in that situation." I met his gaze. "I'm sorry."

He shook his head, lips tight. His eyes didn't quite meet mine, and I wondered if he even felt like he recognized me. Sometimes *I* didn't even recognize me.

"None necessary," he said.

"Thank you for getting me out of there and . . . thanks."

He nodded. I shoved the box of goodies toward him, swiped the credit card, and handed it back. Neither of us made eye contact as he signed.

"See ya, Rachelle. And thanks."

"Yeah. Good to see you again."

He turned to go, stopped at the door, and glanced back, then with one last nod, strode back into the summer sun. My heart followed, as if it wanted to go with him. I sucked in a sharp breath.

"Mira?"

"Yeah?"

"I need a break. I'll be back."

"Sure, honey. Anything."

Without any further explanation, I grabbed my crutches and disappeared out the back door. I sat on the stairs in the alley and let out a long, teary breath. Then I grabbed my phone and dialed the only number I could think of.

"Rachelle?"

Lexie's voice came over the line thirty seconds later, right in the middle of my heavy-breathing-can't-get-air panic attack.

"You all right?" she asked. "This doesn't sound good."

"N-no."

A shuffling sound came over the line. Seconds later, Lexie spoke again, this time with more volume.

"What happened?"

I ran a hand through my hair, then closed my eyes and leaned against the wall. A vise-like feeling held my chest in a tight embrace, as if to squeeze all the air out of me.

"I just saw Chris."

"Chris as in Bradley's old roommate Chris?"

"Yes. He's here for SummerFest."

"Chris that you were madly in love with and wanted to have his babies?"

"That Chris."

"Oh, *sure*. He can hit SummerFest but couldn't come to our wedding."

Her words trailed away, lost in my almost-hysterical breathing. Dots broke out across my vision. When my fingertips tingled, I knew I had to get it under control. I sucked in a deep breath and held it. My thoughts continued to whirl, but the panic seemed to pause.

"Can you calm down?" she asked.

"Y-yes. Just . . . give me a second."

"Want me to talk about how in love I am with my niece? Because they're putting her in a cute baby contest next week, and I *know* she's going to win."

"S-sure."

Lexie prattled on about her niece's latest Shirley Temple dress and the bow that wouldn't stay on top of her head. The sound of her voice, the even flow, started to soothe me. It always had. Lexie talking in order to calm me down was nothing new. After explosive fits of temper when I was a teenager—when Mom and I had screaming matches and I didn't know where to turn afterward—I would call Lexie just to hear her talk.

It worked.

The tension in my chest broke apart, and I took in a deep, cleansing breath. My vision returned to normal.

"... and then she pooped everywhere," Lexie said with a sigh. "*Everywhere.* Kenzie said she was scooping it out of the car seat by the handful. I so wish I had been there. Can you imagine Kenzie dealing with poop *everywhere*?"

"No. But I'd love to see it."

"Me too!"

A long, steady breath flowed out of me. My brain seemed to reset a little. "Your niece is perfect, Lex."

Lexie half groaned, half sighed. "I *know*! It's killing me that I'm not there. Enough of that, now. Sounds like you've calmed down. What's up? It's been a long time since you've had a panic attack like that."

A year and a half, to be precise. I swallowed the hot ball of emotion sitting at the top of my throat. Although my breathing had calmed, I felt as if all the flame had just spread into my chest, where it burned like a flow of magma.

"Yeah."

"Listen, I know you don't want to talk about Chris. In fact, you never even told me what happened that one weekend you went to see him. It's like . . . I don't know. Chris never even told me either. He just got all awkward about it, and the whole thing has been so weird."

"I know."

"Are you ready to tell me now?"

No. I'd never really be ready. It felt so much bigger, so much scarier, when I had to say it out loud. But if not now, when?

"Last time I saw him, Chris took me on a date."

The words flew out of my mouth before I could stop them. But once they were out, they didn't stop. "We were having drinks and, of course, I had too much vodka. Like I often do. *Did.*" I closed my eyes. "I started to sing karaoke."

"That's not so bad," Lexie said.

"There was no karaoke in the restaurant," I said quietly.

"Oh."

"But I was determined to sing, so I . . . I climbed on the closest table, drink in hand, and belted out some horrific, drunken rendition of an Aretha Franklin song. I think. It's all a bit hazy, to be honest. They asked me to leave, but I fought them off. A lot. I may have thrown a napkin dispenser once or twice. A bouncer came in there somewhere. And then—"

My nostrils flared. The memory came so fast it disoriented me, as if I were on a whirling ride that wouldn't stop. Singing from the bottom of my belly. Was I sobbing through the song at one point? Then I was fighting off the manager. Bouncers rushed over. Everything sounded so much louder than normal. In the chaos, I could hear Chris pleading with me to cooperate. There were belligerent shouts. Chris saying we could go somewhere else, tugging on my hand.

"And then . . . the table broke beneath me," I whispered.

Pain had exploded across my back as the table splintered beneath me into two pieces. Some of the shards scratched my legs. My ankles jarred from the impact of hitting the floor. My knees bled a little, even. Everyone in the bar cackled as I rolled off the broken pieces and vomited onto Chris's shoes. My nostrils still burned with the taste of acid and vodka and pure shame. A long silence filled the phone.

"Oh, Rachelle," Lexie whispered.

"I was too heavy for the table. The entire restaurant laughed at me while Chris pulled me to the door. I fought him, too, I think. It's *all* hazy after that." I put a hand on my head. "I can't remember what happened after he dragged me away. I imagine he must have paid for the broken table and all the broken glasses and . . . anyway, suffice it to say that, after that, I returned home and holed up in the trailer for a week because I was so embarrassed. And then . . . I decided it was enough."

"And you started to get healthy and swear off men."

"Yeah."

"I had no idea, Rachelle."

"I didn't want you to." Tears welled up in my eyes. I blinked them back. "It's just all so embarrassing. But I'm never going back there, Lexie. I will never, *ever* be that Rachelle again."

She hesitated, then said quietly, "I know, Rachelle, but the thing is—"

"Never."

My nostrils flared. I made a fist with my hand and swallowed hard. My gaze dropped to my booted foot.

"Never," I whispered again, and felt it all the way into my bones.

Won't Happen Now

After running into Chris, my sprained ankle wasn't my biggest problem. Oh no. Sitting in the house, staring at my ceiling while thinking about how terrified I was about not having worked out in over a week—that was my biggest problem.

The television droned in the background, keying me up when I was already jittery. It used to be a sound reminiscent of my childhood, one that would lull me into a comforted sleep. All my life, I woke to it. Ate breakfast to it. Bonded with Mom over it. Now I loathed it. Heard it while I tried to sleep at night, ate dinner, took a shower, and read the forums.

Tonight, the sound of the television drove me deeper into my own mind. Into my plans. The memory of my last night with Chris played through my mind on a merciless loop. My dreams of the marathon followed. Crossing the finishing line. Running off my anxiety and fear. How I missed it.

Annoyed by my own self-pity, I sat up and swung my bare right foot off the pillows. No more brooding over Chris. No more thinking about what could have been. I might not be able to run, but I could *do* something. And I would. Right here. Right now. The old Rachelle could back off.

I would never be that girl again.

The velcro on my boot made a ripping sound when I pulled it free and carefully slid the boot off. Dr. Martinez had just authorized removing the boot to air it—and my stinky summer foot—out. The rush of cool air on my sweaty skin was my favorite part of the day, so I closed my eyes, tipped my head back, and enjoyed it. Then I cast the boot aside.

"Here we go."

Without touching the floor with my injured leg, I hopped across my bedroom and started up my laptop. Underneath my desk waited two ten-pound free weights. I balanced on one leg, reached down, and yanked them out.

"All right." I drew in a deep breath. "Let's get exercising."

A free exercise video popped up from one of my favorite workout channels. Upper body and core stabilizer. Perfect. I sat on my swivel desk chair and turned it up. Its peppy theme music drowned out the sound of the television that seeped in under the door.

"Ready to work?" a young California-type man in his mid-twenties asked. I eyed his corded arms and perfectly tanned chest rippling with muscles. A woman with platinum blonde hair and another man in short shorts and bright green tennis shoes flanked him on either side.

"You bet I am," I said.

"Let's get you toned and flooded with endorphins. Starting into a warm up."

"Yes," I murmured, feeling a heady rush as I mimicked his movements. "Let's do it."

The first ten minutes of the workout passed easily. I modified each warm up so I could remain in the chair, foot elevated. My shoulders relaxed.

"I got this," I said with a thrill. It was working! Not only could I keep making progress, but my foot was up! The swelling would go down. Muscle tone would rise. The marathon would happen.

Perfect.

"Really elongate that tricep," he said as he pumped his arm up and down behind his head. "Can you feel that burn? Keep going. Push hard for results, and results will come."

I growled in frustration. The padded back of the computer chair wouldn't let me lower the weight more than an inch. When I angled my body to the side, there still wasn't enough room to pump. All three of the trainers in the video stopped at the same time with triumphant smiles.

"Take a break before the next set," he said. "Give that muscle a good stretch."

No *way* was I being left behind.

I snapped the space bar to pause the workout, grabbed the weight in my right hand, stood on my good leg, and hopped toward the bed. There would be plenty of room to move freely there. A wave of dizziness washed over me halfway across my room. Spots of black crept in from the corners of my eyes.

"Whoa."

My left arm shot out to grab the nightstand just as I stumbled forward. In a move born of pure instinct, my right foot dropped to catch my fall. Pain spiraled through my ankle, radiating into my knee and hip. I jerked with a cry. The free weight fell.

Onto my right foot.

Black spots broke out across my eyes again—this time from sheer agony. I dropped to my knees with a gasp. The weight rolled free. A pillow muffled my next scream of pain.

No.

No way.

No *way* that had just happened.

Eternities seemed to pass while my right foot pulsed and throbbed in ways I'd never felt before. Tears smarted behind my eyes. Several long moments passed while I tried to get my breathing under control. The slightest movement sent ripples of pain all the way into my knees. When I risked a peek, the foot was bright red. Already starting to swell. I closed my eyes.

Reaching blindly, I extended my hand, fumbled for my phone on the night stand, and unlocked the screen. After a few awkward attempts at dialing because it was hard to see the screen through my tears, Bitsy's voice came through the speaker.

"Hey Rachelle. What's up?"

"Help?" I croaked.

"What happened? Where are you?"

"Home. I-I need you to take me to the doctor's office."

"What?"

"I think I just broke my foot."

I leaned my forehead against the cool windowpane of Bitsy's car that evening and closed my eyes. The Urgent Care physician's voice floated through my mind, replaying a terrifying refrain.

You broke three of the delicate bones at the top of your foot, called the metatarsals. The swelling you see here? That's probably going to get worse. I think all your treadmill running weakened your bones. Not to mention your sprain. A marathon? I'm sorry, Rachelle, but that won't happen now. With two such injuries, you have several months of recovery ahead of you before you'll be ready for full weight bearing. Of course, your primary physician will have more to say about that when you go follow up with her. Knowing Dr. Martinez? She'll probably have a lot to say about it.

The words repeated like a ticker tape in my mind.

Won't happen now.

Won't happen now.

Tears filled my eyes. What now? No marathon. No proof that I wasn't the same Rachelle. The marathon was the physical proof that I'd never be fat—would never be *that* girl—again. Something I could hold up and say, *See? I'm new. I'm better. I did what she never could have.*

How else could I show it?

I braced myself for Bitsy's damning silence. For versions of *I told you so* from her as she sat solemnly in the driver's seat. When she flipped on the blinker, pulled off onto a residential street, and parked, fear rose hot in my throat. A warm hand rested on my shoulder.

"You okay, Chelle?" Concern filled her gaze.

Hot tears dropped down my cheeks. I hadn't prepared myself for compassion.

"No," I whispered.

She reached over to wrap me in a hug. I clung to her with a half sob. "That marathon was supposed to be my moment!"

"Your moment to what?"

"To prove I'm not that Rachelle anymore. To do something that the old Rachelle could never have done. It was going to show that I'm not embarrassing or overweight or someone to be ashamed of."

"Would a marathon have done all that?"

"Yes!"

She pulled back and put both hands on my face, cradling my tear-streaked cheeks. "What's wrong with the old Rachelle?"

"She was overbearing and loud and . . ."

"And wonderful."

"No. She wasn't wonderful."

"She was. She was fierce and loyal and—"

"She wasn't! She hid from her problems behind her weight. She hid from what she hated most about herself by eating. She acted like nothing was wrong. She even glorified something that wasn't good for her!"

Embarrassment rippled through my chest. Embarrassment I didn't even know was there. Hatred for the girl I had let myself become—then *and* now. It encompassed me like a bath of hot water.

Bitsy released me, reached into her purse, and extracted a tissue. "Maybe you did hide from the truth. Maybe you did the best you could to survive really difficult things. But maybe it's time to face the things you're running from now."

My mind blanked, unable to register what I could possibly be running away from. Weight gain, of course. But that seemed far too obvious. A strange, heavy veil of darkness seemed to draw across my eyes, preventing me from really seeing. Maybe I *was* running.

Maybe.

I mopped my face with the tissue. "What *am* I running from?"

"That's the question, isn't it?"

"H-how do I figure it out?"

A haunted expression rested on her face. She swallowed hard. "You confront the darkness. See what it hides."

"That sounds like a line from a horror movie."

She laughed. "Sometimes it feels like it."

Her amusement quickly sobered.

"Have you done that?" I whispered.

"Yes."

"How?"

She pulled in a deep breath, her shoulders rising and falling with the motion. "For me, it was a matter of finding professional help."

"Janine."

"Yeah. Janine."

"What did she do?"

"She asked me the questions that no one else would. She helped me find the dark spots that I tried not to see."

"Oh."

"Going to therapy was hard. One of the hardest things I've ever had to do. It was also the most liberating. I've never regretted it, though at the time it wasn't easy."

For a moment, I was lost in my own thoughts. They spun back to the day I'd realized I had to change. The dark night that had preceded it. The self-hatred. The fear I had of myself and the lengths I would go to get attention. Could I revisit a time when I felt no hope, no light, no path to redemption?

"What if I just leave it in the past?" I asked. "It belongs there."

"That's what you've been doing. Can you continue like this? Can you continue to hate who you used to be? To stuff it away and live in fear? If you hate who you were then, you will never love who you are now."

The tears brimmed again. "No."

"You *could* ignore it. But you'd live a half life. You'd be running and not know it." Her gaze met mine. "Like your mom."

"I'm not brave enough."

"You are what you have to be."

A long moment passed. Bitsy shifted the car back into drive, pulled away from the curb, and gently accelerated. I gazed on the trees as they whizzed by in fluffy shades of emerald and tucked an errant piece of hair behind my ear. I knew what I had to do, but I didn't want to do it. Didn't want to open the door and step through into something so vast. So dark. An encompassing, terrifying world I wasn't sure I could make it through.

Another tear trickled down my face.

"Will you take me back to Janine?"

Bitsy reached over and clasped her hand in mine. "Of course, Rachelle. Of course."

"Rachelle, it's so good to see you again."

Janine warmly clasped my hand two days later, a genuine smile on her face. There were no signs of gloating, just concern. Maybe some relief that I'd come back. Although Bitsy told me not to, I still felt sheepish. This time, I managed a struggling smile in return.

"Thanks."

"Come on back."

Bitsy waved as I followed Janine, my booted ankle swinging as I navigated the crutches like a pro. Janine wore a plum blazer with a cream button-up shirt and modest pumps. A blast of air conditioning blew across my face when I entered her office. She gestured to the couch.

"Have a seat."

After I situated myself, she glanced at my foot.

"So," she drawled. "I normally use my intake paperwork to give me an idea of where to start, but I think it's clear what we should talk about today. The paperwork can come later."

"Okay."

"Bitsy told me about the weight. Yikes. Your poor foot. Would you like to talk about what happened?"

A hidden implication lingered in her words, but I wasn't sure if I was imagining it or not. Of course, I wasn't *supposed* to be lifting weights then. But how could she know that?

"Not really, but I will. I mean, I should. That's why I'm here, right? Should I just . . . ah . . ."

She smiled in that warm way again. "Go for it."

"Okay. Well . . . basically, I missed working out and accidentally dropped the weight on my foot."

She sucked in a sharp breath. "Ouch. Were you supposed to be working out so soon after an injury?"

"I wasn't using my legs. Just my arms."

She opened her mouth to respond but paused. Even *I* heard the defensive note in my tone. A hesitant beat lingered in the air before I let out a long breath.

"No," I finally said. "I wasn't."

"What drove you to it, then?"

I shoved my fingers under my thighs. How honest was I supposed to be? How honest did I *want* to be? The thought of skirting around the real answer occurred to me, but I shoved it aside. Not here. This time, I had to take it seriously. If I was going to be here, I would *be* here.

"Uh, well, I guess the reason *technically* started a year ago when I . . . when I danced drunk on a table while singing karaoke. The table, uh, broke beneath me. It was so embarrassing. The next day, I resolved to lose weight." I lifted my hands. "Here I am, 110 pounds lighter."

Her brow furrowed. "What was it about that particular instant that motivated you to such a big life change?"

"Oh." My voice shrank. "The guy I liked was there. Everyone laughed at me. It was the single most humiliating moment of my life."

"Ah. So you were embarrassed about what happened and felt that you could avoid it again by losing weight?"

"Extremely embarrassed. If I hadn't been so fat, I wouldn't have broken that table. If I hadn't been fat, I wouldn't have felt like I had to do something outrageous to impress Chris."

"Are you sure about that?"

Her question stopped me. What thin woman broke a table by dancing on it?

"Um, I was until you asked me."

Janine leaned forward and quirked her lips, as if stymied by something. "When you think of that memory, how does your body feel?"

"My body?"

"Do you feel a heaviness in your chest? Does it make you sick to your stomach? Are you lightheaded?"

Several seconds passed while I tried to figure out the question. I'd never thought about how my *body* felt. My mind pretty much controlled my emotions . . . or so I thought. "It feels like . . . I'm not sure. But my heart feels . . . heavy, I guess? Can that happen?"

She nodded. "And what would you call that feeling?"

"Disgust."

"At what?"

"Myself."

"Because you broke the table?"

"Because I acted like an idiot. It's bad enough I broke the table, but to kick the bouncer? To sing karaoke at the top of my lungs? To throw napkin dispensers and vomit everywhere? That's pretty embarrassing."

"I hear that disgust in your voice. I hear resentment, too."

"Yeah. Sure."

"Why?"

Something deep in my chest itched and wiggled like a worm. For half a breath, I almost left the office again. It would be so easy to pick up the crutches and bolt.

But to what?

With a sigh, I said, "I guess I'm disgusted because I was up on a table, totally smashed, hoping to impress this guy. Really, I was . . . I was desperate."

"You felt that dancing on a table would impress him?"

"Er . . . no? I mean, I was drunk at the time, so it's hard to know what my thoughts were."

"You'd be surprised. Alcohol lowers inhibitions. Sometimes the truth comes out when that happens."

My mind flashed back to that night—what I could recall through the haze, anyway. There had been other women there. Sequined tank tops. Thin shoulders. Confident smiles. Everything I wasn't.

"I . . . I wanted him to *see* me. Not the other girls that were there. Just me."

"Was he looking around?"

"I can't remember."

"So you acted out?"

"Yes."

My mind spun with relief to the next morning. I had woken up in my hotel room on the bathroom floor. My shirt was halfway up my stomach, and pieces of hair were pasted to my face with vomit. I'd stood in front of the mirror and stared at myself for what felt like hours. My skin was pale, anemic under those lights. My eyes drawn. Everything moved slowly, like through water. When I finally left the bathroom, Chris was nowhere in sight. He'd left a note on the table, but I had crumbled it up and flushed it, too frightened to read it.

Something I'd always regretted.

I looked down at my hands, which I'd clenched together. One stiff finger at a time, I loosened them.

"I promised myself I'd never be that Rachelle again," I said quietly. "So I haven't been. The other day, I wanted to work out to make sure that I don't gain weight. That I'll never go back."

"You want to be the opposite of what you were?"

"Yes. I want to be thin. Confident. Not loud and obnoxious and opinionated. I thought it would finally make me feel happy."

"Are you happy?"

A long stretch of silence stretched between us, filled with a striking chill. My heart skipped a beat.

"No."

Janine let the quiet ride, and it sank all the way into my soul. When she spoke again, her voice was quiet.

"We create roles for ourselves throughout our whole lives, Rachelle. College student. Best friend. Mother. Daughter. Marathoner. Therapist. There are countless roles and countless ways to place them. The problem with roles is that they aren't really *who* we are. We sink into a role and allow it to define us, but roles aren't solid." She slid her hand back and forth, mimicking a shifting ground. "They move. If we base our self-worth on impermanent things, what happens?"

"It falls?"

"Precisely. At one point, you had an identity of being overweight. Correct?"

"Unfortunately."

"Now you've rejected that and made it about another thing: the marathon. What happened?"

My voice was hoarse when I whispered, "It's . . . gone."

Compassion filled her face when she nodded. "Yes. For now, the marathon will have to be put off. When the roles that define us crumble, what are we left with?"

"I don't know."

She leaned back in her chair. "The first time I met you, I asked you who you were."

"It's haunted me."

"I'm not surprised. I'm going to ask you again, but not today. I'm going to give you homework. This week, take away all your previous roles. Strip them away. Take away weight. Take away jean size. Take away family situations or college degrees or the hours you spend at the gym or what you like to do for fun. Think about who you are without them."

The idea of *stripping it away* made me think of all the plus-sized costumes I'd left hanging in my closet. Sadness had always overwhelmed me whenever I stepped out of them, as if I'd left a piece of myself behind. Embracing the person I *could* be in that costume instead of the person I *was* had been empowering. Left without the layers, who was I?

A deep chasm seemed to stretch out before me, into the beyond.

Into my soul. Into the layers of my heart that drummed a painful song. Perhaps my problems were deeper than I had ever imagined.

"Can you do that?" Janine asked, peering at me with an inquisitive gaze. "Can you think about who you are without roles?"

I nodded.

Janine lifted one side of her lips in a half smile. "You can. I *know* you can. There's no right or wrong answer, either. I want to know who *you* see without outside limits."

"All right."

"I know it feels overwhelming right now, but there is hope. You can find clarity and peace, but only if you show up. Only if *you* want it. Do you want it, Rachelle?"

The answer came from a warm, desperate spot deep inside my belly. "Yes."

She smiled. "Good. Then I'll see you next week."

Roles

That night after talking to Janine, I lay on my bed and watched the shadows deepen in my room. My ankle hovered above me on five pillows. Light from the television flickered underneath my doorway every few seconds. Outside, a mat of slate clouds had drifted in, drizzling rain against the window. Every now and then, a distant ripple of thunder boomed.

Unable to stand it, I pulled my leg off the pillows and sat on the edge of the bed. Fabric spilled out of my closet in gobs, either sparkling, shimmering, or blending in with the growing darkness. The old costumes were a siren song. I stood on my left foot, held onto the side of the closet, and reached out. Velvet, sequins, and tulle trickled past my fingertips.

A wedding dress.

A medieval peasant's garb.

A sequined evening gown. Bright red. It had fallen in layers around my body when I wore it. If I were to try it on tonight, it would be a robe that drowned me.

Bride, I thought, my gaze trailing past the wedding dress. *Peasant from a different time. A beautiful woman on the Vegas strip. Tavern wench. Rainbow Bright. Princess.*

So many costumes. So many . . . *roles.* I'd switched in and out of them like a crazy person, as if I couldn't stand my own life. Were costumes roles, too? Or were they just whimsical dreams of something I couldn't have?

When I settled back into my bed, I tried not to think about the scrapbook lying underneath me, chock full of photos, memories, and drawings of a simpler time. Surely those photographs would betray my roles. Or, more frightening, maybe I'd see what I was without them.

Rachelle as the overweight, plucky kid.

Rachelle as the bold and overbearing teenager who pretended to have no fear.

Rachelle when she was *happy*.

Unable to stop myself, I reached down, grabbed the edge of the binder, and pulled it out. For a long time, I stared at the cover, running the pad of my thumb over the construction paper. The tissue paper flowers we'd glued onto the front crinkled, stained yellow and ripped from years of childhood love. I caressed the pipe cleaners. The gritty glitter.

Two pictures tumbled out from the sides. I pulled them out by the corners. A toothy, chubby girl stared back at me from the top picture, clad in a pink tutu, with thick calves that spilled over her feet. Ice cream smeared her cheeks and ran down her knuckles. Me. Little Rachelle. I'd hated dance lessons. Not only the comments from the other girls about my chubby legs, but the lonely recitals—because Mom never came. I kept with it, though. I wanted to prove I could do anything the *skinny* girls did.

Stubborn, I thought. Was that a role or a trait?

I stroked the side of Little Rachelle's face with my fingertip, then shuffled to the other picture. It was taken two years ago, at my heaviest. I'd stuffed myself into a cosplay costume like a summer sausage. The same hefty feeling of disgust weighted my chest down. My hands burned just touching the photo, where I was smiling. I shoved the pictures back into the photo album, then stuffed the binder as far under the bed as it would go, closed my eyes, and fell into a restless sleep.

Over the past two years, the meetings of the Health and Happiness Society had morphed from a weight-loss accountability group—and the first thing to get me *really* started on the path to health—to a fitness accountability group, then a mostly health- and happiness-oriented one where we updated each other about our lives. Even at the height of my weight loss, Bitsy had refused to do weekly weigh-ins, though she'd never explained why.

When Bitsy perched her laptop on the coffee table across from me, I felt a warm tingle of anticipation. These were my people. My tribe. After all the horrible things that had happened, I just wanted to *talk* to them.

Seconds later, Megan's face popped into view. She wore a white headband, her dark hair pulled back into her usual braid, and a tank top. Sweat glistened across her forehead. She grinned as she slipped earbuds in.

"Sorry," she said, slightly breathless. "Just finished beating Justin in a trail run down the mountain."

A voice from off camera protested. Loudly. She laughed. A landscape of trees decorated the background behind her. From the bright light, it was obvious she sat outside somewhere, at her brother's summer camp Adventura, where she worked every summer as a nurse.

Another face popped up onto the screen next. Lexie. Her blonde hair was pulled back in a messy bun. She was rubbing her eyes, smearing her mascara with a grimace. What appeared to be a cupcake dropped off the screen suddenly.

"What was that?" Megan asked, leaning forward. "Looks delicious."

"Nothing!" Lexie cried. She licked her lips, where I swore a dab of frosting had just been sitting. "Just . . . it's been a bad day, all right! And double yikes. I look like I just woke up."

"Did you?" Bitsy asked.

"No, Mom," Lexie drawled. "But I did just finish a really gnarly test that took me hours. And a really long Zumba class. Let's not talk about it."

She ducked out of sight for a moment, no doubt to eat the rest of the cupcake. Bitsy rolled her eyes, and Megan laughed.

When Lexie reappeared, her mouth was full. She grinned with closed lips. Bitsy settled herself next to me on the couch.

"Mira is in Chicago this week with her brother," she said. "And we're right on time, as usual. It's just the four of us for now. Let's get started." Bitsy turned to me, her determination and verve burning hot as ever. "Rachelle, how was your week?"

Did I imagine the cord of intensity that ran through her question? She'd raised her eyebrows in expectation. Did she expect me to spill everything to them? My brow furrowed. Not that I minded. If there were any girls I could tell, it was them. Still . . . now that the moment was here, how was I supposed to summarize everything that had happened?

"Uh . . . busy?"

"Mira says you've been a lifesaver at the bakery," Bitsy said. "Said it's like you were born to be at the Frosting Cottage."

A knot formed in my chest. Born to be in a house of sugar and sweets? The hair on the back of my neck stood up at the thought.

"The world knows I was born to be there," Lexie muttered. Megan chortled, contorting into a pretzel stretch that I'd *kill* to be able to do right then.

"Bitsy told us about the job last week," Megan said. "Congrats. Seems like a fun time. How are you liking it?"

"It's not so bad, to be honest. But that's not really what I want to talk about. All of you heard I started counseling?"

Bitsy's eyes widened, like she hadn't wanted to bring it up. Lexie gasped. Megan dropped her stretch.

"What?" Lexie and Megan asked at the same time.

A smile twitched on Bitsy's lips. She cleared her throat and leaned back, gesturing for me to take the floor. I leaned closer to the computer screen and licked my lips.

"Let's get into all of that later. First, I need some help figuring something out, so I'm going to ask you a question."

"Therapy by Rachelle!" Lexie cried. "Bring. It. On."

"If you lost everything you had right now, who would you be?"

Megan's brow furrowed. Lexie's eyes widened. "Everything?" Lexie whispered.

"Yeah," I said. "Like, what if you weren't a nurse anymore, Megan? Or Lexie, what if you weren't married to Bradley?"

"I'd die!" Lexie squeaked.

Bitsy's smile became a knowing grin. "Ah," she whispered. "Janine is talking to you about roles."

"My therapist . . ." The words fell off my lips like burned cookies. It felt so *awkward* to say that. ". . . she wants me to imagine who I would be without all the roles I have. Like runner. Marathoner. Cupcake froster. Whatever."

A long silence prevailed—a telling testament. Megan's brow formed deep grooves. "You know? I don't know," she murmured. "I guess I'd still be myself. I'd still be a nurse, right?"

"But that's a role," I said.

"Yeah, but it's also a title. Are they the same things, then?"

I threw my hands in the air. "I have no idea."

"The idea," Bitsy said, "is to stop identifying yourself with what you *do* or what you *have*. All of that could change. You're supposed to burrow past that and figure out what makes you . . . you."

"And doesn't change," I muttered with a glance at my leg.

Bitsy nodded. "Right. So if you take that away, who are you?"

"Grief," Lexie muttered. "That's freaking deep. I'd love to peel away fifteen pounds. Is that the same thing?"

"No," I said, chuckling. "But I wish."

Megan tilted her head and stared into the distance, lost in thought. For a long stretch of time, no one spoke. Their silence was validating. It wasn't just me, then. At least I had that.

Bitsy grinned. "Confusing, isn't it?"

"If you've done it, you must have figured it out!" I said. "Help me, will you? I have no idea how to define myself without . . . roles or accomplishments or whatever."

"To be honest, I'd forgotten about working through this with Janine. I'd also forgotten how long it took me to work out."

"So you know the answer?"

"I know the answer for *me*. But that doesn't mean it will be the same for you."

"Tell me!"

Bitsy opened her mouth, then closed it. She shook her head. "No."

"What?" I snapped.

"No. It's good for you to have to figure it out."

"That's not fair."

"Isn't it?"

She seemed nonplussed in the face of my righteous indignation, and I realized there was nothing righteous about it. In fact . . . she *was* right. Whatever answer Bitsy had come around to, it wouldn't be the same as mine. At least Lexie still seemed puzzled.

"I don't know," Megan said, blinking. "Honestly. I can't think of a single thing or person that isn't defined by at least one role. Bitsy, you're a mama. An exerciser. A woman of power. Are those roles, too?"

"I'm a Little Debbie addict," Lexie said.

"Another identity that defines us." Bitsy's gaze met mine. "Just like being overweight, or a marathoner, or a food addict."

"But how can you just take those away? You can't. They're still definitive." I growled. "What's left? Emotions? Memories? Thoughts?"

"You."

Something bright in her gaze forced me to look away. I couldn't even face it. My life spun backward to the times when I had been happy with Lexie. When we had laughed and giggled over vats of caramel popcorn drizzled with chocolate, and tried to fantasize what it would be like to have Gerard Butler sweep us off our feet.

Being *fat* had been my identity.

"I was happy when I was defined by being fat," I said. The words spilled out of my mouth unexpectedly. Bitsy's eyebrows rose.

"What do you mean?"

"When I was fat, I was happy. At least I . . . was happier than I am now. Than I have been since—"

Since the night I messed up with Chris.

Another stretch of silence fell between all four of us, leaving us to our thoughts. My mind sank even farther into this abyss. Was I happy *because* I was fat? No. Because there had been moments of deepest loathing. Moments I had forgotten until right then. Moments when I forced myself to look in the mirror and see what I had become. But those had been few. Far between. They hadn't been every single day the way they were now. Sometimes every hour. Somewhere in losing weight, I'd started to think that shaming myself for the body I had would motivate me to something better.

No, something *thinner*.

"You were happier in some ways," Bitsy said. "But that doesn't mean you're doomed now."

"You'll figure it out, Rachelle," Megan said.

I didn't tell them that I felt like I was knocking against a darkness that was impossible to see. That I still could barely fathom the idea of not running the marathon, of not being defined by such a big accomplishment.

"Yeah," I whispered. "I know."

"So, you like Janine then?" Lexie asked, a glass of sweating ice water in her hands. "Sounds like you trust her."

"She seems all right."

"You'll keep going?" Bitsy asked. A hint of hope lingered in her voice, and I realized that they wanted me to get better almost *more* than I wanted to get better.

"Yes. For now, I will. I feel like I'm just stumbling around in the darkness, but I guess that's better than nothing."

"Maybe I should go see Janine," Lexie said. "She could finally get me off Little Debbie snacks. Which I only have in moderation!"

Bitsy grabbed her glass of unsweetened tea off the coffee table and clinked it against mine.

"Here's to the darkness."

Megan raised a water bottle. Lexie lifted her glass. We all air-clinked them through the screen.

"And here's to the light," Lexie said.

"So, Rachelle . . . what are your summer plans?"

Sophia propped her hands on the edge of the metallic table in the prep area of the Frosting Cottage. Her black hair fell between her shoulder blades in two braids. She wore her usual white apron, which wrapped around her thin waist. Above it hovered a purple crystal on a silver chain.

I glanced across the table at her. "Not much now that the marathon is off."

"No travel plans?"

"Not really."

"Do you have a job after the summer?"

"Not currently."

"College?"

"I dropped out."

She nodded once, as if considering something. Then she stared at me. Hard. The moments seemed to span an eternity but really must have only been a few seconds. I blinked. *Something* hung in the air between us.

"Ah, did you need—"

"No!" She straightened up with a forced smile. "Nope. Sorry. Just waiting for a bridal consultation. How is the new tip coming along?"

I glanced down. A tray of chocolate cupcakes awaited me, fanned by four bowls of frosting—bright teal, crimson, tiger-stripe orange, and butter yellow. For each color, I used a bag and a generous tip to deposit a large dollop that covered a quarter of the cupcakes' top. I held onto a bag of the yellow frosting, which had a round tip instead of the open star I'd been using the last two days.

"Good. I like the star tips."

"Me too."

I tilted my head to the side. "The round are a little more simplistic. I like that too. I think, with certain flavors, it goes better. Not as much pizazz."

She lifted an eyebrow. "Pizazz? Give me an example."

Heat warmed my cheeks. Was I being too intense about cupcakes and frosting? This analysis felt a little too . . . in depth. I mean, it was *frosting*. Then again, she wasn't laughing at me, so I decided to go with it.

"The white cupcakes with the white frosting and silver ball sprinkles for the little girls' tea party were perfect with the star tip," I said. "The texture of the frosting added just a little more decoration to a mostly uniform cupcake that helped highlight and hold the sprinkles. In these bright numbers, the frosting color makes its own statement. Leaving it rounded helps the colors . . . be themselves."

Feeling really stupid now, I turned slightly to the side. From the corner of my eye, I saw Sophia's brow had furrowed. She stared at the wall with a distant expression.

"You know, Rachelle, you are absolutely right," she murmured. Then she straightened and headed across the room, calling over her shoulder, "Do me a favor? Try this lemonade for me. Tell me what's wrong with it?"

Before I could protest, she reached into the fridge, grabbed a pitcher, poured a bright yellow liquid into a cup, and shoved it into my hand. Her intent gaze intimidated me. I stared down at it, shocked. I hadn't had lemonade—or any other sugary drink—in a year and a half.

I opened my mouth to protest but stopped. Without exercise, the extra sugar would either make me hyper . . . or binge primed. Lexie and I used to drink lemonade by the liter. We'd mix it with Sprite and make slushes out of it. Just the memory of the tart, cool liquid in the summer heat almost made me sweat.

Could I handle it?

"Rachelle?" Sophia broke through my reverie. "You all right?"

"What? Oh. Yes. Fine, thanks."

"You're kind of pale. Is it too hot in here?"

"No, no. I'm fine." I reached for the lemonade and sipped it. A shockingly sweet taste spread through my mouth with a punch. My lips puckered, overwhelmed by the saccharine taste, almost gritty on my tongue. Sophia's shoulders slumped.

"That bad, eh?" she asked.

"Not *bad*. Just . . ." I smacked my lips. "Ah . . . strong on the sweetness."

She frowned. "I can't get the right lemon-to-sugar ratio. Some people like it strong, some like it subtle. It's hard to really get right, especially when making a simple syrup out of it."

"Let the lemon do all the work. It's citrus. Citrus can carry itself with the right ratio. I'd cut the sugar by half and add fresh-squeezed lemon juice if you didn't start with that."

"Sounds simple."

"If you can get it, a drop or two of mint extract. Perfect summer drink."

Sophia leaned back against the counter, arms folded across her slender chest as she chewed on her bottom lip. Her lithe legs and sculpted face and neck always drew my attention. She had such casual grace. A question flowed out of me before I could stop it.

"How do you stay so skinny, Sophia?"

I'd spent enough time here to know that her diet consisted mostly of salads and fresh veggies. Seeing her eat the same thing as me was gratifying, but I cared more about her exercise regime.

"Willpower, mostly," she said with a wry grin.

"Cardio?"

She nodded. "Mixed with weights. I do thirty minutes of each before I come into work every morning."

"That's it?"

"That's it."

That seemed impossible. I'd been doing *hours* of cardio every day for the past three months in an attempt to break the 150-pound weight barrier. Still, I hadn't managed it. Considering my current state of health, I wouldn't for a while.

"Oh."

The tinkle of the door opening broke the silence. On cue, Sophia whirled around with her usual bright smile. A young woman and her mother appeared.

"Come inside!" Sophia said. "It's so good to meet you. I'm Sophia."

They faded into the consultation room amid a chatter of voices. I turned back to the cupcakes, grateful for my simple job. Cupcakes. Frosting. Food coloring. Didn't get too much easier. No doubt Sophia thought I took food a little too seriously. But when you had as much experience with sugar as I did . . .

I stopped to mentally assess my state of mind. No ogre had grown out of my body after I drank the lemonade. I didn't feel like flinging myself across the room, climbing on the counter, and shoving frosting into my mouth by the fistful. I felt . . . fine. In control. No need to rush to exercise every morsel of sugar off.

Reassuring.

The next hour passed in a quiet routine. Cupcakes off the trays. Frost. Decorate. Repeat. Reload frosting. Bundle cupcakes into boxes. Help a customer. Rest my leg for a few minutes while perusing the recipes for the next day. Think about roles and then imagine a lump of color that didn't actually create an actual person but had nothing else defining it. But even then, didn't the color define it? Around two o'clock, a reverberating *boom* came from the back door. I stopped scrubbing a few leftover cake pans and peered over my shoulder. "Hello?"

Four boxes lined the narrow walkway leading to the back door, which opened into a dingy alley that always smelled like garbage. A whiff of hot waste wafted in from the open door. My nose wrinkled. Gross. Who would leave that door open? Who would even *come in* that door? We had to keep the store cool or the cakes wouldn't set right. Four cardboard boxes were splayed across the ground, like someone had dropped them and run. I hobbled over with one crutch.

"Um, hello?"

The silhouette of a slender man appeared with three boxes piled in his arms.

"Who are you?" I asked.

He jumped with a shout, dropping the boxes, one of which fell on his converse sneaker. He flailed and tumbled to his backside, striking the back of his head on the doorframe. I shrieked and dropped my crutch, which clattered on top of his head. One of the boxes had burst open, spilling a plastic jar of edible blue food coloring.

"What the—"

"Who are you?" I cried at the same time.

He scowled and rubbed the back of his head. "I'm delivering Sophia's supplies."

"Oh."

"Who are *you*?"

"I'm Rachelle. Sophia just hired me."

He glanced behind me, suspicion in his bright emerald gaze. His clean-cut blond hair appeared recently tousled. He wore an old pair of jeans and a dirty white t-shirt over his thin shoulders and slender torso. Over his shoulder, I caught a glimpse of the alley, where an old pickup truck with peeling paint and rust spots idled.

"Sophia would have told me if she hired someone else," he snapped. "Where is she?"

"She's busy."

"You're not trying to steal something, are you? One of her recipes? The new lemonade?"

"Ew. No! Have you tried it?"

He scowled. "People are always trying to steal from her. I'm calling her right now."

"What?" I screeched. "No! Stop. She's in a consultation. Do I *look* like someone who's trying to steal from a bakery?"

I spread my arms, drawing attention to the frosting-stained apron. Powdered sugar still dotted the front. The scent of bleach drifted from my hands. His shoulders relaxed a little.

"And a not-very-original bakery at that," I added. "Kate went into early labor, all right? I've just been filling in."

"Fine." He stood up and brushed himself off. "Whatever. I don't have time for this."

What was *with* him? Who was that paranoid about burglary, anyway? He must have some sort of relationship with Sophia. He squatted down to pick up the scattered supplies. I attempted to help by grabbing my crutch. The shoulder padding hooked a bag of baking powder and pulled it my way just as he reached for it. He scowled again and glanced at his watch.

"Late," he muttered. "Stupid—"

"Sorry. Look, I can get this if you need to go."

Grumpy-face didn't answer, but his jaw tightened. He pointed at my boot and crutches. "Can you?"

"Listen, I'm sorry about what happened. I just . . . you startled me. She didn't tell me to expect a delivery and I'm new here."

He said nothing. His nostrils flared as he shoved the rest of the things back into the box and straightened up. Just as I hobbled out of his way, he slid past me, deftly avoiding getting tangled in the crutches. I followed him into the prep area. He started to sling the boxes onto the table, but I stopped him with a cry.

"Wait! I just sanitized that."

He clenched his teeth. The muscles in his neck tightened. "Then where do you want them?" he muttered.

"Just put them . . . over there."

I pointed to the far counter on the other side of the room, then regretted it when he ground his teeth. Almost at a run, he loped across the room, shoved the boxes onto the counter, and dashed back for the others. Even before my injury, I couldn't have moved as fast as him.

"What are you late for?" I asked.

"Class."

My eyes widened. He had to be at least twenty-eight. "You're in *college?*"

The end of a tattoo on his arm peeked out from underneath his long sleeve—which seemed an odd fashion choice in such intense summer heat. When he turned to grab the last box, I caught sight of an old piercing in his right ear. No. Scratch that. Piercings *all* the way up the shell of his ear, in fact. He had to have had eight at one point. Was that the top half of a skull tattoo on the back of his neck?

How intriguing.

"Yeah," he muttered and shoved the last box onto the counter. "In college."

He disappeared out the back and slammed his door before I heard the angry belch of a truck speeding out of the alley.

I drew in a deep breath and let it back out.

What a strange delivery man.

Staring at the close, fading confines of my bedroom the next day left me with a blank feeling inside. This old trailer—which hadn't even been new when Mom and Dad bought it before their divorce—had long been declining. Rusted spots covered the exterior. The windowpane above my bed cracked when I was ten, and we still hadn't fixed it. In the wind, it whistled. Even the carpet seemed dead. Weather beaten. Too tired to fight back.

"Grief," I muttered. "I need to move."

I'd accepted that the marathon wouldn't happen this year. Now, I just yearned for life without crutches. They hurt my armpits and wore calluses on the heel of my hands. Not to mention how much easier life would be if I didn't have to haul them with me everywhere.

The usual murmur of the television filled the living room when I stepped out of my room. Mom sat on the couch, surrounded by a wall of three different bags of potato chips and a plastic cup of sunflower seed shells. The sparkly foil of a candy bar wrapper gleamed from the ground. She normally hid her candy splurges. Maybe she didn't care anymore.

The A/C unit groaned from the window right across from her, blowing with full force. Two other fans were pointed her way, and perspiration still dotted her forehead. She wiped at it with her sleeve.

Mail scattered the floor by the front door. Mom always left it there—she couldn't safely bend over—so I carefully balanced on one leg and lowered myself down. Nothing of consequence. I padded into the living room and tossed the envelopes onto the couch next to her. She glanced at it, then picked up the remote and flipped to another channel.

My stomach growled. Maybe I was hungry. Still, I searched the fridge and settled on some cut-up watermelon and a water bottle. The air was cooler out here than in my room. I relished it while I slurped the slushy fruit pieces. Mom whizzed through the television channels, her legs propped up on an ottoman. Dishes cluttered the sink, and dots of food littered the floor. I frowned.

Why was it so dirty?

Because I'm the one who cleans, I thought. Another role? If so, a stupid one. I blinked. If my role was to clean—which, in hindsight, it absolutely was—then what was Mom's? The sound of her voice startled me out of my thoughts.

"You going to be home tomorrow?" she asked.

I turned around. "No. I have work all day again."

"Oh."

"Need something?"

"Just out of a few things in the kitchen."

My chest felt heavy again. Was it disgust? I couldn't tell sometimes. The sheer fact that I didn't really recognize most of my emotions still startled me.

"I don't think I can get it."

"Why not?"

"My ankle?"

Her brow furrowed. "Oh. Right. How is that, by the way?"

"Ah, it's coming along." I moved out of the kitchen, past the table still piled high with unopened food, and toward the living room. I stopped just behind the couch. "Can you have it delivered instead? I still can't drive. Bitsy has been taking me to work every day, and I have an appointment with Ja . . . I have a thing tomorrow."

Her brow furrowed. "Yeah, I just hate the extra charge."

No, I thought. *You just hate getting it from the porch and bringing it inside.*

Another role? No. That was a chore. Not a role. Perhaps Mom's role was even more subtle than mine. Moneymaker. No, graphic designer? Sort of. Thinking about roles in terms of her life was even more confusing than my own. If I peeled away what my mom did—which wasn't decidedly easy because she didn't actually do much—what was left?

A woman addicted to food?

I shook my head to clear the thoughts. "Sorry about the charge, but I don't think we can avoid it for a while," I said.

She grabbed another potato chip and crunched into it. "You get a new job?"

"Yeah. Temporary. Working at a bakery. I'm done in just a few days."

She met my gaze for the first time. "Oh?" Her voice lifted. "Didn't know that. The food good?"

A rush of something cold trickled down my spine. "Not sure. I haven't had any."

"None?"

"None."

"Well, you'll have to bring home any day-old stuff sometime."

"Yeah." My heart sank, and I didn't know why. "Sure."

The television pulled her back with its tenacious tentacles. My mouth opened, then closed. Words I wanted to say sat on the tip of my tongue. *Did you see me when I was a teenager? Did you know what decisions I was making while you escaped with the television?*

Did you care?

I brushed the questions away. They'd arisen before. I'd never voiced them. Of course she *cared*. It was just different now. It hadn't always been this way, of course. Back when we bonded over food and being overweight, our relationship had been stronger. Intense—swinging from hatred to love like a pendulum—but at least it'd had substance. Losing 110 pounds had changed everything.

Now I wasn't sure that I knew her at all.

"Hey, Mom. What's your favorite food?"

Her brow furrowed in concentration. "Not sure if I could really pin it down. I love pasta in all its many forms. Although a good piece of fried chicken sometimes hits the spot. Then again, Chinese sounds good too." She glanced up at me. "Why?"

"Just curious."

"Huh. What about you?"

Arrested by surprise—this was the first attempt on her part to have a conversation in a long time—I paused. A spark of the mom I used to know still lived within her.

"I'm pretty partial to Thai food these days."

"Chicken pad thai is yummy."

"Hey, did you ever look at the ingredient list for that carrot cake? Still sounds good to me."

She hesitated, a chip halfway to her mouth. "Oh, no. I forgot."

"Okay. Well, whenever you want."

She gave me a thumbs-up, then disappeared back into her television show. I rinsed out the watermelon container, put it into the dishwasher along with the fork, and hobbled back to my room with my water bottle in hand. As soon as the door muffled the sounds of the TV, I breathed easy again.

Forgiveness

The next day, I walked into Wings of Hope Counseling Services alone. Bitsy dropped me off before running to pick up her daughters from soccer practice. The sweltering summer air followed me inside. The receptionist—who I finally remembered was named Margery—smiled.

"Welcome back, Rachelle. Janine will be ready in just a moment."

"Thanks. Oh, I meant to ask, when do I get billed?"

"Billed?"

"Yeah. I haven't received anything in the mail. Bitsy said she'd pay my first one, but last week was *technically* my second. Do I pay as I go? Bill it to insurance or something? I doubt I'm covered."

Her brow furrowed. She tapped on her keyboard, perused something, then smiled brightly again. "It's all taken care of."

"Oh. But . . . I need to pay something eventually, right?"

She smiled again. "All covered."

I squinted. "Bitsy?"

"They asked not to be named and wished to remain anonymous."

"Uh . . . okay."

Before I could make my way to the waiting room, Janine slipped out of her office with her usual warm smile. "Come on back, Rachelle. It's good to see you again."

"Hi."

When I settled on the couch, nervousness fluttered in my belly. I hadn't figured out who I was without my roles. However, I didn't feel the same sense of dread that the last two visits had triggered. That was something.

"So?" Janine asked, eyebrows high. "How are you?"

"Good."

"Did your week go all right?"

She sat in her usual chair, ivory pumps crossed at the ankles, a modest, knee-length skirt and matching teal blazer completing her usual ensemble. She smiled in that non-judgmental way she had. Somehow, I could tell she actually cared.

I shrugged. "I think so."

"A good start. How did your homework go?"

I chewed my lower lip, then stopped. No doubt Janine was analyzing everything—even my nervous tics.

"Ah, I thought about it all the time, it feels like. But I don't really know the answer."

"Good! What did you find?"

"To be honest? Nothing."

"Nothing?"

"Well, if I have nothing to define me, who am I? I mean, how do you quantify or measure that? What am I supposed to picture without accomplishments or roles?"

A ghost of a smile appeared on her face. "An excellent question."

"What's the answer?"

Her head tilted to the side. "It's not an answer I can give you. But for me, I find it's most clear when I'm at my lowest."

Her reply muddled my brain even more, like a kid stepping into an already-murky puddle. Why would *anything* be clear in moments of anguish? I thought back to the night I'd embarrassed myself in front of Chris. No. There was nothing existentially clear or redeemable about myself then. Janine grabbed a pen from a nearby desk and wrote something on the legal pad that rested on her knees.

"Keep thinking on that, Rachelle. Let me know if you make progress. In the meantime, I want to address something we didn't dive into on the last visit. Something about Chris."

I shifted, shrinking back into the chair. My voice felt hoarse. "All right."

"You said you cared for him in a way that you'd never cared for any other man."

"Yes."

"Tell me more about your dating background."

Her request caught me off guard. What did that have to do with Chris?

"Uh . . . okay. It can be summarized by saying that I've dated a lot of jerks. Chris was the first one that wasn't."

"What do you mean by jerks?"

I shrugged. "Losers. I mean, maybe they were just desperate like me. They were someone I could get, at least. That was hard enough."

"You mean get their attention?"

"Or sex."

My mind trailed back to the plethora of gaming geeks, nerds, football players, tattoo obsessers, and other creeps I'd tried out in high school and early college. Something sticky filled my chest at the thought. No wonder they'd always been so eager to get their hands on my chest—I'd basically thrown it at them and acted like I liked it.

"Did you date many of them?" Janine asked.

"I slept with many of them, if that's what you're asking."

Her expression softened. "No, but it's interesting that you say that. Care to elaborate?"

No, I didn't want to. This was another sticky place I hadn't visited . . . maybe ever. The flood of heat that filled my chest startled me, but I pressed on.

"I lost my virginity when I was fourteen."

"Quite young."

"By choice," I said. "I wasn't raped. It was a kid down the street. We were young and stupid, and I was willing and curious, so we did it in his backyard, behind a tree where his parents couldn't see us."

"How does that make you feel now?"

To my surprise, tears filled my eyes. I blinked them back. I *had* wanted to have sex with him. To see what all the fuss was about. To feel . . . *special*. It had been the first for both of us, and had left me a shattered wreck for a week afterwards. Just long enough to clear my head and go for it again when he came back the next week. Our stupid fling only lasted for a few months, but it had been enough to turn the tide. To show me how to get their attention, fat or not. And how to make it worth their while.

"I don't know," I whispered, voice husky. "I just . . . I was too young to know what I was really doing or how dangerous it was. I started my period at twelve, so I could have gotten pregnant."

"How does it make you *feel*?"

"It makes me sad, I guess."

Her expression softened. "That's a lot to take on for a girl that age. Do your parents know?"

"Geez, no! Mom never asked me about that kind of stuff, and Dad left when I was five."

She marked something on her paper with a quick scratch. When she straightened, her gaze met mine.

"There's more at work here than you may think. Anytime you date people that you know don't measure up or aren't sincere, it's because you subconsciously don't want it to work out."

"I never went into a relationship hoping it would die," I said, then silently added, *Never thought it would work, either.*

"On the surface, likely not. But on a subconscious level, pursuing a relationship that's doomed to fail is a safety mechanism. When—or if—they reject you, it's not your fault. You're off the hook. It has nothing to do with *you*. It's all about them and their issues."

"I never thought of it that way."

"We often don't."

"I guess it makes sense. Whenever it didn't work out, which was every single time, I didn't really care *that* much. Beyond being bummed that I'd have to start the chase yet again."

"Self-sabotaging in that way and setting ourselves up to fail becomes a learned behavior. Think about your date with Chris, for example. You self-sabotaged there, didn't you?"

Hadn't there been something inside me that felt no surprise? That was resigned—maybe relieved when he was out of the picture? Perfect, dateable Chris, who would have been a great boyfriend. Chris, who would never have accepted me and all the ghosts I brought with me.

Dear heavens. She was right.

"Oh. I did."

"Why? Why did you sabotage the guy that could have been a healthy relationship for you?"

"I don't know."

"Say the first thing that comes to mind."

For several moments, I mentally cast about, as if groping through the darkness would make it clear. There were tendrils. Brief thoughts. But the moment I tried to grab them, they slipped away.

"I-I don't know. I guess because relationships don't really work, so why even try?"

She straightened up. "Why not?"

"They never have. Except for Lexie and Bradley, but they're kind of an exception. Bitsy's divorced. Mira's husband is dead. Megan went through so many men it's not even funny. Then my parents were obviously failures . . ."

"Tell me about your parents."

"They married. They fell apart. They divorced when I was five after Dad disappeared and never came back. Mom . . . never really left the house much after that."

Her pen scribbled on the legal pad yet again. I wondered if I'd ever get to see the notes.

"What do you think it would take for you to have compassion for yourself?" she asked.

"Excuse me?"

"Would it be difficult for you to look back on all of those times when you dated jerks, when you reached out for attention through sex, when you broke that table with Chris, and forgive yourself for it?"

Was that even possible?

"I-I don't know. I mean . . . I slept with guys that I hated. I let them touch me when it grossed me out. I sabotaged my chance with Chris because it's like . . . it's like I'm afraid to be happy."

Janine pursed her lips together. "Let's take a slightly different tack here. Who is your best friend?"

"Lexie."

"Do you love her?"

"More than anyone. She's always been there for me. Always."

Ferocity resounded in my voice. I felt it all the way to my bones.

"Would you ever tell Lexie that she was disgusting?"

"What? No!"

"Why not?"

"Lexie would never do what I did."

"Let's pretend she did. Swap positions." Janine leaned forward. "Close your eyes, and think about it. It's not going to be comfortable, but it's not supposed to be."

With great reluctance, I obeyed.

"Okay."

"Imagine Lexie so desperate for attention that she'll reach out to anyone who offers it in any form. Imagine her a lonely child. She's lost without her father. Her mother is a single mom. Imagine Lexie breaking a table because she's desperate to impress the guy that she likes. Imagine her filled with disgust and hatred for herself afterward. What do you have to say to her?"

My chest filled with something hot. It rose in my throat, blocking my voice. If Lexie had been so desperate? I'd put my arms around her. I'd love her with the same fierce and protective love I'd always had.

"I . . . would tell her that I love her."

"And?"

"It's not her fault her parents messed up. And her cry for attention was just desperation. It was coping with cards she didn't ask for. She . . ." My throat bobbed up and down. I swallowed back tears. "She was doing the best she could."

"Is it possible to feel compassion for Lexie? Even though she feels embarrassed and ashamed?"

"Of course."

"Now, remove Lexie. Go back to that fourteen-year-old Rachelle so desperate for attention that she turns to the neighbor boy even when she hates it. The girl who feels she must do those things in order to be loved and special. Can you describe her to me?"

Picturing myself at that age came easy. Jeans. Tank tops even though my arms had rolls. Long hair. Too much makeup. Constantly chewing gum and talking too loud, as if no one could hear me. Instead of obnoxious and larger than life, I just looked . . . lost.

"I'm—or is it *she*?—is sad. Maybe confused. She keeps looking around, like she's waiting for someone to show up."

"Can you see that fourteen-year-old Rachelle acted out of desperation?"

"Yes."

"Can you wrap your arms around her in compassion and tell her that you love her?"

Just thinking about it felt strange. Out of sorts. But in that tangle of awkwardness lurked a desire to do it.

"I can try."

"Love that scared teenager, Rachelle. Because you *are* her. And no matter what you've done, you deserve love. No matter who you are, you deserve love. You have value just *being*. You deserved healthy, compassionate love, and you can give it to yourself now."

An eternity seemed to pass while I tried to imagine myself holding the frightened, vulnerable version of me. Memories rolled through my mind. The night after I gave my virginity away, I'd bled. I'd never known I would bleed. Terror had filled me. I'd cried for an hour, too scared to tell Mom. Instead, I'd called Lexie. Whispered what had happened. She reassured me. Googled it. Told me it was normal. I held onto that desperation, remembering how lonely it felt to be in that trailer. My hands tightened into fists. My eyes flew open. Janine watched me with a mixture of concern and compassion.

"It wasn't my fault," I said.

"No. It wasn't."

"I always thought it was."

"It was a cry for help from a little girl who desperately needed it. That's what I want you to do for your homework this week. Think of all the times you hated yourself. Think of times when you felt you'd done something unforgivable. Then let it go. Forgive yourself."

A feeling of dubious uncertainty crawled over me. "I guess I can try."

"That's all I ask."

Late that night, Lexie's groggy voice answered the phone.

"'lo?"

"Lexie?"

"Chelle?" A note of panic awakened in her voice. "Everything okay?"

A rustle moved in the background, as if she were climbing out of bed. I glanced at the alarm clock next to my bed. 12:34 a.m. I grimaced.

"Yes. I'm fine. Nothing bad's happened. Maybe I shouldn't have called. I'm sorry, I—"

She yawned. I thought I heard a door close. "It's fine. What's up?"

"I, uh . . ."

The words that had once been so clear suddenly thickened. I

swallowed hard. The session with Janine that afternoon still lay heavy on my mind. Compassion. Forgiveness. Roles. False blame.

Attempting to straighten it all out had just led to a sleepless, frantic night with no treadmill in sight. Without my injury, this would have been an eight-mile run kind of night. In desperation, I'd reached out to the person who'd always been there.

"I wanted to call and thank you," I said, swallowing hard.

"Thank me?"

"I just . . . I had to call. I had to."

Her voice was clearer this time, even though I could tell she was fighting off a yawn. "What's going on?"

"Thank you for being my friend."

She paused. "Rachelle, you aren't dying or something, are you?"

A long breath whooshed out of me. "No. It's Janine, Bitsy's therapist. And mine, now, I guess. I've only been to two full sessions now. I haven't told you many details about it because . . . well, I guess I'm still trying to figure it out myself."

"That's all right. You gotta do this on your own terms. You told me at the meeting that you were seeing her."

"Yeah, but Lexie, we're tight. We're sisters. I always tell you everything. It's been killing me to keep it from you. That's . . . that's why I had to call tonight. I had to tell you what we talked about today and thank you for all you've done for me. I need to just . . . I need to repeat what Janine told me. I think it will help. Can we do that?"

"Heck yes we can. Tell me everything."

"It started when she asked about Chris."

For the next half hour, I relayed everything I could remember in a haphazard tangle. She interrupted only to ask a clarifying question or react to something. By the time I ran out of steam, a stunned silence filled the phone. I pressed the phone harder into the shell of my ear.

"Lex?"

"Goodness, Rachelle. I don't know what to say."

I let out a long breath. That, in itself, was validating. "Me neither."

"That's only been *two* sessions? Yikes. Can you imagine what it'll be like when you've gone ten times?"

"Some people do therapy for years."

She laughed. "I'll probably end up being one of them. So, what is it?"

"What is what?"

"What's going to be the hardest thing for you to forgive yourself for?"

I knew the answer right away, even though I didn't want to say it. A lot of water churned under this bridge.

"Chris," I whispered. "Messing up with that."

"What's it going to take for you to forgive yourself?"

"I don't know. I really don't."

"I mean, how do you feel now after talking about it? I've never thought of forgiving myself, and my mind is still reeling from that whole roles thing you brought up. I can't imagine how you must feel right now."

"I don't know. I don't feel any different. Just more confused, I guess. I've been thinking a lot. That maybe if all of these things I did was just me trying to get attention and survive, then I guess this means that I'm not despicable? Is that a totally weird conclusion?"

"No! Of course you aren't despicable. Did you really think that?"

"It seems so easy for you to know that, but it never was for me. I thought . . . I thought I was just . . . someone who didn't deserve any better. But that wasn't true. I was actually just scared."

"You just wanted to be special."

"Yeah."

"You *are* special, Rachelle. You are. I hope, through working with Janine, you'll be able to see that. It's so clear to me and Bitsy and Megan and Mira. Always has been. Maybe you'll get to understand that too, eventually."

I didn't. Not yet. But I felt one step closer. Like I'd advanced farther into the darkness, although the light in the distance seemed so dim and cold still.

"Me too."

"I love you like crazy, Chelle."

"I love you too, Lex."

"Please keep calling me about this?" she said, a note of pleading in her voice. "Only when you want to, of course. When you're ready. Being married to Bradley doesn't change the fact that you and I are sisters. I'm here for you. You are special to me. And I will never let you stray too far away."

Tears clogged my voice. "Love you."

"Love you too."

"We'll talk soon. I promise."

"If we didn't, I'd hunt you down so fast . . ."

After I hung up, the phone clattered back to my nightstand. I stared at the dark ceiling. A storm brewed outside, blowing the lilac bush into a tizzy. Light flickered under my door. Mom had stopped going to her room to sleep for the last week. She just camped on the couch now, propped up by pillows. The resonance of her deep snores often woke me up. I didn't think she *could* sleep laying down now, with the weight of her body pressing on her.

The distant sound of thunder mingled with the laugh track of a late-night comedian. I closed my eyes and slipped into a deep sleep.

Mira picked me up the next morning with a broad smile, her eyelids lined with taxi-cab yellow eye shadow.

"I'm back, sugar!" she cried.

My crutches clattered against each other when I tugged them inside her car and balanced them between my knees. The scent of potpourri filled the car with a cloying smell. Mira grinned, her lips stained with pink lipstick.

"I'm so glad!" I tugged the heavy Cadillac door shut. "It's good to see you again. How's your brother recovering from the surgery?"

"He's good. My sister-in-law can handle it all now that I got the house cleaned. Bitsy would have had a seizure if she'd seen the place. How'd things go at the bakery?"

"Seemed fine."

Mira's gaze tapered. "Did she push the lemonade on you?"

I laughed. "Yes! It was disgusting."

"I know. All belted up? Let's go!" Her tires shrieked as we peeled away from the curb. "She really needs to listen to me and stop trying to make it work. It's like she's serving concentrate, but she just can't bring herself to water it down."

While we careened through the streets, I held onto the seat and braced myself at every turn. Mira chatted about a bad drive and her eagerness to get back to her shop again.

"Can I ask you a question?" I asked when we stopped at a red light.

"Sure, honey."

"Have you ever made any big mistakes?"

She tilted her head to the side. "Of course I have."

"Would you mind if I asked what they were?"

"No." She paused, blinking. "I guess my biggest mistake was getting into an argument with my husband right before he died. Of course, I didn't *know* he was going to die the next morning, and he could be a very ornery man. But still . . . that stung."

"Does it sting anymore?"

"No. Not really."

"Why not?"

"Because I moved past it."

"How?"

"You know . . . I don't know."

"I mean, did you feel like you had to forgive yourself for it?"

"Hmm . . ." Mira made a sound deep in her throat. "I suppose I did. Although I never thought of it in those terms."

I leaned closer to her. "How did you just forgive yourself?"

"I think it happened when I realized that my guilt wasn't actually making me feel any better. Seemed silly to hold onto it if I didn't control the outcome. I mean, my husband had already died, and it had just been an argument. We had them all the time. I loved him, he loved me. That argument didn't define our whole relationship."

That argument didn't define our whole relationship. Just like, on some level, my past didn't define my entire personality, I presumed. I sank deeper into the chair, riding that thought out.

"Thanks, Mira."

"Anytime, honey."

By the time we made it to the Frosting Cottage, the *open* sign had already been flipped over and a customer was walking out of the shop. With a sigh of relief that I'd survived the trip, I climbed out of the car. Inside, Sophia stood at the prep table, a plethora of papers sprawled around her. She wore no hat today, which meant Mira and I would be running the food prep. Or would it just be Mira? Or just me? Now that Mira was back, I wasn't sure what would happen. The thought that this might be my last day felt a little . . . empty.

Fatigue lines rimmed Sophia's eyes when she glanced up at us, which seemed an exceptionally bright hazel color without the brim of the hat in the way. She perked up when she saw Mira.

"You're back!"

"Just to drop Rachelle off. I need to head into the sewing shop."

"That's right. I almost forgot. Time moves so quickly." Sophia turned to me. "Might as well get this over with, then. You want a job, Rachelle?"

I paused halfway into the prep room, stunned by the unexpected question.

"Me?"

"Yes, you. I used last week as a test to see if we would work well together. I definitely think we would."

"Oh. I hadn't expected this. I . . . really?"

Sophia laughed. "A promising start."

Mira nudged me from behind. "I know you're afraid of all the food, but it's not going to eat you. The reverse, actually. Besides, you'd be working in a bakery. That's Lexie's dream! You were made for this, Rachelle."

She had a point. No one knew sugar the way I did. Well, maybe Lexie, but she wasn't versed in the technicals. If Mom had given me anything, it was the knowledge of how to putter my way around a kitchen and make food that was worth the time. Especially baked goods. Before she went on her Italian spree, I had years of growing up on homemade cakes, muffins, scones, and just about any pastry with sugar in or on it. We never bought donuts—we'd always made our own. Maple frosting and all.

"I-I just mean . . . I didn't know you were looking," I said.

What I meant to say was *I didn't think you could afford it,* but luckily I restrained myself. Cupcake bulks sales had been slowing down in the past few days. Now that SummerFest had ended, only a handful of events would crop up here and there. If anything, it would make more sense for her to call me to fill in when she needed extra help.

Sophia sighed, eyeing the paperwork sprawled across the table. "I'll be honest—I can't guarantee how long we'll be open. Things aren't going well right now. The only thing keeping this place alive—and my mortgage from crashing into the fiery pits of hell—are the wedding cakes."

My gaze drifted to the glass display. Her offerings lacked pizzazz in a desperate way. She donated food to the homeless shelter more than any business owner should have to.

"It doesn't bother you that I dropped out of college and used to be fat?" I asked. "I could go on a rampage one day and clean you out."

She tilted her head back and laughed. "I have my doubts that will happen. For what it's worth, I dropped out of college too. Twice."

My eyes widened. Twice? The word *unforgivable* filtered through my mind. Once felt bad to me, but to drop out twice was serious business. How did she ever get through the third attempt?

Or did she?

"Seriously?" I asked.

"I eventually went back when I hit my mid-thirties. Got my master's in business once I figured out what I wanted to do."

"Was it hard to go back?"

Or to accept that you'd failed twice? I'd been drowning in the shame of letting college go just once.

"Yeah. Worked out great."

Her laissez-faire attitude hit me like a cream pie. She just . . . let it go. Forgave herself, just like Mira. It didn't make *sense*. How could it be so simple for them?

"Admittedly," Sophia continued, "I probably should have at least taken a few classes in culinary science." Her rueful gaze trailed back to the counter. "I think my recipe creation skills lack a little flair."

They definitely did.

The idea of working full time here would have terrified me a week ago considering my historical love affair with baked goods. Aside from the lemonade, I still hadn't broken my streak and eaten anything she'd offered. Not to mention that fifteen dollars an hour was more than I'd ever made. Once my ankle healed, I could still exercise before and after work, which meant training wouldn't have to stop. I chewed on the inside of my cheek.

What other prospects loomed ahead of me, anyway?

"What are the details?" I asked.

"Comes with full training on all of the desserts. You'd run the kitchen while I did the business and the cakes. Depending on how things go, we could have an eventual transition into the cakes. Pay's $15.00 an hour. More as your skillset increases. Hours from 10-6. My hope is that turning my focus away from production will help me pull my marketing together."

"Sounds like a dream," I murmured.

She grinned. "It's not so bad." Her smile fell. "Assuming we stay open, that is."

"I'm not kidding about the fat thing. I could have wiped your store out for breakfast and come back for brunch."

She belly-laughed again. "Trust me, Rachelle. I'm harboring an inner fat kid too. Every now and then, she comes out. It's all good."

"Then . . . yes. I'd love to work here full time."

To my surprise, a thrill of excitement fluttered through me. One I hadn't felt in a long time. Mira clapped, and Sophia let out a long breath of relief.

"I can't tell you how relieved I am. Thank you *so* much. I'll do my best to make sure you have a sustained job here, I promise."

I had no doubt she'd try.

I had major doubts she'd succeed.

My first few days as an official employee crept by.

Not only had cupcake orders slowed almost to a halt, but it seemed as if everyone had left town in the middle of the week. Despite the summer tourism into downtown, no one wanted to stop in. Sophia stood at the window often, fists propped on her hips. Wedding cake orders came in at a steady trickle, so she trained me on three different types of frosting and, in the quiet hours, had me practicing piping techniques on pieces of cardboard.

"It's time you learned how to make macarons, Rachelle," Sophia said as I walked into work one bright, hot morning. "I got a special order for a wedding. Isn't that great? They want over a thousand French macarons. What do you do with a thousand macarons?"

A giddy thrill put a high pitch in her voice. I almost choked on my own spit. Over one *thousand*? It had been well over a week since we'd seen much activity beyond three very elaborate cakes I couldn't do much to help with. The money would be good—maybe even push us through this month and into the next one—but it would require a *lot* of delicate French pastries.

That I had never attempted.

"Ah . . . sounds great," I managed to say as soon as I realized she was waiting for me to say something.

Sophia reached into the fridge, extracting several things at once. "Ever made them before?"

"Nope."

"Know anything about them?"

"Not really."

"There's an ingredient you'd never guess."

"Oh?"

She yanked a large white bag out from the bottom of the fridge and set it in front of me. Words in black marker were scrawled across the front.

Almond flour.

My eyebrows lifted. "Really?"

"Really. The trick to a good macaron, in my opinion, is to beat the sugar mixture until it's shiny. You'll see what I mean. Grab an apron. See that paper over there? That's the recipe. Bring it with you."

Without a beat of hesitation, Sophia dove into a speedy masterclass on French macarons. We made foamy egg whites, dumped in food coloring, discussed the importance of a white, peaky froth, and sifted through almond flour and confectioners' sugar.

I tried to keep my head from spinning.

Sophia moved at light speed, her movements instinctual in the kitchen. Her recipe creation wasn't exciting, but her culinary skills were undeniable. By the time she'd used a frosting bag to form a circle of dough on a piece of wax paper, the smell of sugar in my nostrils and the number of instructions whirring through my head made me dizzy. Just as she slipped the first batch into the oven, the bell on the door tinkled. Two forty-something women strolled in, peeling their sunglasses off.

"Sophie?" a platinum blonde squealed. Sophia's head snapped up.

"Adrie?"

"Sophie!"

The woman, clad in flip flops, a brown tank, and a bright, gauzy pink skirt shuffled into the back at a half run. Sophia collided with her, and they spent twenty seconds in a squealing embrace. By the time they pulled apart, the other woman had entered the prep area with a beaming smile. Soon, all three of them were chattering like a flock of birds. Finally, Sophia put her hands on their shoulders and drew in a deep breath, calming the frenzy.

"Okay, ladies. We have to calm down and start talking *cake*. All right? Because you're getting married, and we have so much to catch up on!"

Adrie squeaked. Her eyes filled with tears as she flashed a massive engagement ring on her left hand.

"Everything!" she cried. "I want *everything* on this cake!"

Before I could say a word, Sophia's two friends—and apparently new customers—followed her into the consultation room. The door closed with a firm *snick*. I blinked, staring at the mess in front of me. Well, that was an unexpected deterrent. How hard could replicating macarons be anyway?

> Almond flour.
> Sugar.
> Egg whites.
> Blending with aeration.

Sophia had already covered everything. With it fresh in my mind, I had this in hand. One deep breath and a nod later, I cracked my knuckles, re-situated my right leg on the chair, and faced the cacophony of ingredients.

"One thousand French macarons," I said. "Here I come."

I messed it up.

The thought ran through my mind a million times as I stared

at the disastrous pile of confections, if they could be called that, in front of me.

Sophia's macarons—that I'd pulled out of the oven at the timer's insistence—were picture perfect. I'd lined them up on a fresh piece of parchment paper and studied them. Next to *them*, mine looked like gobs of colored mashed potatoes or crooked muffins. They billowed and peaked and bulged in all the wrong places.

"Yikes," I muttered again.

I straightened, frowning. Not only were my macarons twice the size of Sophia's and decidedly pink instead of red, but the bottoms had turned a toasty brown even though I'd kept the oven temperature and the cooking time the same. Yet another glance at the recipe confirmed that I'd done nothing different. Almond flour, confectioners sugar, and food coloring littered the table around the mixing bowl where I'd worked. Frothy white eggs still dripped off the hand mixer and onto the gleaming table.

With a growl, I shoved away from the prep table, using it as my crutch when a customer stepped up to the counter.

Totally failed. Messed up yet again. Can't even make a batch.

The thoughts whirled through at a million miles an hour, so fast I almost didn't hear her ordering. Three attempts to ring her up later, I managed to shove the thoughts aside just long enough to complete the purchase, thank her for coming, spin back around, and glare at the atrocities on the other side of the room.

"Can't even finish college, either," I muttered as the bell announced the store door closing again.

As if on cue, Janine's voice floated through my head. *Think of all the times you hated yourself. Think of times when you felt you'd done something unforgivable. Then let it go.*

I scowled. "This isn't unforgivable," I said out loud, as if she were there. "This was just a stupid mistake that I shouldn't have made."

But still . . . something about it *did* feel unforgivable.

No response came, but I felt an unsettled stirring in my chest all the same. If this *wasn't* an unforgivable thing—stupid and small, really— why did it matter if it had happened? I thought back to my second meeting with Janine, when she framed everything in terms of Lexie. Would I be annoyed with Lexie if she'd messed up a delicate recipe?

My nostrils flared as the answer struck me.

No.

In fact, I'd probably laugh at the decrepit-looking cookies that seemed more like mushrooms and tell her to start over. She must have missed a small detail, which was understandable with such a finicky dessert. *Let's do it again,* I'd tell her. *It will be fun.*

If Mira could let go of arguing with her husband before his death and Sophia could move past dropping out of college twice, surely I could *let go* of a bad batch of macarons.

However I was supposed to do that.

"Fine," I muttered to the macarons. Then I closed my eyes, channeled my inner Megan, and tried to tap into yoga breathing. I let out a long breath. "I made a mistake. I don't know how to stop beating myself up about this, and I feel crazier than ever because I am talking to *air,* but I choose to, ah . . . let this go? Yes. I'm letting this go. I choose to forgive myself and attempt another batch."

When my eyes fluttered open, nothing had happened. The same empty bakery stared back at me. No swelling of love bloomed in my chest, reassuring me that *everything was all right now that you've reached self-acceptance.* But when I looked back at the macarons, my lips pressed into a thin line to stop a smile. They were pretty ridiculous looking. Maybe we could start a discounted rejects pile and sell them at half price.

Or give them away, if anyone would take them.

With a half chuckle, I grabbed my phone, pulled the parchment paper closer, and snapped a picture. Then I texted it to Megan, Lexie, Mira, and Bitsy in our group chat with the message *#nailedit.*

When I shoved the phone back in my pocket, a little of the tension had left my chest. Moments later, Lexie replied with a giggle emoticon. Mira LOL'd. This time, I did laugh. Out loud. Into the strange air. I faced the recipe with renewed determination, feeling oddly better for having laughed about it.

"You and me, macarons," I muttered, snatching the eggs. "You're going down."

Two hours and the littered corpses of four different batches of poorly shaped macarons later, the consultation door opened. Sophia and her friends spilled out, giggling about something. No doubt having recently sampled some celebratory champagne that I knew Sophia kept in there. I straightened up from placing a frosted macaron top on a flat, rounded bottom just as Sophia waved goodbye to Adrie and the other woman.

Sophia spun on her heels and headed toward me, then stopped halfway. "Whoa."

The prep area had become a disaster zone. When the second batch didn't work out, I consulted the internet. When that batch came out runny, I went to YouTube. The fourth batch was burned and lay in scattered remnants across the table. Still, I felt triumphant when I planted my hands on the counter.

"I did it," I said. "I *finally* figured it out after five batches. See?"

Sophia blinked. The arrested, blank expression on her face alerted me to a new worry: had I just wasted too much food? Any ingredient I used was money out of her pocket. Would she be upset that I couldn't figure out a recipe she had just shown me on the first try? Almond flour couldn't be cheap.

For a long eternity that was probably only five seconds, Sophia's gaze swept the prep table, finally landing on the perfectly sandwiched, frosted, and developed French macarons sitting right in front of me. Red, this time, not pink. Then her eyes met mine.

She grinned.

"Well done, Rachelle. Five batches isn't too bad." She reached over and gave me a high five. "Not bad at all. Now, get back to work. You have nine hundred and ninety more to go."

A couple of days later, Dr. Martinez tipped her head to the side and frowned, sending a waterfall of ebony hair cascading onto her shoulders. My bare ankle lay open on the awkward patient bed. The bruising had receded into swirls of green and yellow. Still as hideous as before, if not more so.

I really should have shaved my legs.

"I'm sorry, Rachelle. There is some progress in decreased swelling at the top of the foot, but not enough for your broken metatarsals to support weight yet."

Disbelief swelled in me. "But I've done everything!"

"I believe you."

"So why . . ."

"Sometimes you can do everything right and it still doesn't work out the way you want. We can't force the body."

My shoulders slumped. There was a life lesson to write on a cake. A thousand rebuttals came to mind, but I stifled all of them. None of it was Dr. Martinez's fault. It was mine. The heavy weight loomed large. Sometimes, it really sucked being the person who had to learn things the hard way. *Perhaps I should forgive myself for this too,* I thought, but the idea felt too heavy in the moment. I let it go and sank into the sadness instead.

"Yeah," I sighed. "Fine . . ."

Dr. Martinez pulled her glasses off her face. "Are you still hoping to run that marathon?"

"No. I've given that up for this year. I just miss being able to move freely. These crutches are really annoying."

She put a hand on my shoulder. "I'm sorry, Rachelle. It'll heal eventually, even if it's not as fast as you want."

"Yeah. Me too. Well, thanks for looking at it. Want me to keep the boot on?"

"For now, yes. "

I managed a vague smile in response. After Dr. Martinez shuffled out with her clipboard under her arm, telling us her nurse would see us to the front desk, Mira stood up, eyebrows high in silent question, as if asking, *You okay?*

With a sigh, I grabbed the crutches and slid off the chair.

"Let's go."

That night, I lay in bed, thinking about the binder.

It sat underneath me, its siren song whirling over and over again in my head like cinnamon rolls. The sound was a mere hush in the background of my thoughts, really. A quiet whisper. That's all I heard from it. But it seemed to thunder.

Face me again, coward.

If Janine truly wanted me to confront my past and forgive myself for things I still hated myself for, that would originate in the binder. All my secret lives were chronicled there. A list of boyfriends on page forty-two. The Hollywood crushes I used to drool over while eating Muddy Buddies and drinking an Orange Julius—Mom's favorite drink. Pictures. Drawings. Letters to Lexie. Notes we'd passed back and forth in sixth grade.

The idea of broaching that wall overwhelmed me.

Because I don't deserve it, I thought. Didn't I deserve to lose the marathon? To have to fight, tooth and nail, to feel good about myself? Because I'd brought this all upon myself.

Was there really another way?

I shoved Janine's challenge away. Tonight, it was too much to think about. Too much to broach. Instead, I sank into sleep, dreaming of macarons, and powdered sugar on my hands while I tied my tennis shoes, the sounds of the TV twining through it all like a soundtrack.

Attractive

"So?" Janine asked, a trailing question in her voice. "How did things go this last week?"

I sank onto the couch, controlling the motion more with my legs than the crutches, and leaned back. Stories of macarons, car-ride conversations with Mira, and long nights contemplating and ignoring my past rushed to the forefront of my mind. Explaining seemed like too much work when I really hadn't figured out anything, so I let it all float away.

"Pretty good."

"Did you make any progress on learning who you are without roles?"

My nose scrunched. "Not really. The whole you-are-still-worth-something-even-if-you-messed-up thing has me reeling." My brow furrowed. "I'm not sure I was ready for that."

"For what?"

"To forgive myself."

Her eyebrows shot up. "Really?"

I shifted in my seat, attempting to find a spot that felt comfortable. "Yeah."

"Want to explain?"

I blinked. Of course I didn't. "I guess I just wasn't ready."

She paused, no doubt waiting for more, but I didn't offer it. "Meditation helps," she said when the silence stretched too long. "If you do that sort of thing. So does journaling. Writing helps a lot, actually."

"Okay."

"Keep working on it. You'll figure out something."

I wondered if she could detect the lack of certainty in my response. This whole thing was getting a bit too uncomfortable. I'd only shown up for this appointment because Bitsy had been my ride.

"Sure," I said.

"In the meantime, I have an idea to work on your self-hatred."

She pointed to her toes, then elevated her feet off the floor. "My father always told me that I had weak ankles. Apparently I tripped a lot. We had gophers in our backyard, so I think *that* had more to do with it than my body structure, but that's a different story."

She had *great* legs, actually. Her ankles were svelte, slipping into her heels like a model's. Despite all my work, my calves still looked like bowls of lumpy gravy.

"Anyway," she said, "I grew up thinking there was something wrong with me. There wasn't. As I said—gophers. It took me years to realize that my ankles weren't only just fine, they were wonderful. They're strong, just like my calves. They carry me everywhere. They hold up with heels. And because of them, I've been able to travel the world."

"They seem perfect to me."

Her nose wrinkled. "Isn't it funny how easily we assign such words to other people but not ourselves? I digress. I want you to go through your body, one piece at a time. Tell me what you're grateful for about it and what's attractive about it."

I blinked. "What?"

"For example, my toes." Her foot slipped free of the shoe. Five perfectly normal toes wiggled in the air. "They're cute. Small. Slightly chubby but perfectly tailored to my foot shape. Because of them, I have greater balance when I walk, which takes me places."

She made them dance for a second longer, then tucked them back into her shoe. With a gesture of her hand, she motioned to me.

"Your turn."

"We're really going to talk about my toes?"

"Why not?"

Why? I tossed the hair out of my eyes.

"I don't see anything attractive in my body."

"Nothing?"

"My hair is okay sometimes. But my ankles? No. I've never thought any part of my legs attractive. Why lie?"

"It's not lying."

"But . . ."

She waited as my response trailed off, then died. How was I going to believe that every part of me was lovable and attractive?

I'd spent the last year trying to perfect my body into being *acceptable*. Whenever I got there . . . there was always something I hadn't noticed before. Extra skin. Cottage-cheese arms. Flabby butt. It seemed like being overweight never really went away.

"Tell me something about your toes," she said when the silence continued to swell in the room. "Anything."

I lifted my left foot and peered at my toes peeking out of my flip flop. "They're normal?"

"How are they attractive?"

"Well . . . they aren't hobbit toes."

She tilted her head back and laughed. "Non-hobbit toes are a plus. Tell me something about them that you're grateful for."

"About my toes?"

"Yep. Gratitude is one of our most powerful tools."

"Oookay. Well . . . I guess now, more than ever, I'm grateful that I can walk? Or will eventually be able to again."

She beamed. "Me too. Mobility is an underappreciated gift. Now your feet."

"You're serious? We're going to do every single body part?"

"All the way to your hair. Every single one."

Feet, toes, fingers, wrists—those I could get around. But thighs? Stomach? Breasts? How on earth would I lie my way through *those*?

"I am grateful for my feet because they wear shoes," Janine said, tapping them together. "And I *love* to wear shoes. My closet is testament to that. They're attractive feet, too. I love the shape of them."

This was getting absurd.

I cleared my throat. "Uh, all right. I-I like my feet because sitting all day would be miserable and . . ." My voice brightened. "I love to run. Without my feet, I couldn't run."

A smile illuminated her face. "And they're attractive because?"

"Gross. No feet are attractive."

Janine laughed. "Okay, that is the *only* one I will let slide. Now let's talk about your ankles."

We ascended our way up to my dreaded thighs. My mouth turned to cotton. No way I could lie my way through this one.

"Why are you grateful for your thighs? And how are they attractive?"

I avoided glancing at them by sheer willpower. The only words that came to mind filled my cheeks with heat. Lumpy gravy. Cellulite. No gap. Nor did I want to admit that this conversation had been getting a little bit easier—at least being grateful had. Every response about why my body was attractive felt forced. But there were things to be grateful for.

"I'm grateful my thighs can run."

"And they're attractive because?"

Another long silence prevailed. In vain, I cast about for something. My legs were less than half the size they used to be. Maybe even a third. But even then, they weren't totally straight, were they? They weren't tan.

They weren't bump-free.

"I-I . . ."

To my horror, tears filled my eyes. I blinked them back, mortified. Crying? Why was I crying about my thighs?

"I can't think of anything," I snapped.

"Nothing?"

In shame, I shook my head. Was this what it had come to? Had I thought so little of myself that I couldn't conjure one sincere, accepting thought about my own legs? Was the hatred really so strong?

Yes.

And it burned.

"I see tears in your eyes, Rachelle," Janine said, breaking the silence. "Can you tell me what you're feeling?"

"Overwhelmed."

"By what?"

"How much I hate my body."

My nostrils flared in an attempt to draw in a deep, slow breath and keep the tears at bay. How would I ever battle out of this? How would I ever be able to look at my thighs and feel anything but disgust?

"Why do you hate your body?" she asked gently.

"Because it's . . . it's not perfect. I've tried so hard. I run so much. And it . . . it can't ever just look *right*. It's always wrong, no matter what I try."

"Could you run a marathon without your body?"

I glanced up. "No."

"Could you hug Lexie without your body?"

"No."

"Could you enjoy the way a hot bath feels at the end of a long day?"

I barely heard my own whisper. "No."

"If you're chasing perfection, you'll chase it the rest of your life. It doesn't exist. Even if you *did* somehow get the perfect body, you'd never recognize it as such. When we live our lives around roles and conditions, we never measure up. Think of it this way: if you lost all ability to move on your own tomorrow, would you have a different definition of perfection?"

"Of course."

"Do you think you'd appreciate the way your thighs moved? Crave them no matter what they looked like?"

"Yes."

She smiled in her off-center way again. "Yeah. You would. This is the power of gratitude. It takes our mindset off of what we don't have and puts it on what we do have."

The simplicity took my breath away. Sure, Bitsy had always said *be grateful for what you have* and *perfection isn't real*, but until that moment, I hadn't appreciated it. Right then, I thought I saw understanding glimmering in the distance. Just a wisp, but something flickered out of the darkness.

"I . . . I think I know what you mean."

"Don't think I've forgotten. You're still on the hook. Butt is next. Make it good. Then we're moving into your waist, and I won't take anything that's not sincere."

By the time we made it through my body—even though I felt like a fraud the entire time—I was emotionally wrung out. Training for the marathon hadn't ever made me so exhausted. No, this seeped deeper than my bones and all the way into my heart.

"I know how hard that was for you, Rachelle," Janine said once I finished. By the look in her eyes, I could tell she meant it. "But thank you. We can retrain our brains once we've learned a new skill. Time for my homework for you. I want you to write a letter to yourself."

"A letter?"

"You can share it with me next week if you want, but you don't have to. It can be just for you."

"What am I supposed to say?"

"I want it to be something that you read every morning and every evening."

"I'm going to forget."

"Not if it's important to you."

"What is it supposed to say?"

"Write down your own self-love and acceptance as if it's already happening. Phrases like *I am beautiful right now.* Or *I love myself just the way I am* or *I am happy with the person I am becoming.*"

"You want me to lie?"

Her gaze tapered for a second, and I felt a flash of guilt. We had just spent an entire hour working through this. Did she have any other clients this difficult? She shook her head, any shred of judgment disappearing.

"Put yourself in the position of wanting to believe it. Don't you want to believe you're beautiful? Don't you want to love the person you're becoming?"

"Of course."

"The mind is an amazing thing. If you focus on something for seventeen seconds, your brain will start to find evidence of it. For example—you wake up, look in the mirror, and think, *How did I get this overweight? I will never be happy. I will never love myself. I'm doomed to the life that I'm in now and I might as well accept it.* Do that for seventeen seconds, and when you walk out of the bathroom, your brain is going to find proof that that's true."

"That's insane."

She smiled. "That's powerful. Where you think, there you go. You may not believe in this yet, but I'm going to ask you to have some faith in me and try it."

"All right."

"Good luck with the letter. I look forward to your report next week."

The next morning, I stared at myself through the fog of the bathroom mirror.

My hair hung in limp, dark strands around my face. I had a towel wrapped around my torso, a novelty I'd discovered only after I'd dropped below one hundred and eighty pounds. I held my right foot, boot free, off the ground. The hot, steamy shower had felt wonderful despite the rippling summer heat outside.

"I can do it," I murmured. "I can say something nice about myself."

Another long stretch of time passed before I felt the words rise in my throat and sit there.

I have nice eyes.

What did *nice* mean anyway? Kind? Not ugly? No one had ever said that I had kind eyes, and I figured *that* made sense. My mouth always got me in trouble. In fact, I probably hadn't come across as kind much when I was overweight. I was probably too concerned with being right, or obnoxious, or overbearing.

My brain started to wander, into memories of high school when I stood up for Lexie and myself against the cheerleaders. The teachers who wrote me off as inconsequential and stupid just because I was loud.

"I was loud for a reason," I muttered to the mirror. "I wasn't stupid."

Roles. This time, the word didn't seem so foreign. Being loud and proud had been my role. It's who I had embodied all through high school. Then it all shifted the night I got raving drunk with Chris.

What was my next role? Exerciser. Weight-loss guru.

For some reason, the thoughts seemed to settle in my head better. It just . . . made more sense now. I'd thought that those things were what defined me, but they didn't. *Something* defined me.

I just wasn't sure yet what it was.

With a shake of my head, I turned away from the mirror and reached for the door handle, then I stopped.

No.

I turned, faced the mirror, and said, "I-I have . . . strong legs."

My nostrils flared. I *did* have strong legs. Nothing compared to Megan's, but strong nonetheless. That was something to go off of. "This is crazy," I said, shaking my head. "This will never feel normal."

But even as I said the words, I felt a niggling doubt. Maybe, one day, it would feel normal. This time, I grabbed the door handle and pulled it open. When I turned back toward my room, Mom blocked my path. I reared to a stop. Her head jerked up, startled, eyes small in her thick face.

"Oh," she said. "Sorry. Didn't see you there."

"No problem."

A tense moment passed while she attempted to sidestep out of my way, but I blithely slid aside instead. There wasn't much room in the path. Not enough for both of us to wiggle by at the same time. Her cheeks reddened. She didn't quite meet my eyes.

"Three chins moving through here," she quipped. "They take up more space than you'd think. Almost need a wheelbarrow."

With that, Mom disappeared into her bedroom. I stood rooted to the spot, my mind whirring. When had Mom started making fun of herself? Memories whipped through my mind, taking me by surprise. Mom on my birthday at twelve, calling herself a cow for eating half the cake—I polished off almost the other half. Eating an entire bowl of pasta, then cracking a joke about eating for three and not being pregnant.

Always. She'd always made fun of herself.

I sucked in a sharp breath, washed through with something heavy. Not disgust this time. Not even annoyance. Sadness. Pure and utter sadness. Only this time, it wasn't just for me.

Opportunity

The next day, I left Sophia's office with a recipe for petit fours she wanted me to attempt. The paper wrinkled in my free hand. The close proximity of things in the prep room—and my skills with using only the crutch on my right side—gave me a free hand these days. A little piece of freedom that I appreciated more with every passing day.

I came to a dead stop just inside the preparation room.

Neatly stacked boxes filled the far counter.

A head of blond hair appeared just over a tall cardboard box. The delivery boy from a few weeks ago.

"Hello, William!" Sophia called from behind me. She waved. "Great to see you again."

Huh. He didn't look like a William.

William lowered the box to the ground with a wide smile that extended all the way to his eyes. "You too, Miss Sophia."

Our gaze met. He ran a hand through his tousled hair. "Hey," he said to me. "Listen, sorry about last time. I was late for a class. Which doesn't really justify being rude but at least explains why I was so . . . grumpy."

Ah. Not *too* intense on the bad attitude, then. A refreshing change. I smiled and shrugged.

"No problem. I was the one who scared you."

He waved to Sophia again as she slipped back into her office, then motioned with his hand to the boxes. "I figured the counter was the best place. What with your leg . . ."

"It's perfect. Thanks. Sophia puts all the big stuff away, anyway. I just sort through it."

He nodded and moved to the back door while I reached into the nearest box and pulled out containers of rainbow sprinkles and candy stars coated with edible glitter. By the time he returned, I'd already unloaded a new assortment of frosting tips, food coloring, and silicone cupcake liners onto the prep table. I tossed the cardboard box to the ground. William paused in front of it, head tilted to the side, then grabbed the box.

"Does Sophia use these?"

"Not that I know of."

He eyed the boxes. "Mind if I take them?"

"I don't care. I think she just recycles them."

"Sweet." He stacked his hands on his hips and looked around. With his long-sleeved gray shirt, his bright eyes appeared more seafoam green than emerald. "Look," he said, "I have some extra time. Do you want help unloading all this? Then I can get these boxes out of your way."

"Sure."

For the next couple of minutes, we didn't say a word. William worked at lightning speed, like he'd been a grocery bagger for years. Each box I unloaded he happily bore away.

"Sophia gave me some of the macarons you made last week," he said, breaking the silence. "She dropped them off a few days ago."

"Oh?"

"They were really good. Rivaled Sophia's, and I don't say that lightly. Seems like you're a good fit here. She said you're working full time now. That's pretty cool."

A rebuttal surfaced. *You're just saying that about my macarons,* I wanted to counter, but I stopped myself. I thought of my last session with Janine, when I complimented her perfect calves and she smiled. *Isn't it funny how easily we assign such words to other people but not ourselves?* At the time it had seemed like an easy way to defer my compliment, but now I wasn't so sure. Because I easily accepted that Sophia's macarons were perfect. By the end, mine looked just like hers.

Maybe Janine was trying to teach me something *then* as well.

Deciding to be kind to myself and accept what he said at face value, I forced a smile. "Thanks," I managed to choke out. "If I have to make another macaron, I think I'll throw up."

To my surprise, he laughed. Some of the tension drained out of my shoulders. When was the last time I'd been in the room with a man I wasn't trying to seduce or ignore completely? Far too long.

"So, what are you going to do with the boxes?" I asked as I loaded two-pound squares of butter into the fridge. He used a box cutter to break a box down, tearing through the package with quick *zips*.

"Recycle them."

"Oh."

A hint of a blush appeared at the top of his cheeks. He ripped the tape off of one box and broke it down into a smaller, thinner piece. "I'm around boxes a lot because of how many deliveries I do. So I started asking people to save them, and I haul them away. The recycling center pays for it. Some of my customers are so happy to get rid of them they actually pay me to take their recycling away. Works out in my favor."

"Hard up for money?" I quipped.

"Yep."

His reply, so utterly without apology, silenced me. My expression fell. Although I hadn't meant it in a bad way, I certainly felt like an ass.

"Oh," I said. "Sorry if that—"

"It's fine."

"Good for you for finding opportunity."

He shrugged and grabbed another box, as if entirely unbothered by what I'd said. "There's money everywhere. Not everyone sees it."

"Are you using it to pay for college?"

"Yeah."

"What's your major?"

He hesitated for a beat, and I couldn't fathom why. Did he think I'd eat him if he told me? Finally, the ice thawed.

"I want to get my PhD in cancer biology."

"Whoa. You want to cure cancer?"

He shrugged, brushing a stray lock of hair out of his eyes. Even though I saw a hint of nerd in him, I still had the feeling he'd been more of a punk than a debater in high school. Not to mention how hefty a major and career field that would be for a guy well past his mid-twenties.

"Yeah," he said. "Seems pretty cool. I mean, it would actually do something to improve the world. Instead of take away from it."

That piqued my curiosity, but I silenced my questions. Instead, I shifted to safer ground.

"Why do you want to cure cancer?"

He blinked, his brows growing heavy. For a moment, I could see a troubled bass player in his eyes, but it disappeared. "Because . . . I have a goal."

"Did you have a family member die from cancer or something?"

"No."

"Did you have it?"

"No."

"So you just want to cure it?"

"Yeah. I mean, go big or go home, right?" His eyes didn't quite meet mine. "If I'm going to make something of my life, I'm really going to make it. Even if I have to recycle cardboard to do it."

He'd worn long sleeves again, though I knew what to look for. Curls of his clearly inked wrists showed when he moved. What were the tattoos? Why was he hiding them? The day was hot for a long-sleeve shirt, even if it was cotton and decorated with a surfboard and a few waves across the front. He didn't strike me as the surfer type. Was *he* trying to be someone he wasn't?

Maybe William didn't know how to be kind or forgiving to himself, either.

"I've never met anyone so motivated," I said. Although Bitsy posed a close second. Before he could respond, Sophia appeared.

"Will, can you make an extra trip here next week?"

"Probably. What day?"

"Not sure. What's your schedule look like?"

"Just a second."

Although I couldn't be sure, I thought I saw a hint of relief in his eyes. Probably glad to get away from my grilling, but I couldn't help myself. *Money is everywhere.* And *go big or go home.* In my extensive experience with men of all kinds, I'd never heard a guy say things in such a humble way. There was more to this paradox of a man than I'd first imagined.

Maybe he could be my first male friend.

When he returned, he held a rectangular office calendar, the kind that hung in a bland office with a receptionist who always had her hair in a bun. He set it on the table between bottles of vanilla and rum. Words filled the boxes, color coded with at least five different colors. Arrows raced from one day to another, sometimes for a whole week.

I hadn't seen anything this organized since I'd opened Bitsy's coupon binder. He pulled a pen and a highlighter out of his pocket.

"I'm open here and here." He pointed to two different days. "But the rest is pretty booked. If you stay open late, I can come before my night class. Or, if you're here late working on cakes, I could come after my night class, too."

For all his perfection in scheduling, his handwriting looked like chicken scratch. I could just make out a few words. *Class* and *Homework* and *Visit Grandma*. Was this guy for real? He couldn't be much older than me. Maybe twenty-seven. He was like the male version of Bitsy.

"Friday is perfect," Sophia said, straightening. She hooked him in a side hug that he seemed to melt into. "Thanks for working me in, and tell your grandma that I said hello."

Before I could say another word, he grabbed a box filled with the broken-down boxes and deftly avoided my gaze.

"Thanks for the boxes, Sophia. See you in a week. Bye, Rachelle."

With that, he disappeared into the alley. The door squeaked when it closed behind him. I watched him go, startled.

He remembered my name. Then I turned back to the petit fours, my head filled with thoughts and questions I didn't quite know how to pinpoint.

Jealousy cut through Lexie's voice with oozing intensity later that week. "Are you loving your job at the Frosting Cottage?" she asked through the phone. "Because I hate you for it. Even when you send me those fail pictures. The macarons were funny, but it was the demented eclair that had me *really* giggling."

I lay sprawled on my bed in my underwear, my ankle propped up. I twined a piece of hair around my finger while we talked. A fan blasted at me on full speed, but it didn't change how stuffy the room was. The A/C had never reached in here, but the moving air made it seem less suffocating. If I opened my bedroom door, cool air would drift in, but so would the television.

"It's really fun working at the Frosting Cottage, actually," I said. "Just learned a few tips on the perfect cinnamon roll."

"Anything life changing?"

"Nothing Mom hadn't already taught me."

"Sweet! Send me one?"

"Sure."

"That's my girl, Rachelle. But only ship like one. Or two, then I don't have to share with Bradley. That's understood, right? I'm still engaging in portion control. And you'd be proud—I worked out six days last week. None of them on the treadmill. For obvious reasons."

I laughed. "Of course."

"It's so funny looking back on our childhood because you always were talented with food. It's just . . . you working there makes sense. Like maybe you didn't finish college because this is your thing."

"As opposed to all eight majors I attempted?"

"Yeah. Sometimes we take the long road to get where we're going."

"Yeah," I said. "Maybe."

The idea of working with food for a living still sent a shock of panic through me but not one that paralyzed me anymore. So far, I hadn't sampled anything beyond the lemonade. Which had been more of an exercise in self-control to make sure I wouldn't revert back to my old ways. I didn't fear food as much as not exercising—but even *that* hadn't killed me.

Perhaps that fear is just a result of my role as marathoner. I scowled and pushed the thought aside. If nothing else, I knew I could work around food without becoming old Rachelle again. Not that Janine would approve of me still hating old Rachelle so much.

"I'm dying to know how it went with Janine last time. I feel like maybe I can get pseudo-therapy through you. Are you up to talking about it?"

"Oh, sure." A ripple of guilt moved through me. My homework to write a letter to myself this week had all but faded from my mind. The idea of writing to myself was too much when I was still attempting to say nice things about myself—and believe them. "It was . . ."

Annoying.

Tough.

Strange.

"Different."

"What's *that* supposed to mean?"

"I don't know," I murmured. "She had me do this thing with gratitude and attractiveness with my body. It was weird. I felt like I was lying the whole time."

Lexie didn't say a word as I elaborated on what we'd discussed, and I was grateful to air it all out. When I finished, silence reigned. To my relief, though, I felt better. Something about speaking the thoughts helped me line them up better. When Lexie said nothing, I pressed the phone harder to my ear.

"Hello?"

"Sorry. Just looking at my ankles and trying to figure out if I adore them or think they could use some work."

"See? It's not easy."

"You're right. It's not. But how cool."

"Cool? I was lying almost the whole time."

"You have adorable toes!"

I wiggled them on my left foot. "Yeah, I mean, they're cute. But the point is that it's really hard to be that kind to myself. And that's sad."

"You really didn't find a single thing you felt was attractive?"

"Well . . . I mean . . . my calves aren't bad, either."

She snorted. "I'd kill for your calves. Look, even if you're struggling through your self-hatred, I just think it's great that you're doing something different."

"Way different."

"Isn't the definition of insanity doing the same thing over and over and expecting different results?"

"Yes."

"So? Now you stopped doing that. You looked for happiness in food, didn't find it. Looked for it in guys, didn't find it. Looked for it in weight loss, didn't find it. Looked for it in intense exercise and didn't find it. Now I get the feeling you're looking in the *right* places."

Then why did I still feel so lost?

"You're doing what no one else in your life—Bitsy aside—has ever done. Not even me. You're actually getting help to fix a problem, not just putting a Band-Aid on it. Good for you, Rachelle."

Her observation gave me pause. I'd never thought of it that way. Most of the time when I spoke with Janine, I felt like I was floundering and hoped that she had the life vest. Not to mention how depressing it seemed that I *had* looked for happiness everywhere and still hadn't found it.

"It's just . . . I feel like I'm waiting for something to click, you know? From the outside, it probably *seems* like I'm doing something great. But inside? I'm just . . . I feel lost."

"I'm going to do it with you then!" Lexie cried. "I'm going to find things I think are attractive about myself and that I'm grateful for. And I'll write myself a letter, too. Maybe it'll click if you have someone else to commiserate with."

I sat up. "Really?"

"Yeah! Pseudo-therapy, remember? Honestly, the more we talk about your sessions with Janine, the more I think *I* need to get out there and find me a Janine. Does she do it over video chat? That'd be awesome. There has to be gobs I could talk with her about. Starting with how smelly male laundry is."

"But you don't need to go to therapy."

"So *you* say."

"Enough about Janine." I flopped back to the pillow. I heard the couch groan—Mom must have stood up. "Tell me about married life."

"Blissful in some ways. I really miss home, though. I'm so disoriented here. Like, where's the Chipotle? Oh, it's twenty miles away! We only have one car, and Bradley has to take it most of the time while he helps his dad in the fields. That math doesn't work out well in my favor. Actually, it does. My clothes are fitting better. But *still* . . ."

I laughed, and the feeling of it rolling through my belly sent a shot of euphoria through me.

"Oh, Lexie."

"Bradley is great, though. I may not like living with his parents, and the area is pretty remote, but it is wonderful being with him every night instead of having to be apart. Also, I adore his mom. Still trying to figure out where I fit with his dad, though."

"Not to mention you get unlimited sex."

"Yeah. But, you know, he's tired after working in the fields all day. Practice is going to start in August, so he'll *really* be gone then. To be honest, when he's out with his dad, I think he forgets he's married sometimes."

"I highly doubt that."

"For all our sakes, let's hope."

"You sound happy."

She sighed again, and I could picture it ruffling her blonde bangs. "I am."

"Good. That's all I want."

"Listen, I gotta go. His mom fixed stew and cornbread for dinner, so I need to eat. We'll talk later?"

"Right. Of course. Love you, Lex. Thanks for talking with me."

"Thanks for the pseudo-therapy. I can't wait to get started myself. I'm pretty positive I'll love everything about my forearms. Not to brag, but I have lovely hands. Love you, Chelle."

Once we hung up, the quiet aftermath rang like a gong. Even through the fan whirring next to my bed, I could still hear the ceaseless drone of the TV in the background. Mom had settled back in. The channel changed.

I drew in a deep breath and thought of what Lexie had said. She wasn't seeing Janine, and even *she* was going to say nice things about herself and write a letter.

I glanced at a notebook on the bottom shelf of my nightstand. With a rueful sigh, I grabbed it, fished for a pen in the drawer, and yanked the cap off with my teeth. Before I changed my mind, I started to write.

Dear Rachelle,

I paused, already at a loss. Janine had said to act as if I were already the girl I wanted to be. As if I already loved myself. Me, the girl whose father left and mother *never* left. As if I could love and respect the girl who used to act like she was proud of her brash, outspoken, overbearing personality.

I slammed the notebook closed around the pen and shoved it under my bed. Far under my bed. Then I closed my eyes, threw my arm across my face, and let my whirling thoughts subside into the safety of sleep.

"Marriage has changed nothing about my appetite."

Lexie peered out of the computer at Bitsy, Mira, and me, a scowl marring her fair skin.

"Did you think it would?" Bitsy asked, amusement in her voice.

"Hoped, I guess." Her shoulders slumped. "I thought once I'd really captured him, it would take the pressure off. I mean, he married me imperfect body and all. But noooo." She tilted her head back with a sigh. "Sometimes I feel the pressure more than ever."

"You know what you need to do," Bitsy said.

"I know. I know." Lexie straightened her head back up and let out a long breath. "Journal it. Talk to Bradley about it. Don't eat my emotions."

"Very good!"

The pursed-lip smirk on Lexie's face meant she'd almost rolled her eyes but stopped herself at the last moment. I stifled a grin—Bitsy could see me through the video-chat screen.

"Megan?" Bitsy asked. "How was your week?"

Bitsy and Mira perched on the couch behind me, while I sat on the floor with my back propped up against the couch's arm. The heavy boot still kept my right foot prisoner. It was itchy in the summer heat, but I didn't hate it as much as I used to.

Or perhaps I'd just forgotten to hate it.

In the background, Bitsy's two daughters giggled from somewhere outside. The smell of freshly mown grass drifted in from the open back door.

". . . then the stupid little twelve-year-old thought it would be funny to throw a rock at the moose. It charged." Megan sighed, blowing hair out of her face. "Luckily the idiot had enough sense to run into the lake and swim as fast as he could. Moose didn't get him, but it was close. Anyway, that was *my* week at work. In between cooking meals and taking care of first-aid problems, I managed to get in three lifts and four trail runs."

Lexie's eyes widened. "Whoa. Back up. The kid was almost killed by a moose?"

Megan waved it off. "He's fine. The moose was probably just bluffing. Now my brother has to make a protocol for moose attacks, though. He's not too happy about it."

I snorted to hide a giggle, but Megan was smiling, so I didn't feel too bad. Bitsy, who was holding onto a water bottle, turned to Mira.

"And how was Chicago, Mira? We haven't met since you've been back."

Mira used a hand to push her curling bangs off her sweaty forehead. Bitsy's window air conditioner worked hard in the background, chugging out tepid air that didn't really cool things down.

"Hot," Mira said. "And busy. I did more cleaning than a woman should have to do. Don't know how you run a cleaning business these days, Bitsy. I was proud of myself, however, to abstain from all the plain Pepsi in the fridge!" A mild cheer went up from all of us. "Yes, I drank diet. Sorry, Bits. But I figured not spiking my blood sugar was better than throwing myself into diabetes."

Bitsy managed a smile, even though I could see a flicker of something in her eyes. No doubt she wanted to give Mira a lecture on the horrors of artificial sweeteners—and probably thought that plain sugar would be better—but she abstained.

"Do you feel good about it? Because that's the most important thing," Bitsy said, somehow with full sincerity.

"I do!"

"Then good! That's what's really important."

Lexie cheered. Megan applauded. I whistled, then shifted back off my sit bones just as Bitsy prodded me in the spine. Even knowing this conversation was coming didn't prepare me for it."

"How about you, Rachelle?" she asked. "How did the week go?"

"Can you go next?"

"We'll get to me later. You girls always come first."

I opened my mouth in rebuttal, but decided against it. Last week, we'd glossed over Bitsy, who surely noticed but hadn't said anything. Come to think of it, Bitsy *often* avoided recounting her week.

Megan leaned closer to the camera, her chin propped on her palm, distracting me from my train of thought. "Yeah," she said. "I've been looking forward to hearing about how things are going with your therapist. What therapy can you give the group tonight?"

A thousand replies flooded my mouth. *It's insane. It doesn't make any sense. I'm not sure I'm making progress.*

Instead, I said, "Well, this week I'm having a hard time liking myself."

Through the computer screen, I could see Bitsy's eyebrows rise. "What is it you don't like?"

The question—though so simple—gave me pause. At first, I'd just assumed *everything about my body*, but careful thought throughout the week made me realize it was more than *just* my body. People had always underestimated me because I was overweight. They made assumptions the moment they met me: I wasn't smart. I wasn't athletic. I wasn't able to do things that skinny girls could do. I hated that I let myself act stupid, flamboyant, and bitter. Or maybe I still was that. I couldn't tell anymore.

"My body, for one," I said, opting for the safest, most true answer. "I'm still having a hard time loving myself. But I also don't like that I acted stupid and didn't care about anything but boys. Anyway, Janine is trying to help me conquer my self-loathing." The words came out heavy and filled my throat like custard. "Obviously, I struggle with it. I just . . . I guess it's stronger than I expected, and it's been harder to get over than I thought. I can't even do the homework."

Mira's lips turned down a little. Despite our morning car rides, I hadn't confessed this to her yet.

"What is your homework this week?" she asked.

"I'm supposed to say nice things to myself every day and write a letter to myself as if I'm already the person I want to be."

"That sounds awesome," Megan said, eyes tapered. "I should do that."

"Scared?" Bitsy asked me with a nudge in my ribs.

I hesitated. "Yeah, actually. I kind of am."

"Of what?"

"I don't know!" I cried. "I just feel like I'm lying. I'm *not* that girl yet, so why would I pretend to be?"

Megan straightened up. "I can appreciate that on some level. I don't hate my body, but I hate that people judge me in my career field."

"What?" Lexie asked. "Why? You're so clearly awesome."

Megan shrugged. "I haven't gone to grad school or done advanced education. Some people think I gave up career progression because I left the ICU and didn't become a flight nurse. It's just weird."

Lexie raised a hand. "I don't hate my body, but I hate worrying about what Bradley thinks of it all the time. He so clearly thinks I'm the hottest thing since man discovered fire, but it doesn't stop me from worrying. In fact, everything I used to struggle with I still do." She scowled. "That really kind of sucks."

"I've stressed over my body in the past," Mira said. "But I always hated that people found me airheaded or annoying. When I was growing up, I always hated my personality."

"What?" I shrieked. "Mira, that's insane. You're the best person I've ever met. Who thinks you're annoying?"

"I know." She spread her hands. "I don't get it, either. I've come to terms with it in the past couple of years, though."

"I hate that I only liked myself if a man liked me," Bitsy said, her lips pushed to one side of her face. "I had to deal with a lot of self-loathing if I didn't have a boyfriend or someone who wanted to be with me."

"Wow." Lexie reared back. "I didn't know that, Bitsy."

Bitsy waved it off but didn't quite meet anyone's eyes.

"I would never think that about any of you," I said, running a hand over my face. "Megan, I never once thought of you only in terms of your career. And Mira, I never thought you annoying or airheaded."

"Same," Megan said. "Especially with you, Rachelle. Not once, even before you lost the weight, did I feel like your body had anything to do with *you*. You were strong and determined and knew who you were. I don't think that's actually changed all that much—even if it doesn't seem like it right now."

"Same here," Bitsy and Lexie said at the same time, then laughed.

Mira put her hands on her thighs. "Then why do we think this about ourselves?" she asked through a laugh. "It's the silliest thing I've ever heard."

There was a question I hadn't stopped asking myself since I started working with Janine.

For a moment, everyone else giggled at the absurdity. I adored these women. The idea that they didn't see themselves as clearly as I saw them was . . . disconcerting, to say the least. Maybe a little freeing.

It gave me a push of courage I didn't know I needed until right then. I didn't feel so alone.

"Well," I said with a sharp intake of air. "I guess we all have some work to do."

"Letters to write!" Lexie cried.

"Amen," Mira said.

"I'll second that." Megan cracked her knuckles.

Bitsy rapped on the table. "Third. That's the challenge this week, ladies. Write a letter to yourself as if you're already the person you want to be. Can you do it?"

"Got it," Megan said with a thumbs-up.

"On it," Lexie said.

Mira matched Megan's thumbs-up.

All of them turned to me at the same time, and I nodded once. "All right. I'll do it."

While Lexie and Megan fell into a discussion of what they'd say, I rubbed my lips together, lost in thought. Clearly, whatever I saw in myself wasn't what others saw in me. Even if I was confused and lost and uncertain about myself, so were women I admired with every fat cell in my being. Perhaps there was something universal in seeking validation.

"I found a new lettuce-wrap recipe that all of you need to try out," Bitsy said, grabbing a magazine off the coffee table. "Instead of soy sauce, I've been using coconut aminos. Love them. Plus, it gets a little more soy out of your life. We could all use that. I bought small bottles and am shipping them to you girls, Megan and Lexie, to try out. Should arrive within the next two days. The recipe is copied in there, too. All right, we've already set our challenge for next week. Megan, what's your goal?"

The next time I stared into the mirror, I met my own gaze.

Thoughts about my eyes ran through my mind. My body. My strong legs. But, I rolled them away, peeling back to the one thing I *really* wanted to say.

"I am smart."

The three words fell like bombs in the stillness of the bathroom, punctuated by the drone of the television in the background. With a deep breath, I said it again.

"I am smart."

Several seconds of silence passed. I sat in it for a moment, then said, "I am not just a drunk college student that doesn't care. I have passion and courage."

That felt good.

Not overwhelming, not life-changing, not encompassing. Just good. Finally, with a last push of courage, I said, "I'm more than my roles made me out to be."

I am . . . something.

Satisfied, I nodded once, flicked the light off, and shut the bathroom door behind me, as if I could trap old ghosts back there, too. Maybe Janine was right.

Maybe there was power in new ways of thinking.

Wicked Smart

The longer I stared at the glass display case in the Frosting Cottage, the more convinced I became that the bakery had no hope.

"Sophia?"

Her name echoed through the gleaming prep room. The expansiveness of the bakery was what I loved most about it. The front of the store had a wide view of the prep room in the back, which made everything feel open. The ceiling spanned two floors—what used to be a flat had been torn down to open up the space. Today, sun streamed in through the windows in long, glimmering banners that illuminated dust motes floating in the air. The smell of Windex lingered amid the dry grit of flour—a comforting smell I'd started to get used to.

Sophia sidestepped out of her office, a pair of black glasses perched on the end of her nose. "Yes?" A handful of receipts filled both hands. I'd just closed the shop door and flipped the sign. Mira would arrive any minute now to pick me up in the back alley.

"You're too . . . normal," I said.

The papers rustled as she put her hands on her hips. "I've been accused of many things in my life, but that isn't one of them."

"The offerings." I spread my hands. Scrumptious desserts filled the display—cookies, cinnamon rolls thick with frosting, and slices of pillowy tiramisu. Desserts that hadn't sold in days. Nothing that Mom couldn't buy at every other bakery. "They're . . . normal."

She pulled her glasses off. "What do you mean?"

"Have you heard of Marco's Bakery?"

"No."

"It's like five miles away from here. He sells every one of these things, and he's been here twenty years. Kind of a community figure now. Might run for mayor. Anyway, if you want to analyze an ideal client, you'll need to meet my mom. She orders from him once a week because he delivers."

Her forehead furrowed into deep lines. "So? This is a bakery. Bakeries sell baked goods."

"Yeah . . . but no."

"You want me to start delivering?"

I shrugged. "It's an idea."

"What do you suggest?"

"That we spice it up a bit. If my mom can order all this from Marco's, she will. She's loyal, like a lot of people in this city. So maybe we need to think outside the box."

"How would you spice the offerings up?"

I blinked. "Well, I hadn't really thought that far. I'm just thinking out loud here. I mean, the food is all delicious, I'm sure."

"Have you tried some?"

Heat bloomed in my cheeks. "Oh, no. I-I haven't. Yet." I hastily continued before the awkward silence engulfed us. "It's just what everyone says. William talked about your fruit tarts for twenty minutes last time he stopped by. But none of what we offer really stands out. The cupcakes are pretty normal, right? Strawberry. Vanilla bean. Double chocolate."

She stepped closer to the display case. "The cinnamon rolls are our biggest sellers."

"We had to offer them at a discount two days ago because they were starting to get stale."

She frowned.

"The eclairs?"

"I've sold three in the last week."

"What about the macarons?"

"I've only sold five of the batch I made four days ago, and that was to the same customer. Your bank account can't be as happy about all this as the homeless shelter is. I sent William there with a huge box of food three days ago. Which maybe isn't the worst thing, but . . ."

Her frown deepened. "I suppose I could take a look at what's selling best in division, apart from bulk sales." She bit her bottom lip and followed my gaze. "I've just been looking at numbers overall recently because I didn't have time once Kate left."

"I'm willing to bet none of these pay themselves back," I said with a wave at the case. She stared at me uneasily, so I continued. "We need to start bringing people in because we have what no one else has."

Finally, after a long stretch of silence, she pointed one of the arms of her glasses at me.

"I agree. Great idea, Rachelle."

"Thanks."

"You have three days."

"What?"

"Come up with at least ten different ideas—and recipes so we can start right in on it—and we'll talk again. Maybe we can throw a special party or something."

"Wait."

"Outside the box," she murmured, tapping her chin. "I like this. It feels right."

"Oh, no. I didn't—"

"Three days." She poked me in the shoulder. "I can't wait to see what you come up with."

"That's a little *too* much faith in me."

She laughed. "Nonsense. You've long since proven that you have an eye for color and decoration. If anyone can do this, Rachelle . . ."

"But I'm not really sure how to do it. Just that we need to. I mean—"

"You can."

"But—"

She tilted her head to the side. "Don't you trust me?"

"Of course!"

"Then maybe you don't see it yet, Rachelle, but you've got a steel core in that mind. You're wicked smart. If anyone can do this, it's you. Now, get to work and sprinkle some magic around here. We need it."

I opened my mouth to reply but shut it again. *Steel core. Wicked smart.* She backed up two steps and held up three fingers.

"Three days."

She disappeared back into her office. A gaping hole seemed to have opened in my chest.

You're wicked smart.

No one had ever said that to me. No one had ever said it when I was overweight, and no one had said it since I'd lost all the weight. It wasn't something that came up—that I knew ever mattered.

Until now.

A whisper moved through me. One I'd never heard before.

What if she's right? What if Janine is right, too? What if all your friends are right about you and you are the one who is wrong?

A cold waterfall trickled down my spine. Sophia was right about my eye for visual decoration. I could feel it in my bones. In the way my toes curled. The way my heart pounded just thinking of it. My suggestions were spot-on. They were instinct—I'd started talking before I'd fully thought them out—but they were right.

They were *damn* right.

That meant something inside of me had value to give to the world. That I could draw conclusions to improve the way things were. I wasn't stupid, or subpar, or weak, or a vapid, oversexed, drunk girl.

Sophia was right.

I was wicked smart. I did have a steel core. I'd never considered it before, but that didn't make it any less true now. All of those things belonged to me. They were me, part of me, like breath, and lust, and life.

My breath caught just as Mira honked from the alley out back. I grabbed my house keys and wallet, shouted a goodbye, and hobbled out the back door as fast as my crutches would carry me.

I had to find Janine.

Now.

When I burst into Janine's office a few minutes later, Margery stared at me with wide eyes from where she stood bent over at the fountain, as if to turn it off. The overhead lights were off, and the water began to still. No music played overhead. One of the blinds was drawn.

"Oh," she stammered, hands poised halfway above the fountain. "H-hello, Rachelle. I don't believe you have a—"

"Where's Janine?"

Sweat trickled down my back, dripping down the ridges of my spine. Outside, the sweltering heat had kicked up a notch, welcoming in the intense humidity of the evening. My foot sweated in the boot.

Every now and then, it twinged with pain. Mira stepped into the office behind me, still appearing ruffled. No doubt from my demands to get to Janine's *as fast as you possibly can.*

"Janine is in her office." Margery glanced over her shoulder at the closed door. "But—"

I stormed toward the door amid the *thunk thunk thunk* of my crutches and threw it open.

"I've been wrong!" I cried.

Janine's head shot up. Sitting across from her was a man with jet-black hair and a pointy nose, his hands gripping the cushions. I stumbled back a step. *Whoops.* Janine rose to her feet, her expression hard with a blend of concern and annoyance.

"Rachelle?"

The whole drive over I'd pictured the way this would go down. I'd calmly walk in, request to speak with Janine, wait in the waiting room if necessary, and then tell her I needed help unraveling something.

"I-I'm sorry. I didn't . . . I've been wrong. I-I've been wrong, and . . . and I have to talk to you because Sophia gave me a compliment and now everything has changed and I don't know what to do."

Janine's lips tightened. In a firm voice, she said, "I'm with another client right now, as you can see. Step back. Take a deep breath."

Like an obedient child, I shuffled out of sight of the other client, pressed my lips together, and sucked in a deep breath through my nose. Janine nodded, seeming more composed herself.

"Once more."

I followed again. The wild edge of hysteria faded slightly.

"Step back into the waiting room and wait for me there," she said. "This is not acceptable behavior."

Without a sound, I retreated. A wave of embarrassment tore through me, but I didn't care anymore. Didn't care that that had been an overreaction. Didn't care that I'd probably broken some privacy law. In retrospect, it just didn't matter.

Because I was *wrong* about myself.

"Sorry," I whispered to Margery, who glared at me.

My mind whirled while I sat in the chair next to Mira. My left leg bounced up and down. Mira eyed me but said nothing. My every attempt to pay attention to the television screen—which Margery must have turned back on—met with failure. Ages passed before the man slinked past us with a scowl aimed at me. Janine stood at her office door.

"Rachelle, you may come in. Margery, you may go. I can handle this from here, thank you."

"I'm sorry," I said once I settled on the couch across from her. She regarded me with steep concern. Who could blame her? "I'm sorry. Really. Really sorry. Are you even open anymore?"

Her eyes flickered to the clock. "I'm not supposed to be, but I can make an exception. This sounds quite important."

"Thanks. I-I didn't mean to barge in or lose my head. I just . . . something happened, and I don't know how to process it, and it all just . . . happened."

"Tell me."

"My boss gave me a compliment."

She lifted one eyebrow. "Must have been some compliment."

"That's the thing. It was. And it was right."

Tears bubbled into my eyes from deep in my chest, blurring Janine's worried face. This time, I didn't try to blink them away. They dropped onto the backs of my hands as I recounted the whole week—all my struggles, my concerns, my fear of lying to myself. By the time I finished, Janine's shoulders had softened. She looked at me with compassion.

"I see."

"Sophia was right!" I cried, wiping the tears off with the back of my hand. "I am wicked smart. And I really do have a steel core."

"Did that scare you?"

"No. Maybe? I don't know." I wrestled with my own thoughts for a moment. "It's just . . . if she's right about that, and I know she is, that means I've been wrong about myself all along."

"Like what?"

"I never believed I was smart. I tried eight different majors in college for five years before dropping out. I dated arrogant guys I hated. But . . . maybe I was just telling myself I wasn't smart or worthy of better." The tears welled up again. "Maybe, all that time, I really was smart and worth it. If that's true, then . . ."

I wasn't sure I had the strength to finish my thought.

"Then?"

"Then maybe everything I believe about myself is false. Maybe I do . . . maybe there is value in . . . in *me* after all."

Janine tilted her head to the side, as if in deep thought. A silence followed, allowing me to gather my emotions.

"Let me ask you a question," she said quietly. "What are little babies worth when they're born?"

I blinked and wiped the hot tear trails off my cheeks. "Babies?"

"Do you know any?"

"Lexie's niece."

"How much is she worth?"

Being an only child with a mother who never left the house had kept me separated from babies pretty definitively. But Lexie's little niece was a darling girl with chubby fists and a squeaky cry. My brow furrowed.

"She's worth . . . everything."

"Why?"

"I mean . . . she's just this little ball of instinct. She's lovely and sweet, and I can't imagine she *didn't* have worth."

"At what point will she lose that value?"

"Never."

"Never?"

A careful question lay in her words, locking me into some sort of trap. No, Lexie's niece would never be less-than. She wouldn't be perfect, of course. Maybe she'd one day even make bad decisions the way I did. But I wouldn't think less of her.

"Never," I said, more firmly this time. A smile twitched at the edges of Janine's lips.

"Then why have you?"

A long moment passed while I absorbed that, at a loss for words. Tears trickled down my face. "Because I've made mistakes," I whispered, voice hoarse.

"So will her niece."

"I-I was really obnoxious and selfish."

Janine gave me a soft smile. "So are babies. But that doesn't devalue them, does it?"

"No."

"We think our worth is tied into what we do or the roles we play. That's not true. We have worth simply by being. Just think about the wonder of your body. When you tell your leg to move, it does. When you want to recall a memory, your mind will do so. Humans do impossible things every day just because they're alive. Isn't that worth something?"

To peel back the layers of life and look at it with such deep intensity caused me to pause. Of course my body responded to my commands—that's what it was supposed to do. My gaze drifted to my right ankle and the heavy boot that held it prisoner. Now, of all times, I could better appreciate the value of a body that worked unimpeded. The miracle of breath, thought, emotion.

Everything.

"I guess that is pretty cool," I murmured.

"Your body doesn't have to be perfect or work perfectly for you to have value. You have it because you *are*. Close your eyes and ask, *Could I be wrong about my own worth?*"

A ball bubbled up in my throat, nearly cutting my breath off. I barely managed to whisper the question.

"What's the answer?" Janine asked.

My eyes opened again. I leaned forward and covered my face with my hands as a sob burst from my chest.

"Yes," I whispered. "I've been wrong my whole life. Because of that, horrible things happened. If I had just . . . why didn't I know? Now I feel like I've been living a lie."

"Was it?"

"No."

"Can you forgive yourself for making the mistakes that have haunted you? Can you have compassion for yourself?"

Something felt like it slid into place in my mind. Forgiveness wasn't excusing my behavior. It was removing it as an obstacle. It was compassion.

Love.

"Yes," I whispered, my lip quivering. "I can. I think I finally can."

Janine's warm hand rested on the middle of my back a few moments later. Heavy sobs unleashed themselves in a torrent of tears, emotion, and ugly, ugly memories that I'd been holding back. Ages seemed to pass. When the sobs turned to sniffles, Janine passed me a tissue and met my watery gaze with firm compassion.

"You may have believed the lies others—probably unknowingly—told you about yourself. You may have believed you were less-than when you absolutely were not. That is something to grieve. But you face a choice that many don't know they can make. There's a fork in the road for you, Rachelle. You can continue as you have been, or you can fight for more."

Her hand dropped away from my back.

"What are you going to believe about yourself now?"

That night, I sat at my desk.

Crickets sang outside in a sweet summer serenade as I gathered my notebook and a pen. A listless breeze whisked into my room, carrying the quiet shuffle of leaves with it. My lamp cast a warm light, countering the flicker of the television under the door. I stared at a blank piece of paper and tapped my pen against the desk.

I had to do it.

I had to.

For an hour I'd sat there, staring at the paper, still feeling drained from my emotional meeting with Janine. Now, I needed to act. With a pained breath, I put the pen on the paper and began to write.

Dear Rachelle,

This letter isn't going to be perfect. And for the first time, I think that's okay.

I paused, read back, and sighed.

First, I want you to know that you are beautiful. You don't see it yet. It's like it's hidden. There's a tapestry in your mind that's keeping you from the truth. But the truth is there, and this is it: you are worth something. One day the tapestry will shift, and you'll see it.

You'll see that you're wicked smart and have an eye for business and all things pastry. Don't be afraid of that so much. You're stronger than

> you think. You have laugh lines around your eyes because of your great sense of humor. Really strong shoulders—in more ways than one. These are some of my favorite things, but they aren't everything.

Strong shoulders. That was something positive. I glanced down. Thanks to Megan and lots of overhead squats, I *did* have strong shoulders. The pen stopped, hovering just over the page. Did drawing attention to my body count as loving myself? Then again, hadn't Janine and I just spent an entire session doing that?

> But you are more than those things. You are more than the "roles" you play. (Which, right now, you think your roles are college dropout, runner, daughter, best friend, and girl-that-doesn't-know-what-she-wants.) But it's not who you are, even if you don't know who that is yet.
>
> You are powerful. Maybe you don't see yourself as powerful in the same way that you see Bitsy as powerful, but you are. Didn't you lose over a hundred pounds? Didn't you make a hard life change?
>
> Didn't you seek help?

The words spilled out faster now, as if they came from a different place in my mind. From someone that wasn't me. Someone that directed the pen and the pain, pushing them both along. I let them flow, feeling a catharsis in the release.

> It's not easy to face the darkness, but it's worth it. You are confident. You are brave. You are a warrior princess—the exact one you dressed up as no less than fifty-four times in your teenage years. You wanted to be her so badly that you didn't even recognize you already are her.
>
> You're strong, Rachelle. You'll never know how strong until you let yourself. It's time to be that girl.
>
> Love,
>
> A Wiser Rachelle

Before I could go back and read a single word or comprehend what I'd said, I closed the notebook and stuffed it back under my bed. Then I lay on my mattress, stared at the ceiling, and drew in a long, shuddering breath. Janine's challenge ran through my mind.

What are you going to believe about yourself now?

Rearranging

A flash of a long-sleeved bright green shirt slipped past the prep room the next day. William gave me a quick smile and wave before disappearing down the hall. I watched him go, startled. He came and went pretty often—deliveries or not—but today seemed particularly unexpected.

"Sophia," he called. "I think I found a new distributor that could get you supplies for ten percent cheaper."

I pulled my thoughts out of the baking magazines I'd been perusing all morning, hoping for inspiration to create exciting new recipes but finding none. Grateful for a distraction, I grabbed my crutch and worked my way toward the hall.

When I peered around the corner, William had thrown his lean body into a chair across from Sophia's desk. She sat with a cup of coffee and a harried expression, her eyes half on him, half on the computer screen. She'd been wandering around all morning, expecting a call from someone at a bank, alternating mumbling to herself and staring at the wall. I'd let her go, not certain I wanted to know why.

"Oh?" she asked absently.

"They're the same brands that you order now, I checked. But I was able to talk them down a bit in order to get them some business."

"Mmm-hmm . . ."

A giant calculator sat next to her computer. A negative number appeared on the screen when I shuffled closer to her door. William glanced at me and managed a small smile but couldn't hide the stress in his eyes.

Sophia's office reminded me of a wedding cake. Light peach walls. A couch with silver and white ruffled pillows—I suspected she slept there some nights. Gauzy white linens hung from either side of two tall, thin windows. They fluttered whenever the air conditioning flipped on. Her deep mahogany desk was adorned with pictures of young kids—I presumed her nieces and nephews as she'd never mentioned having any of her own—in gilded white frames. The only thing that didn't fit was the collection of decorative knitting needles that lined the wall behind her chair. The rest of it was elegant, simple, and understated, like Sophia herself.

"Oh, and I finished mowing your lawn and walking Braveheart," William added, rubbing his hands down his pant legs, as if to get rid of grass stains. "He didn't eat breakfast again."

"Braveheart?" I asked.

Sophia glanced at me, then back down with a frown. "My dog."

"He's a total chicken," William whispered. His gaze returned to Sophia, who muttered under her breath as she studied a spreadsheet on her computer. A bridal consultation was coming in in twenty minutes, and she was still haphazardly put together with a skewed bun, glasses half on her face, and no makeup.

"Fifteen-minute warning," I said. "You need to get ready for your next consultation."

Sophia growled deep in her throat and shoved away from the computer. "Right. Consultation. Oh, thanks William on the tip. Can you bring me the details tomorrow? I'll be able to look into it more then. I have a few things on my mind today and won't really be able to give you the consideration you deserve. That okay?"

"Of course."

"Thanks." Sophia walked around the desk, bent down, and pressed a kiss to his cheek before leaving the room. The bathroom door down the hall closed, followed by a rush of water.

William met my gaze. "Do you have a minute?"

"Sure."

He reached around me and closed the door behind us. I opened my mouth to protest, but he instantly stepped back, putting six feet of space between us. Whatever this was, it couldn't be good. He swallowed hard, nostrils flaring, like a kid on too much sugar.

"You okay?" I asked.

"Is there anything I can do to help Sophia?"

"With the store?"

He nodded, so eager I thought of a puppy. My mouth opened, then closed.

"I-I don't know. She's never told me numbers."

"She's drowning. I can tell. I haven't seen her like this since . . ."

He sucked in a sharp breath and shook his head. "It's been a long time. I have to be able to do something to save her."

"I'm going to create some new recipes."

"Okay."

"We're hoping they'll appeal to a new client base. Bring some people in, at least. I think if we can get the store selling better, it'll take the pressure off."

"Great." He nodded. "What can I do?"

I blinked, taken aback by his sudden ferocity and curious again about his relationship with Sophia. Just like every time he slipped in, which was more and more often these days, it seemed like too much to ask him.

"I don't know yet," I said. "I'm supposed to propose some new recipes in two days. I guess we'll need help selling them?"

"I can do that. People?"

"Yeah. Sure. We'll need people."

"I have people."

"Good."

An awkward silence stretched between us. It wouldn't be enough to bring people the day we launched the new recipes. We needed a steady stream. But the exposure would help. He let out a long breath, appearing less cagey. I peered at him. "Are *you* okay?"

"Fine."

"You seem—"

"Sophia means a lot to me. The Frosting Cottage has been her dream for years. She started it after the accident, and I don't want it to fail. It *can't* fail." He stepped forward and grabbed me by the shoulders. My breath nearly stopped. "If there is anything I can do to stop this from caving, please let me know. I will do whatever it takes to make it happen, so don't be afraid to think big."

"O-okay."

He opened his mouth to say something, then decided against it and shook his head instead.

"Thanks."

When his hands fell away, something seemed to go with them. The air in the room felt a little stuffier, close. He stepped back again, looking sheepish.

"Sorry. Sometimes I get too intense," he said. "I'm just worried."

I managed a half smile. "I think it's sweet. I'll think about it, all right? I promise."

He dug into his pocket and pulled out his phone. "Will you give me your number? Then you can text me any idea you have."

"Sure."

He unlocked the screen, pulled up a new contact page, and passed it to me. I filled it out, sent a text to myself, and gave it back. The text came through, vibrating against my back pocket.

"Thanks," he said again.

"Sure."

William slid past me, then stepped into the hall and disappeared into the prep room just as Sophia came out of the bathroom, looking like her normal self, even though I saw the strain behind the shadows in her eyes. She gave me a bright smile. I returned it, then hobbled back to the prep room. My gaze flitted around, and William's determination infused me with new spirit. I grabbed all the books I'd gleaned from Mom's bookshelf—which had been surprisingly full of recipes—and spread them out in front of me.

I'd make new recipes.

Then we'd kill it on the new launch.

"Lexie, I need you to tell me everything you remember about me when we were little."

Lexie paused. I pressed the phone harder to my ear, as if that would encourage her to respond sooner, but she said nothing.

"Uh, okay," she responded. "Right now?"

"Can you? Are you busy?"

"No. I'm definitely not standing outside a gas station talking myself out of a donut because it will only make me feel sick to my stomach. Good timing. Really glad you called. Hold on, let me get back in the car."

The rustle of movement and the sudden chime of a bell rang in the background. I heard a door shut and keys clink together. She sighed.

"Okay, I'm back. What's going on?"

"It's something I'm doing with Janine."

"Can we do this over video, then? Way more effective when I can see your face."

"Sure."

Lexie's face appeared on the screen with a bright smile seconds later. Her blonde hair fell into her cornflower blue eyes. She blew it out of her way with a light raspberry.

"Thanks," she said. "You helped save me from a really bad decision."

"Chocolate-covered?"

"No. Just glazed. I don't think I would have bought it, but the temptation is real. I—whoa. Chelle. What's going on over there?"

Hundreds of photos fanned the floor around me, cluttering the old carpet in my bedroom. Images of a doll-faced little girl with liquid chocolate eyes and brown hair. Princess tutus. Tiaras. Cheesy smiles. Sticky fingers. Me dressed as Sleeping Beauty at Halloween. Mom and me sitting on the couch together when I was three or four. Pictures from my first prom.

"I'm rearranging the way I think of myself," I said, glancing at the photos. "It helps to remember who I've been."

"With baby and prom pictures?"

"How else?"

"Fair."

I cleared my throat. "You love your niece, right?"

"That *squish*!" she cried. "Yes! I could eat her for—wait. Why? Of course I love her. You know that."

Lexie listened with rapt attention while I recounted the last session with Janine. She frowned, gasped, teared up, and stared hard at me at all the right moments. Just talking to Lexie was validating.

"Whoa," she said.

I flapped a picture so she could see it. "That little girl had value, so why don't I? Just like your niece. It's like I think I lost value along the way, but that doesn't make sense either. I don't think *you've* lost value."

"Have you pulled out the pictures of five-year-old Rachelle yet?" she asked quietly.

An icy shiver shot through my chest.

I swallowed hard. Of course Lexie would go there right away.

She'd open the path to the place that I'd been seeking through these pictures but not actually wanting to find. Wasn't this really why I'd called her?

Five years old meant she was thinking of the day Dad left. I picked up a glossy photo of me as a toddler, my brown hair curled at my neck, mouth spread in a gummy giggle. Two paces away, arms outstretched, was my father. He had thick black hair, dark skin, and a bushy mustache. I couldn't believe Mom hadn't burned it with all the others. It was the only shred of evidence I had that Dad was actually real. The vague memories, mere wisps, weren't just my imagination.

"No," I finally whispered.

"Why not?"

"You know why!"

"You're trying to figure out if your father leaving is the reason you feel you lost your worth. Like it was your fault that he left. Am I right?"

That's exactly what I'd been trying to do. My heart paused for half a beat. "Was it my fault?"

Her expression softened. "Of course not, Rachelle."

"What if he left because of me? What if me being born was the wedge that pushed him away from my mom? Lexie, this could all be my fault."

"Could it?"

The intensity of her question reined in my wild, hysterical thoughts.

"I-I mean . . ."

"Could an adorable little five-year-old who loved her father and her mother, who played in the kiddie pool and ate ice cream, really have caused issues between her parents that drove them to make really rash decisions?"

"No."

"Think my niece could do that?"

"No."

"No way, Rachelle. If that happened to my sister, it would be all about her and her husband's issues, not baby girl. Your father leaving and never coming back had nothing to do with *you*. It speaks nothing to your worth but to his issues. His desperation. His fear. Not yours."

"Then what could have haunted him?" I asked. "What could drive someone to leave and never return? Never call? Never write? Never do anything?"

"It's a good question."

"I don't think there's an answer."

"Oh, there's an answer. You just may not like it or understand it or ever get it, really. You can talk to me anytime, Chelle, and I'll be here. But I'm not the person you should be talking to about this. I think you know that."

A cold fist of dread settled into my stomach like an icee. Lexie was right. I didn't want her to be, but she was. My gaze flickered over to the door just as Mom laughed. The unmistakable sound of *Seinfeld* drifted into the room.

Mom. I needed to talk to Mom.

"Think she'll tell me?" I asked.

"Are you going to ask her?"

"Yes."

Lexie's eyes widened. "Really?"

With a deep breath, I nodded. "Really."

"I don't know, Rachelle. I've never really heard your mom talk about anything except food and television."

"Me neither."

"Maybe she'll surprise you."

I mentally steeled myself. Dad didn't leave because I suddenly lost value. He left for *something*. As his daughter, I deserved to know. Yearned to know. *Had* to know.

Right now.

"I'm going to talk to her right now while it's on my mind," I said.

"Good. Then you won't back out."

I managed a half-hearted smile. "Let's hope not. I'll call you back later, that okay?"

"Always."

"Thanks, Lexie. Love you."

"You too, Chelle. And seriously, call me back ASAP! I'm dying to know what you find out."

With one more round of promises, I shut off the phone and slowly stood up. Photos fluttered back to the ground like sheets of tissue paper. My lungs expanded with a deep breath.

The time to confront Mom had finally come.

My stomach growled when I swung my way out of my bedroom. Night had started to fall, leaving the corners of the trailer swathed in shadows. An almost-empty bowl of Muddy Buddies rested at Mom's side. I opened my mouth to speak, lost courage, and continued into the kitchen. It was past 8:00 in the evening, and I still hadn't eaten dinner. A quick search through the fridge revealed nothing appetizing. I grabbed an apple from the crisper and a water bottle from the door and shoved both into the pockets of my sweatpants.

"So, Mom, how was your day?" I asked while I hobbled over to just behind the couch. The cap of the water bottle cracked when I twisted it open. Mom glanced up, then back to the television.

"Uh . . . fine."

"Finish your projects?"

She lifted the remote and flipped the channel, eventually settling on an old rerun of NCIS. Trying to predict the killer had been one of our favorite games. Actually, she seemed to have a knack for it.

"Yep," she said.

The usual silence fell. My throat thickened. Could I really do this? Talking to Mom about Dad was the epitome of desperation and need. She never spoke about him. Not even when I'd asked. I felt like this was last-straw kind of stuff. I cleared my throat.

"Hey, Mom?"

She glanced up, as if surprised to be addressed a second time. Was it so unusual to hear my voice? Had it been that long since we'd spoken? Losing weight had certainly driven a wedge between us, but this seemed more like a mountain. I shrugged it off. Surely the hours at my new job had something to do with it.

"Yes?" she asked.

"I need to talk. Ask you some questions, if I can."

"Talk?"

"Yeah. Um . . . can we talk without the television on?"

Her throat bobbed as she swallowed. She moved aside the mixing bowl filled with powdered-sugar memories and sifted through the crumbs on the bottom. She often ate an entire batch of Muddy Buddies herself. I used to make my own batch. We'd sit on the couch together, eating out of our own mixing bowls while falling into unending Netflix series or RedBox rentals. The conversations hadn't been all that in-depth, now that I thought back on it. Chatter about school. Lying about my current boyfriends. *No, Mom,* I'd say in horror. *I would never let a guy sneak into my room. You must have heard the wind last night, or me talking in my sleep.* She always seemed relieved enough when she heard what she wanted to hear.

Mom motioned to the couch with a limp wave.

"Uh . . . sure," she said. "Have a seat."

She muted the television and turned to face me, except she stared at my shoulder. The words stuck in my throat. How could I ask her about Dad? I racked my brain, trying to remember the last time she'd even left the house. Three years ago, the power had been out for six hours. She'd been in a sheer panic without the television for that long, so she went to the grocery store, then quickly came back because her hips ached.

"I . . . uh . . . I just had a few questions for you," I said as I moved around the couch and sat across from her. The crutches clattered a little as I set them aside.

"Okay," she said.

"How have you been?"

Her eyes darted to mine, looking small in the folds of her face. "Fine," she drawled. "You?"

"Fine."

Panic made me hot. If I asked her questions about Dad, I'd have to explain why I was asking. What would Mom say about Janine? Would she think I was crazy? Mom's gaze flickered to the TV. For some reason, asking about him seemed like too much. Far too personal when we could barely handle small talk.

"What was your question about?" she finally asked.

"Dad," I said, blurting it out like I was giving birth. "I have questions about Dad."

Her head jerked back to face me, mouth open. She readjusted, as if she'd had to compensate for the world suddenly shifting, and looked away.

"Oh."

"Look, I know it's coming from nowhere, but . . . I've been thinking about how we've never really spoken about him. I mean, the last time I can remember is when I was in high school. And I think you just said that he left and, except for divorce papers, you haven't heard anything."

"What questions do you have?"

Her even cadence, the unruffled tone, all took me by surprise. Had I expected her to burst into flames? Hysterics? Tears? Dealing with her so calm and in control seemed too easy. I didn't know what to do next. Couldn't we just resort to yelling at each other the way we did when I was a tween?

"Well, to start, I guess I was just curious about what happened between the two of you."

She shrugged, her face deadpan. "We grew apart. He was pretty closed off for most of our marriage. Didn't like to talk."

"How did you meet him?"

For half a breath, I thought I detected a softening. A fissure in her icy wall. But it hardened. She blinked.

"I can't remember."

"How long did you date before you got married?"

"Three weeks."

I reared back. "That's all?"

She shrugged. "Felt good at the time. I didn't have any other offers and didn't think I likely would."

"Oh."

Her eyes narrowed. She folded her hands in front of her, threading the sausage-like fingers together. "I suppose it *was* fast, and there were issues I should have known were red flags, but that didn't seem important at the time."

"What issues?"

"Can't remember." She reached blindly for the bowl of Muddy Buddies and, finding it still empty, frowned.

"Nothing?"

"I guess money? He was really tight with his money and was always blowing up about the grocery bills. And we used to fight about food." Her shoulders tightened. "All the time."

"Food?"

"At first we didn't really argue, but then we got pregnant with you. I put on a little more weight than he would have liked. Once you were born, he was really controlling about how much you ate and would always get angry with me if I fed you certain things, like ice cream. I thought it was okay to have a treat every now and then, but he didn't."

Something wrinkled inside me. So I *was* the cause? *No,* I thought, blinking with the power of a sudden memory. The day Dad left they had argued . . . over me eating ice cream. No.

A *second* ice cream.

"Do you remember the day he left?" I asked instead, pushing that away to analyze later. For some reason, the details seemed intimately important, as if I could extract the story from them alone.

If possible, her eyes grew even more distant. I fought off panic. This was the most I'd ever gotten out of her. Whatever magic existed today would probably never happen again. I couldn't lose the thread now.

"Yes," she said. "I remember when he left."

"You were fighting, right?" I asked gently. Snippets of memory continued to flit across my mind. A pool. Hot sunshine. Something sticky on my hands. The sounds of screaming from the house. I was outside?

"Yes," she said.

"About an . . . ice cream cone?"

Her eyes returned to mine for half a breath. "Yes. Something like that, I'm sure. It was always something with him. I forgot a bill once, and he freaked out. So controlling."

"Do you know why he left?"

"I can't remember."

"Is there anything you *can* remember?"

She blinked once. Twice. Even though the room lay oddly quiet, I felt as if something loud filled it. Perhaps my pounding heart. Or the heavy sound of silence.

"I remember that I did love him once. I think. It's so hard to remember anymore. We were very young. And then . . ." Her voice trailed away. She turned her head, angling it back toward the television.

In a shot of desperation, I said, "Mom, I've been blaming myself for your divorce."

She sucked in a sharp breath but didn't move.

"I-I think I've . . . I thought he left because of me. Is that true? I mean . . . if I had just done or acted differently, somehow, would things have worked out better? Is this my fault?" I asked in a small voice.

I couldn't help it—I sounded like a lost little girl. It had been years since I'd been this honest with her. Ten years since I'd admitted anything real to her. The words left me feeling raw and exposed in a way I'd never felt before.

Her brow furrowed into deep grooves. Beneath all the layers of her body—her graying hair, her muumuu, the shield of skin and girth she wore to protect herself, I wondered if she even knew who *she* was anymore. What were her roles? What did she believe—probably falsely, like I did—about herself? If Mom asked herself these questions, what answers would she find?

She reached over, putting a thick hand on my knee. Tears sparkled in her eyes. For the first time in a long time, the little girl inside me stopped screaming.

"Whatever your father was or wasn't, Rachelle, had nothing to do with you. It may not seem like it, but he loved you very much."

My eyes watered. "Then why did he leave?" I whispered.

Her lips hardened. She leaned back, and her hand fell away, taking any trace of the mom I once knew with her. This time, she angled her body away as much as she could and sank back into the couch cushions.

"Because of me."

With that, she turned the volume back on the television—so loud it hurt my ears—and I returned to my room, my thoughts spinning.

Inspiration

The door to the Frosting Cottage tinkled behind me when I shut it the next day. I stepped into the warm aroma of fresh cinnamon rolls and confectioners sugar, hung my bag on the peg in Sophia's office, and hobbled into the preparation area.

"Sophia?" I called.

"Coming!" she sang. Flour dusted her cheeks and apron when she appeared. A beautiful tower of cake, tulle, and glittery perfection sat on the far prep table. "I'm just about to finish up the McArthur cake. What's up?"

I passed her a crumpled piece of paper.

"Here. Sorry it's so wrinkled. Mira drove me today, and I thought I was going to die. But I had a few strokes of inspiration on the way, thanks to Mira talking nonstop about her Pepsi addiction unraveling."

She unwadded it and leaned back against the counter with her hip. I held my breath at first.

"Cupcake ideas," she murmured. "Sweet potato with cream cheese frosting. Pineapple lemon lime. Bacon and maple. Grapefruit with buttercream. Dr Pepper flavored?"

"That was actually Mira's idea. I think she wanted to say Pepsi but didn't dare in case Bitsy's bugged her car."

Her head tilted to the side as she continued without further comment. "Healthy cupcake ideas: Green tea. Earl Grey. Low sugar. Lavender. Gluten free. Java. Cappuccino. Cupcakes sweetened with—or made from—beets. Carrot-cake cupcakes. Zucchini cake."

She glanced up, eyes wide. The list fluttered in her hand as she shook it.

"Whoa."

"It's just a starter list." My cheeks flared. Why was I so self-conscious? With the last of my courage, I extended a second sheet of paper. "These are my other ideas that aren't cupcakes. I came up with them last night when I couldn't sleep."

Mostly because Mom banged around the kitchen like a mad hatter and cooked until four in the morning, but I left that out. I feared my questions had broken her. Sophia snatched the paper out of my hand and continued to read out loud.

"Loose tea in glass jars. Crazy lemonade flavors: Tangerine. Blackberry. Currant. Gooseberry. Dessert ideas: Fruit pizza. Peanut butter cookies filled with actual peanut butter. Gingerbread brownies instead of normal brownies. Rice Krispie treats with different flavors. Chili. Pickle. Lemon lime. Bite-sized cookies instead of really big ones. Buy by the dozen and have a variety of at least twelve. Brilliant," she murmured under her breath. "Like a cookie bar."

"Yeah! Except less guilt because they're smaller. So people just looking for something small could buy those."

"Yes, yes. Brilliant." She tapped the paper again. More ideas trailed down it that she hadn't read out loud. "I love the movie-themed mini-cake ideas too. Wonder Woman. Deadpool. Market it to the what's popular. We can tell them that they can have the cake for the first time they watch the movie! We'll patrol Netflix and new releases . . ."

"Yes! We could coordinate the flavors, colors, and piping to match the movie style."

"Yes!"

My heart pattered a little in my chest, but I forced myself to stay cool. I cleared my throat instead of hopping up and down on one leg. Sophia bit her bottom lip and kept perusing the ideas. There weren't many more, but her eyes darted around the sheet, going back over the ideas she'd already read. Then she paused, eyes glued to the paper in an unseeing gaze.

"It may not be as branded as you wanted," I said. "I mean, if you wanted to be a bit more niche, we could work with that. I—"

"Stop."

She held up a hand. My mouth snapped shut.

A grin crossed her face. "Rachelle, this is wonderful. These ideas would set the Frosting Cottage apart and bring new people in. The cookie bar especially. We could rotate cookies each day and charge by the bag. No! By the dozen. We could offer bulk orders as well. Holiday themed! Then they could sample . . ."

She trailed off, mumbling under her breath as she paced the kitchen. Seconds later, she yanked supplies out of the cupboards and shoved them onto the prep counter. Sprinkles. A cake-frosting knife. A bag of flour she used to make small, experimental batches. Food coloring.

"What are you doing?"

"We're getting started."

"But—"

She reached into her pocket, pulled out a wad of cash, and tossed it to me. "Call William. He doesn't have class today. Tell him to get a twelve-pack of Dr Pepper. Pepsi. Coke. Sprite. What are other big flavors? I love the soda cupcake ideas."

I caught the cash mid-air but hesitated. "I haven't worked out the recipes yet. These were just ideas. I was going to kind of refine and test from there."

"No, no. This is the fun part!" She reached into the pocket of her apron, pulled out her black hat, and slid it on. "We get to play. Bakers rarely take enough time to play. We get focused on the next batch, the next cake, and rarely take time to just frolic with ingredients and make something fabulous."

"The McArthur cake—"

"I'll get to it." She waved a hand. "They won't pick it up until tonight. Would you like to learn more about recipe creation?"

Anticipation streaked through me like wildfire. Not only would it be fun to *try* something new, but I hadn't felt this excited about something since I signed up for the marathon. It had been a while since I just . . . let myself be happy. Embraced food in my life.

Did something new.

"Of course!" I cried. "That sounds like a blast."

"Then call William. Tell him whatever you think we'll need to try this out, and I'll get started with a base. We'll have to be careful about the liquid-to-flour ratio in the soda cupcakes . . ."

Unbidden, a giggle rolled out of me. Sophia glanced up, then grinned. Within moments, both of us were laughing. It felt so good to release all the heavier emotions of the past three days. I laughed until my eyes watered. The weight on my shoulders disappeared. Oh, how I missed laughing.

Sophia tossed me an apron. "Put this on, Miss Martin, and make that call. We have lots to do today."

Reframe

Janine glanced at the scrapbook on the couch next to me. "What is this?"

I'd carted the old scrapbook in a backpack to my next session. It sat there like an innocent little thing even though I knew it was a time bomb. Given one good opportunity, that combustible collection of memories would explode and rain sugar cereal and sprinkles.

"It's a scrapbook my best friend and I assembled when we were young."

Janine's eyebrows rose. She held out both her hands. "How lovely! Would you mind if I looked at it?"

"It's . . . well, no. Of course not. You can look at it all you want. But I brought it because I hate it."

"You hate it?"

"Well," I mumbled, "I hate the pictures of me *in* it. This binder is why I'm struggling to really accept myself."

"Because of a photo album?"

"Because of what's *in* the photo album. Mainly pictures of me when I was loud and obnoxious and overweight. Every time I try to love myself, I end up thinking about this binder. It represents the worst parts of me."

"Ah."

"So . . . I brought it. Thought maybe we could start here."

She smiled warmly. "I'm so glad you did. Let's start at the beginning and see what is so terrible that you don't want to face."

My stomach churned when she carried it back to her chair. I didn't care if Janine saw the pictures—*I* just didn't want to see them. Long months had passed since I'd convinced myself that being fat was better than being thin. Now, I had no idea what I felt. I just knew that these pictures stood in my way of figuring it out.

Janine pointed to the first one.

"Can you tell me about this picture?"

Lexie and I were sitting at the table, a pizza box open in front of us. The late-summer humidity left blooms of color on my cheeks. I wore a tank top and had plenty of arm fat spilling out the side. I swallowed. My hair stuck out in two braids on either side of my head, like Pippi Longstocking.

"That was the summer before eighth grade. What you can't see is the empty pizza box off to side. Mom and I had finished that one off, and then I was helping Lexie with the second one. That night, we had a marathon watching romantic comedies."

Janine flipped the binder around so I had to face it straight-on. She grabbed a piece of paper and covered me, leaving only Lexie.

"Take yourself out of the spiral of shame that I can see on your face. I want you to see just Lexie."

"Okay."

"Describe what you see."

I blinked, already prepared for something like this. Seeing myself through the lens of Lexie had been easier, even if it hurt that I still couldn't look at myself.

"I see a girl having a good time."

Janine smiled. "It does look like a fun time! Pizza and romantic comedies with your friend? What a perfect summer memory."

The corners of my lips tugged up slightly. It had been fun staying up late with Lexie, giggling over boys and pizza. It always felt as if I belonged somewhere, with someone. The smile spread, a bit sheepishly.

"I always tried to get Lexie to do burping contests, but she wouldn't. She knew I'd win."

To my surprise, Janine laughed. "A proud trophy, I'm sure." She slipped the paper away. "Keep that perspective. Now, tell me what you see."

A lump rose in my throat. I saw bright eyes. A true, wide smile. A girl who, although she'd just eaten more pizza than two girls her age should have, had a spark of something in her. Was it strength? Was it fun?

Buried beneath the smiles in that picture was something deeper. Something haunted. Maybe frightened. A girl who felt as if she were careening out of control, hurtling down the tracks of her own life, and didn't know how to stop. No one, it seemed, reached out a hand to slow her.

"I see . . . someone a little bit frightened," I said.

"Of what?"

"Herself. Her love for food. Her ability to hide in it. I was terrified because I couldn't stop, and no one seemed to be stopping me."

"Interesting."

Tears clogged my throat.

Janine's brow furrowed. "What are you feeling now?"

"I don't know," I whispered. "Sadness? I . . . I was so lost. I mean, I was happy but . . . I felt so out of control. So confused and alone and . . . food was the only compass I had. The steady thing that made me feel good. For a while, anyway. Afterwards, I felt worse."

Her expression softened. "Food was a link to happiness and love."

"Yeah."

Tears brimmed in my eyes and dropped down my cheeks one at a time. I wiped them off with the back of my hand as Janine motioned back to the picture.

"When you set aside self-hatred, what do you think is the truth?"

The photo seemed to fade into mere pixels as I stared at it remembering the damp, cheap trailer. The rickety old table. The greasy pizza box. Even Mom had seemed happy that night, perched on the end of the same couch we still had.

"I think I was lonely, and I . . . survived through food."

"You survived a very lonely and frightening situation. Food was your friend. It prevented you from coping through worse means and helped you get through. But you aren't that young anymore."

"Why is it so painful now?"

"The mind is a lot like the body. When we get a splinter that isn't removed, what happens?"

"It hurts?"

She put her hands in the shape of a circle. "It forms a protective little ball that isolates the splinter from the rest of the body, protecting us from infection. The mind does the same thing with difficult memories. It creates pockets of pain. When we see them and remove the emotional splinters, it's going to hurt a little." Her hand opened up. "But then the pocket is gone, and it won't affect us anymore."

"So I'm popping pockets of pain?"

She nodded, her lips pressed together. "Yeah. It takes time. They'll appear unexpectedly, but then you deal with them. You look at them as an adult with a new, wider perspective and see the truth."

Janine brought the photo album back to me. "Leave it open," she said. "Now I want you to see the picture and tell me what you want to see."

My eyes skimmed the memory. Lexie's wide grin, full lips, bright blue eyes. She wore a baggy t-shirt and shorts. The night had smelled like pizza and root beer and sunshine. I could still remember the cold root beer trickling down my throat. I didn't want to see shame in my eyes or a girl who hated herself.

"I guess I want to see two best friends having a good time."

"Then close your eyes and count to five. Now, open them and look at the picture. Instead of thinking, *I'm so chubby* or *I wish I hadn't eaten so much*, I want you to remember how fun it was. For example, you could think, *That was really fun* or *I'm so lucky I had a good time with my best friend*."

With a deep breath, I obeyed. When I opened my eyes, I said, "I'm really lucky that Lexie and I could have such a good time."

"And that you had such a great best friend!"

"Yeah. It was easy to hang out with her because she never cared about how I looked." I tilted my head to the side with a smile. "It really was a fun night."

"Very good." Janine smiled with a knowing grin. "Yes, horrible memories happen. No, we shouldn't stuff them aside or act as if they didn't. We move through them, process them, lance that pocket, and reframe in a positive light. Can you give that a try this week?"

My gaze dropped to the picture. I managed a haphazard smile. "Yeah. I can. And I *am* pretty lucky to have someone like Lexie."

Janine beamed. "Good, because that's your homework. Reframe your memories, reframe your thoughts, and you'll reframe your life."

"Rachelle, your ankle has shown marked improvement."

"Really?"

I perked up out of my half-comatose state. After working a full day at the Frosting Cottage on chili-flavored Rice Krispie treats, I worried that my ankle would be swollen. But Dr. Martinez stared at it with a tilted head. Her warm fingers gave me some hope because the ankle didn't hurt when she touched or rotated it. I leaned forward to see better. Most of the swelling had disappeared, leaving only gentle streaks of color that had once been marbled bruises. The swelling had receded enough that I saw veins in the pale skin again.

"You dropped the weight on your foot over a month ago. Healing seems consistent. Overall, a marked decrease in swelling and bruising. Better range of motion, for sure."

"So I can start exercising?"

"No." She straightened up and met my hopeful gaze. "But you can start weight bearing."

My shoulders slumped, but I forced them to straighten. Disappointing, to be sure, but far better than nothing. Surely Janine's *reframing* lesson could pertain to more than bad memories. Perhaps I needed to start *reframing* my current attitude.

"That's great news," I said. "I'm just happy to be doing something."

Dr. Martinez studied me. "What? No complaints? No frustrated sighs?"

"I'm happy to move forward."

Which felt true.

She paused, then nodded once. "Good for you. Yes, this is a great step. We'll start with toe-touch weight bearing, which means we'll swap the boot out for a simpler brace."

"Hallelujah!"

She pointed a pen at me. "Toe touch means you can only touch your toe to the ground as you walk. Nothing else. Let's see how that goes and then move from there in a week. Then we'll talk physical therapy for rehab."

I smiled. "Thanks. That sounds great."

"You can drive now, as long as it doesn't feel like too much movement and doesn't hurt. The brace won't restrict that."

Relief coursed through me. Even better than expected! I'd have a modicum of my life back.

"Thanks, Dr. Martinez."

She winked. "I'll see you in a month. My nurse will come in soon to demonstrate toe-touch weight bearing with you. Don't get crazy, all right? Your bones need time to adjust. If it hurts, stop."

Twenty minutes later, Mira pulled up just as I worked my way back out. *Toe-touch* weight bearing wasn't as easy as it sounded. Putting some weight but not too much felt like a moving mathematical formula. Still, having that boot off felt divine. The blast of air conditioning that hit my face when I slipped into Mira's old Cadillac revived me.

"Good news?" she asked.

"Yeah." I grinned. "Starting toe-touch weight bearing and will start with a physical therapist in a week. I can drive again!"

"Great!" Mira's expression dropped. "Are you okay with that? It's not as much as you wanted, is it?"

I drew in a deep breath and paused. How did I feel? I felt . . . okay. Unconcerned, even. Now that I had some space from what had happened, I could see that running the marathon really hadn't been the most important thing in the world. Healing my ankle thoroughly so I could continue to move without pain was more important.

"Yeah," I said with a smile. "I'm very happy with that."

Mira patted my knee. "Good on you, girl. Let's get you to work. Sophia said she needed taste testers for a lemon-lime cupcake? What brilliant genius came up with that? Leave it in the Sprite bottle, sister. That's all I have to say."

She winked at me. I tilted my head back and laughed.

Water, cool and clear, lapped at my feet.

For a moment, I stared at it, transfixed by the play of light in the pool. It rippled like ribbons dancing in the breeze. The sun bore down hot—at least, I thought it did. I couldn't really feel it, just saw the brightness. Then I noticed that my ankle was naked.

Why wasn't I wearing my new brace?

Where was I?

The happy shriek of a child brought me out of a confused daze. I looked up to see a little girl only a few feet away, splashing in a kiddie pool. Surrounding us was a familiar, weary fence and a rubbery hose that snaked through half-baked grass. A few lawn toys littered the area. My heart tied itself into a knot. That little girl's face was familiar.

Too familiar.

That little girl was me.

I was five years old, wearing a lime-colored swimsuit and a fluffy tutu. An ice cream cone dribbled down my knuckles, sticky sweet. The sweet taste of vanilla bean lingered on my tongue. I reached out to touch the water but felt nothing. This had to be a dream.

Behind me—us?—came the sounds of a familiar television show. *Eureeka's Castle.* My childhood favorite. The opening song played. Angry shouts followed on its heels. Little Rachelle glanced up, her intent gaze on the back door. Her forehead furrowed into a deep groove as the livid voices escalated.

"One ice cream cone is enough!"

"She's a little girl."

My heart trembled when I recognized the voices. Mom and Dad. How could I remember this day so vividly even though I'd been so young? Everything from the spray of sunshine in the water to the heavy blanket of summer air was vividly real. As if it came through the lens of a detailed camera.

"Exactly!" Dad yelled. "What little girl needs three ice cream cones?"

"They were small."

"That's not the point, Melissa!"

"Nothing I ever do is good enough. Did you even mention the fact that I gave her a good lunch? Or got up with her last night when she wet the bed? No. You don't care! You slept through everything just like the pathetic drunk you are."

Little Rachelle sucked in a sharp breath. A bead of ice cream rolled off the cone and down her knuckles. Something inside of me turned cold.

Fish sticks littered a plate next to me on the grass. Splotches of water from my small swimming pool sparkled on the half-dead lawn. A flash of heat warmed the bottom of my feet. Little Rachelle shifted to stand in a different spot, her eyes glued on the house. A little whimper escaped her lips. On instinct, I stepped forward and put a hand on her shoulder. Her tense muscles relaxed.

Could she feel me?

Was this . . . real?

"That's not what I'm trying to say," Dad said. "I just . . . feeding her nonstop ice cream is no way to raise a child."

"Don't be dramatic! It hasn't been nonstop."

"She needs to learn portion control. Look at her!"

"I suppose you're going to say that I need it next, right?"

"Don't put words in my mouth."

Two figures appeared in the window. One agitated, pacing back and forth as he rammed his hand through his thick black locks. The other throwing her hands in sharp gestures.

"I don't need to put words in your mouth!" Mom cried. "It's written all over your face. You're ashamed of me just like everyone else. You're so concerned about what I feed her? That's rich coming from you. You're never here! When you actually put some face time in with your child, you can critique the way I raise her."

The ice cream fell from little Rachelle's cone with a plop and melted into the grass. Little Rachelle frowned. Her body trembled. I crouched next to her, tears welling. Heat washed through my heart in long, sonorous waves when I saw the pain in her eyes. I remembered.

Oh, how I remembered.

"Oh, no," little Rachelle whispered.

A door slammed inside. Light flashed, as if someone had thrown open drapes. Mom screamed.

"Don't you walk away from me! If you walk out that door, don't bother coming back. We don't need you! We don't even want you."

"Why would I?" Dad shouted. "You don't respect me. You don't appreciate the twelve-hour days I work to pay the bills, to buy the food you stuff in your face every other minute. You don't even let me have a say in raising my own daughter! You just throw it in my face that I'm never enough."

"We'd be better off without you!"

Little Rachelle shoved the rest of the cone into the ground and darted across the lawn.

"Daddy," she whispered. "Daddy, no."

I followed close behind.

She ran to the back door and attempted to open it, but her sticky hands caught on the doorknob. It was locked. With a chubby fist, she banged on the door.

"Mom!"

Another door slammed—the front door. Shouts followed, unintelligible and fast. Everything seemed to blur. The world slowed. Panic surged through my veins. Something hung in the air. Something frightening. She could feel—we *both* could feel?—that something was wrong. This fight was different.

"Mom!" she screamed through a sob. The door trembled under her pounding fist. "*Mom!*"

I dropped to my knees next to her. Tears fell down my cheeks when I gently grabbed her shoulders.

"Rachelle," I murmured, "it's okay."

She didn't stop, but her frantic punches slowed.

"Mom!"

Distant shouts. A car starting. More screaming, sobs from somewhere else. Rachelle stopped and cocked her head to the side. In the booming silence that followed, my eyes darted over the trailer. It was so much younger. The paint hadn't peeled. A latticed skirt circled the bottom. No rust spots dotted the exterior. Little Rachelle rubbed her wrist under her nose. I turned back to her, my hands still on her shoulders.

"It's okay, Rachelle. This isn't your fault."

She sniffled. "They fight all the time."

For a moment, I froze. She heard me. Could I really talk to her? Was this a chance to recreate what had happened? To tell her the truth—not let her believe the lies she'd gathered like flowers in a field? A thousand thoughts whirled through my mind until I forced them to calm.

"I know they fight a lot. It's very scary, isn't it?"

"Daddy hates me."

My hands tightened on her shoulders. "No, sweetheart. Daddy doesn't hate you. He . . . he hates himself. He hates that he doesn't . . . ah . . . he doesn't know how to be a dad."

The moment I said the words, I knew they were true. Something in my heart seared, as if knitting back together. She turned to me, her bottom lip jutting out, and stared right into my eyes. Until I saw her, I hadn't realized how much it had hurt that day. The heaviness sank into my heart like a stone.

"Mom hates him," she whispered. "She says he's . . . he's gone too much. That he's trying to control us the way Grandpa controlled her. She says he'll hide the food and we won't be able to eat."

My voice was husky when I said, "She doesn't hate Daddy. They loved each other once. They've just forgotten how much. Sometimes that happens when you grow up. Things aren't always easy. But they both love *you* very much, even if they don't get along very well."

"Then why do they fight?"

"They fight because they're angry."

"At me?"

"Definitely not. At . . ." I paused. Was there a right answer? Their voices had been livid and tinged with desperation. Maybe even rage. Definitely pain. Mom had sounded like a mama bear. Not weak or frightened or small.

She had once been mighty.

"They're angry at themselves," I finally said. It felt right. "At each other. At really difficult adult things that they have to face. But not at you. Absolutely not at you. They're both trying to protect you. Just . . . in their own way."

"I want them to stop."

"I know you do. I know."

Rachelle stared at the back door. Her jaw tightened. Her steely gaze didn't waver. She stared at the door, nostrils flared. But her shoulders relaxed beneath my hands. Did I dare tell her that things wouldn't get better? That it would be difficult for many years? That she'd never see him again, and Mom would slowly fade away into a shell?

"It's not your fault," I whispered again, feeling desperate. "If there's anything I want you to understand, it's that none of this is about you. None of it! You are beautiful and good and kind and worth so much more than you believe. Can you believe that, Rachelle?"

The back door opened. I straightened, coming face-to-face with Mom. She didn't seem to notice me. She was young. A little overweight but not frighteningly so. She still moved with ease. Her hair hung in thick waves onto her shoulders. Tears sparkled in her eyes when she pushed open the back door. Little Rachelle shuffled back to allow space for the creaky screen door. She tilted her head, eyes sparkling.

"Mom?"

"Come inside, baby girl," Mom whispered, not seeing me there. "It's just you and me now."

Tears glimmered in my eyes when I reached out to touch Mom, but my fingers traveled through air. She didn't feel my touch on her arm. She didn't see me—didn't know how similar we looked. Twins. We could have been twins.

"Rachelle," I whispered and dropped back down to her. Time seemed to pause, elongating to give us space. A tear dropped down my face when she glanced back at me, solemn and wide-eyed. "I'm sorry this is happening to you. But I love you. They love you. It's not your fault. Please remember that? Please?"

Little Rachelle stepped inside with a sniffle. The door shut behind them. I stood on the porch, my heart a burning coal. The quiet backyard turned into waves. The heat abated.

My heart paused with a hiccup, then I streamed into the darkness that waited behind the memory.

I woke up with a gasp.

Sweat coated my face and neck. I sat up, sticky from the night humidity, my cheeks wet with tears. My heart raced until the endless drone of the television in the background reoriented me. My breathing slowed. My heart calmed. I collapsed back to the pillow and shoved the hair out of my sticky face.

Then I closed my eyes and fell back to sleep with a little girl on my mind.

The sound of a lawn mower ushered me out of sleep.

I emerged to life one layer at a time. My muscles felt as heavy as my thoughts, as if they wanted to stay in the safety of the darkness. Despite the strange fog that pervaded my mind in the wake of such a strange dream, there was something else that had changed. Space had opened up in my brain. Had my heart grown? Or had weight simply flown off of it?

I felt powerful.

Different.

When I stepped out of my room, Mom occupied the couch. She skimmed through the commercials, remote in hand. After a few seconds, she stopped on an old black-and-white movie. A plate full of sausages and scrambled eggs sat on the couch next to her. She grabbed a sausage and brought it to her lips. I thought of the fierce mama bear she'd been that day and wondered where she'd gone.

I thought she'd never really tried to be my mom, but she did once, I thought. *She wasn't always like this.*

With a shiver, I recalled the haunted expression in her eyes when Dad left. I went to the bathroom and cranked up the hot water. One could certainly argue that I'd *reframed* a massive memory last night. Perhaps the darkest of them. Janine's voice played through my mind while I stood beneath the warm spray of the shower on one leg.

Reframe your thoughts. Pull out the positive. Don't focus on the negative.

Once the water turned lukewarm, I stepped out. My hair felt silky when I pulled a comb through it, brushed my teeth, strapped my brace back on, and hobbled out with one crutch. Steam billowed out with me despite the sultry day. Mom didn't look up from the couch as I walked past. My gaze dropped to the food surrounding her like a wall.

She doesn't care, came the thought. *She doesn't care about anything but food and television.*

No, countered another thought. *I'm reframing. She does care. She did care. She does care about things.*

But that thought sputtered. I couldn't bring myself to believe it. If Mom cared about anything, I had no idea what it was. Food, maybe. The television schedule. Herself, too. Janine would say that Mom was hiding. That the pain she felt interacting with life on any level was too great. When did Mom ever speak about herself? Happy memories? Good times? Her parents? Her childhood?

Never.

I couldn't help but wonder what my grandparents had been like. Then I wondered if I wanted to know.

While I scrambled an egg, the dream-not-dream replayed through my mind. It hadn't been a dream. That had *really* happened. Every scary, frightening, real detail. The temptation to ask Mom about it filled me, but I forced it to pass. Not now. It wouldn't be fair to her.

Wild thoughts filled my head until I grabbed my car keys and my purse. Relieved for a break from my own mind, I slung my bag over my shoulder and headed for the door. Once there, I stopped, hesitated, then called, "Bye, Mom. I hope you have a good day."

She paused, a sausage link halfway to her mouth. Then she chomped off the end, lifted a hand, and kept watching television.

A Long Time

The movie theater dimmed into near darkness.

An ad for a free diabetic screening popped up first, cloaking the theater in pale shadows. Bitsy and I were the only ones in the room, so I propped my ankle up on the chair in front of me and reclined back. Getting away from the Frosting Cottage—and the numerous failures on our new recipes—felt almost as delicious as the smell of buttery popcorn in the air. Bitsy had insisted on bringing snacks for us instead of buying. *Much cheaper,* she said. *Healthier, too. A tub of that popcorn would set your heart health back eighty years.*

Bags of kettle corn, carrot sticks, and frozen grapes were tucked inside her purse.

"Channing. Tatum." I whistled. "Hello, old friend. Cannot wait to see you again!"

The wolf cry felt pitiful without Lexie giggling at my side. I glanced at the empty seat next to me with a sigh, reassured that she was watching with her sister-in-law in a different theater but at the same time.

It keeps us connected, she had said. *Through Channing Tatum. This is important stuff, Rachelle.*

Bitsy snorted. "Channing Tatum isn't that cute."

"You lie!"

She sucked in a drink of water through a straw and set it in the armrest. "He's overrated."

"Let me guess, you're a Rhett Butler type?"

"Definitely."

"You prefer older men?"

"Preferably sterilized older men. Two kids is plenty, thanks." I laughed as she wiggled deeper into the seat. "Mira said the debut on the new flavors is coming up in a couple of days," she said. "You nervous?"

"Definitely."

"Ready?"

I shook my head. "Not even close. We've perfected the easy recipes, but we're still trying to find a unique version of the soda cupcakes. She's putting most of her hope in those, though I think the cookie bar will dominate. At least we have a plan for the cookie bar. It's not easy thinking of a dozen variations of cookies. Just saying."

"I plan on bringing the girls."

"Thanks. We'll take whoever will come. Sophia's optimistic for a lot of people, but I'm not."

Bitsy's gaze darted around. Her nose wrinkled. I counted under my breath.

"Three . . . two . . . one . . ."

Right on cue, Bitsy leaned down, pulled an antibacterial wipe out of her purse, and started to sanitize the chair. She cast me a sidelong glance promising steep retribution if I teased her. I held up two hands in surrender.

"So." She scrubbed the arm rest at her side. "How are things?"

Weeks had passed since we'd had a chance to connect with just the two of us. In some ways, I'd appreciated the space. The last three days, though, I'd been desperate to talk to her about the dream and what I'd seen in my mom afterward. A whole new world had started to unroll around me, littered with memories, photos, and long nights spent with my eyes closed while I imagined pockets of yellow pain bursting when I squeezed them in my fist.

"Intense," I finally said.

"You're obviously going to Janine still. Good."

"Yes, still going. Feel like I'm finally making some progress, but it's hard to tell. Listen, I had this dream, and I wanted to see what you thought of it."

Finally satisfied that her environment wasn't fostering contagions, she sat back, tucked the wipe in her bag, and nodded once.

"Ready. Spill."

While a movie trailer for a romantic comedy flickered across the screen, I caught her up. Having to review the dream out loud made me feel like I'd finally processed it. By the time I finished, the opening credits had started.

"And then I went to work. The dream was so real, Bitsy. I just . . . I didn't even know what to think at first."

"You did the right thing."

"What do you mean?"

"You comforted little Rachelle. Did Janine tell you how that works? That our subconscious doesn't know time?"

I frowned. Janine had told me many things.

"No?"

"When we have a traumatic memory, it gets stored in our brain."

"Right. Pockets of pain."

Bitsy nodded once. "Yes, but our subconscious doesn't recognize time. Little Rachelle needed someone to tell her it wasn't her fault. You did that. Now your subconscious just knows that you received what you needed. Pocket of pain destroyed. If you ask me, it'll probably change something. They often say that inner-child work can heal almost instantaneously."

My thoughts sank into that as the lights dimmed, coating the room in darkness. So *that* was inner-child work? Comforting little Rachelle had been a natural reaction. What else would I have done? Perhaps it had shifted something, though. I felt different. Less . . . frantic, perhaps.

Bitsy leaned closer. "It definitely gives you some insight on your mom, though."

"How?"

"The whole food thing. Sounds like she's had a food addiction for a long time. Not only that, but little Rachelle said that she was afraid Dad would hide the food just like Grandpa did and they wouldn't be able to eat. Now *there's* a fear that originated in your mom. Wonder what she's been through."

Despite saying it out loud, I'd missed that little detail. Mom loved her food. There had always been a strong argument for an addiction, but I'd always assumed it was television. Overeating seemed like a natural byproduct of sitting around all day. But perhaps it was the other way around. Or maybe they both affected each other.

"Look at it from both sides," Bitsy said as Channing Tatum flashed across the screen for the first time. I ignored him. "Your father probably felt intense frustration that his wife wouldn't listen to his concerns about your health. Your mother sought connection through food, and he was critical of it. Maybe food is the only way your mom feels safe. Explains why she never leaves and always has food with her, doesn't it?"

"Yeah."

I'd faced Mom's issues every day of my life but never thought of them that way. Until the dream, I hadn't remembered the source of their anger at each other. Now, I couldn't imagine it being anything else. If I had been Dad, I would have been worried, too.

But I wouldn't have just *left*.

"He couldn't have left only because of how much ice cream my mom gave me," I said, leaning toward her. "Right? That's just stupid."

"I'd wager there was more going on. A lot more." Bitsy shook her head with a frown. "I worry about your mom. She breaks my heart."

"Why?"

"She's hiding from the world. And me. Which, you know, I can't blame her. I'd probably hide from me, too. It seems like she spends most of her energy fighting herself. Denying her problems instead of facing them. She lives a half life. She's blind to her problems. She never leaves the house. She medicates with food. Heartbreaking, isn't it?"

That my mom had issues was nothing I'd contest; she clearly had her demons. But I'd never thought she lived in denial. Nor had I found it heartbreaking. It was her choice. No one forced her in front of the television and no one forced corn chips in her mouth. Even now, I had a hard time conjuring up pity. Everything just felt hollow inside.

"I hadn't thought about it like that," I whispered. Channing Tatum popped up on the screen again, but I didn't care. I couldn't even remember the name of the movie.

Bitsy leaned in.

"You know what you're really doing when you go see Janine?" she asked. "When you're pulling the ghosts out of the darkness?"

I met her gaze.

"No. What?"

"You're learning how to live as you. That's worth all the pain. Trust me, Rachelle. You're doing the right thing, no matter how much you question it."

The movie shuffled onto a new scene, illuminating the theater in bright light. I hardly saw it, focused on the new, whirling revelations that spun through my mind like birds in flight. Central among all of them was one guilt-ridden question.

Why couldn't I feel compassion for Mom?

The end of the day settled on the Frosting Cottage with a gentle sigh.

After flipping the sign, locking the front door, and turning up the music, I sank into my next task alone: start three hundred cupcakes.

Sophia had taken off to find antique furniture that could double as the new cookie bar. She had some sort of funky twist in mind. Hundreds of cupcakes awaited me. I'd put off making them so I wouldn't have to go home. Each of the past three days, I'd spent over twelve hours at work and dropped to sleep in exhaustion each night. Tonight, however, was going to be late for both of us.

Tomorrow was the big Summerpalooza and Bake Sale event.

While I shuffled around the kitchen on one crutch, my mind still spun with images of Mom when she was young. A wave of guilt that I didn't understand flowed over me. An empty mixing bowl clanged when I set it on the metallic counter, pulling me out of my thoughts. Seconds later, a knock on the back door reverberated through the kitchen. I paused. The store was closed.

I ventured toward it with both crutches, then called through the thick door, "Hello?"

"Hey. Just me. The door's locked."

The door cracked opened when I pulled the handle, revealing William's bright eyes. He wore a long-sleeved shirt, like usual, and a pair of old jeans.

"Hey."

I pulled the door open wider. His delivery truck wasn't in the alley, just a beat-up old Cadillac with streaks down the side.

"Hey. Sorry about that. Sophia must have locked it." I shuffled back to let him in.

He slid past me.

"What's up?" I asked as the door shut behind him.

He rubbed the back of his neck with a hand. "Just stopping by to talk to Sophia. I take it she's gone?"

"Yeah. Had to go shopping for the party."

He grinned. "Right. Can't believe it's tomorrow."

"You're still bringing people?"

"Don't you worry about that. This party is covered. It's going to be way above what you expect."

"I hope so."

An awkward pause filled the air. I motioned toward the prep area. "I have hundreds of cupcakes waiting on me. Want to come in? She might not be too much longer."

His eyebrows lifted. "You sure?"

"Just making cupcakes."

He stepped inside with a little hop. "Sounds like a better Friday night than hanging out at home with my grandma. How long does it take to make that many cupcakes, anyway?"

"Couple of hours, if you know what you're doing. Sophia has all the equipment to make ginormous batches. It's not the making that takes up the most time. It's the frosting."

"Sweet." He rubbed his hands together. "Put me to work."

I nodded toward the metallic countertop. "See that laminated recipe?"

"Yeah."

"Check how many pounds, then start dumping flour into that really big mixing bowl."

He eyed the massive bowl and grinned.

"Sweet."

"Just do one recipe at a time. I need one hundred cupcakes with a vanilla cake base. The rest we'll have to make individually."

At first, we worked together in silence, interrupted only by the gentle *poof* of flour and the occasional question as he sought ingredients. I grabbed bricks of butter from the countertop where they had been coming to room temperature and slid them to him across the table. Then I flipped the ovens on.

"So," he said, "you can make cupcakes, injured your ankle, and just started working for Sophia. Anything else I should know about you?"

"I dropped out of college."

"Really?"

"Yeah."

I waited while sifting through confectioners sugar, wondering when he'd start judging me for it.

"How does it feel?" he asked.

"Honestly? Not as freeing as I'd expected."

A thread of amusement colored his tone. "What did you expect it to be like?"

"Less stress. College and I didn't get along. I was constantly trying to figure out what I wanted, but I never did. Such a waste of money. I was nowhere near a degree after five years, so I left."

"What did you do afterward?"

Lost the weight of another person. Started teaching Zumba. Lost myself and didn't even know it.

"I found a job and focused on myself for a while."

"Good for you."

A beat passed between us. I glanced over my shoulder to see him studying the recipe. "The baking powder is in the cupboard below the ovens," I said, anticipating his question. "Sugar is just above it. What about you?"

"Me?"

"Yeah. Why are you in college so late?"

He didn't meet my gaze. "Stuff. What else goes in?"

Instead of pushing the question, I motioned toward the fridge. "Eggs."

The conversation shifted forward to other topics slowly. First to his job as a food-service delivery man, then to where we grew up—both of us were locals—and finally trailed off to our favorite dessert.

"Definitely cupcakes," I said with a wistful sigh.

"Fruit tarts for me."

"A good choice. Can I ask you a question?" I asked. "It's been bugging me for a while."

He briefly met my eyes. "Sure."

"You work as a delivery guy, collect recyclables to help save money, have to be over twenty-five, and you want to go into a degree field that will take a ridiculous number of years to complete, right?"

"Uh..."

"Why? It just doesn't all quite add up."

His nostrils flared, and I realized, probably too late, that I'd hit a sensitive nerve. A habit from my past, for sure. He swallowed.

"It's a long story."

"You don't have to tell it."

He put both hands on his slender hips. "No. I will. You seem trustworthy."

"Trust me. There's no dark secret you have I couldn't match," I muttered.

He leaned back against the counter and folded his arms across his chest while I peered into the mixer and turned it on. The arm ground at first when it started to spin, then smoothed out.

"A few years ago, I was in a car accident," he said. "A really bad one. Took me two or three months to recover. Sort of changed my life. Ever since then, I decided to do something to improve the world."

"Were you drunk?"

He hesitated, then nodded once. "Yeah. I was coming home from a concert and had had one too many."

"The other person okay?"

"Barely. Pulled through at the last minute. Took her four months to get out of the ICU." His jaw tightened. "Helped me get a job, find a purpose, leave the band I was in that wasn't good for me. Instead of hating me the way she should have, she sort of adopted me."

Something struck me all at once. I turned to face him.

"Sophia?"

He nodded.

"Whoa. No wonder you're so protective of her."

He drew in a great, shuddering breath. "I didn't deserve forgiveness, even, and she gave me a lot more than that. It's a complicated story, but suffice it to say that I will owe her for the rest of my life."

Perhaps great pain *could* be overcome. Forgiveness could be granted. I turned away. "You said band? You were giving the concert?"

"Yeah."

"How big were you?"

He hesitated. "Big enough. Nothing international at the time, but plenty of people knew us in the state. We'd booked out gigs for almost a year. Had swelling popularity. They're on a nationwide tour now, supported by a label."

"Did you like it?"

"Yeah. Part of it." His head tilted to the side. "I loved the music. Just *playing* was my favorite. I'd rather play for fun and do everything without a plan instead of having a staged jam session. I didn't really care about all the rest, either. Groupies. Fans. Sales. Whatever. It came with the territory. Seeing people respond to the music, though, that gave me a physical high. Even if it was a dangerous world to dabble in, there was something magical about it."

"You seem to miss it."

"I do. I miss bringing people together for a common purpose. I miss playing my guitar."

My eyes flickered to his wrists, then away. "Rock, wasn't it?"

"How'd you know?"

"The tattoos."

He glanced at his wrists with a frown. "I cover them up."

"I've noticed."

"People judge me. I don't want them to think I'm the person I was before. I'm new. Better. I can't remove all the old scars . . ."

My eyes met his. "Trust me, I understand the feeling."

Another silence fell, and I could sense no more would be said, but he could see my sincerity. I wasn't on this path alone.

That meant something.

"You've been eyeing the glass display for a while," I said to break the sudden tension. The mixer stopped when I pushed the arm back and unhooked the bowl. "Do you want to eat something?"

He smiled, looking relieved at the change in subject. "Dumb question. I always want Sophia's food."

"Grab a fruit tart, then."

He hesitated. "All right. Split it with me?"

I hesitated. The fruit tarts weren't that big. Barely wider than my fist. A vanilla, cookie-like crust framed the bottom, scooping under a fruit base with a shiny glaze. To be honest, I'd been glaring at them for weeks. They looked entirely too delicious.

"Ah . . ."

He lifted an eyebrow. "What?"

"I just . . . haven't tried them yet."

"Food allergy or something?"

The temptation to use that as an excuse almost overwhelmed me, but I pushed it off. Old Rachelle had lied her way out of many situations. I couldn't even fathom the thought anymore.

"No."

He scooted toward the display. "Great! A perfect time to try it."

My track record since starting work at the Frosting Cottage had been perfect—except for an occasional, small taste of frosting or custard while we tested the recipes, I hadn't tried a single dessert. Before I could stop him, he returned with one of the fullest tarts. The arrangement of the fruit and the thickness of the glaze were admirably perfect.

William lifted an eyebrow in an adorable, boyish kind of way.

"Ready?"

"Yeah."

What would one bite hurt? I didn't have to devour the whole thing. He grabbed a knife from near the sink and brought it over. A few pieces of the crust crumbled away when he sliced into it and pushed half my way.

"Here you go."

My hand picked up the tart of its own accord. I couldn't deny a little thrill deep in my belly. How long had it been since I'd had a treat? A long time.

Maybe too long.

William tossed half the tart into his throat, then closed his eyes with a groan. "That," he mumbled, "is one of the most delicious tarts I have ever tasted in my entire freaking life."

The crust crumbled in my mouth, dissolving along with the fruit in a sugary landslide. I closed my eyes and savored the moment. No tart had ever tasted so good. When I opened my eyes, William was grinning.

"Pretty good, huh?"

I smiled. "You'll never know just how much."

Slatted light fell through the window and illuminated Sophia's face the next morning. The early summer sun already felt broiling hot, the humidity thick on my skin. The sound of people rushing around outside in a Saturday frenzy already sounded from the sidewalk.

A good sign.

I tested my weight on my right foot. *Half weight,* Dr. Martinez had said only thirty minutes before, at an early appointment. *See how it feels, then schedule your appointment with the physical therapist.*

Felt like a step toward freedom.

"Do you think this is going to work?" I asked Sophia.

She quirked her lips and stepped away from the window. "Let's hope. My usual taste testers loved all of the cupcakes and the cookies, but they aren't who matter."

My gaze swept over a congregation of cupcakes and new confections. William, Sophia, and I had stayed up until two o'clock perfecting each batch, cleaning the store, and putting up the final flourishes. Glitter streamers. Oversized folded bows. A table filled with miniature taste-tester cupcakes. Another table piled with tiered layers of cupcakes and other treats. Everything gleamed, from the preparation area to the glass display case to the front windows, which were amply painted with bright letters.

Soda Pop Cupcakes!

Cookie Bar!

My stomach threatened to flip flop inside me. I couldn't bear the thought of this not working. I'd failed college. The marathon. Dating. The thoughts muddled my brain. I paused. Wait.

What was I thinking?

No, I commanded myself. *Reframe.* I had to reframe this negative view. I thought of what Janine would say. *I am not valued by what I do. My worth and happiness do not depend on external success.*

"This will be great," I said. Strength infused the words. "Everything is going to go fine. Even if no one likes the flavors, we'll readjust. At least then we'll know, right?"

Sophia's worried frown straightened. She nodded once, jaw tight with resolution. She didn't have to say it for me to know it, but we didn't have a lot of wiggle room here.

"Yes. You're right. Lots of good things that we can't track may come from this, like exposure and brand recognition and people coming inside who may not have come in before."

I grinned. "It will."

"Do you know when William is supposed to be here?"

"No."

"He said he had some big idea. Hopefully he comes later, when traffic is heaviest. Everything is slow before noon."

Thirty minutes later, we threw open the doors.

Hot air streamed inside. A little flicker of disappointment erupted in my belly when no one came in with it.

No adoring fans waited on the curb, rushing in with frantic energy the way I'd secretly hoped. Of course they wouldn't, but I couldn't deny some disappointment. Sticky heat filled the store, so I shut the door again to protect the goods. Sophia puttered around the prep area, pulling flour, scraping pans, and humming under her breath. I envied her chance to distract herself with wedding cakes.

Ribbons on the nearby table fluttered in the A/C. I spotted a smudge on the glass display and promptly cleaned the entire thing. The tang of window cleaner filled the air. The oven beeped when Sophia turned it on. I swept.

Again.

An hour passed.

Two girls in flip flops walked by, glanced at the window, and kept going. A young couple did the same. My brow furrowed. Almost 11:00 already. Certainly late enough to visit a bakery—we had plenty of brunch offerings. Free coffee percolated off to the right with a delicious warmth. I bit my bottom lip.

Eleven o'clock passed.

Then noon.

One o'clock slid by, and we hadn't had a single customer. I feared I'd die of boredom. Sophia kept glancing at the window with a frown. I cleaned the glass display for the tenth time. Straightened three cupcakes that looked as if they'd moved. Then folded my hands and waited by the windows. Streams of people strolled past. Where was William, anyway?

Why didn't anyone want cupcakes?

When two o'clock inched closer, I set aside one crutch. This slow day was getting ridiculous. With a clatter of pans, I grabbed a cookie sheet, loaded it up with fifteen different taste-tester cupcakes, and stepped outside with a single crutch. The bell dinged as the door shut. Traffic was starting to pick up. Cars were parked in every other spot, and pedestrians filled the sidewalks.

"Are you brave?" I called. "Do you love cupcakes?"

An elderly woman turned to me with a startled expression, a hand on her chest.

"Sorry," I whispered. "Didn't mean to frighten you."

She scuttled away with a scowl.

"You'll never find cupcakes like these anywhere else. Strawberry rhubarb and lime. Sweet potato cinnamon. Don't forget tangy, delicious vanilla Sprite. Get cupcakes inspired by all your favorite sodas. Coca-Cola. Pepsi. And my favorite . . . Orange Fanta!"

Two boys slipped across the street and headed for me. I recognized the gleam in their eyes and set the tray on a small wrought-iron table. Then I tapped into full-scale Rachelle charm.

"Let me guess," I pointed to the one on the left. "You're a Pepsi man."

He grinned. "You got it."

I shoved a sample sized cupcake at him with a wink. "I dare you not to love this. And you." I pointed to the other. "Fanta?"

"Sure."

"A man after my own heart. More inside, boys. They're on sale for a dollar a cupcake today. Limited supply."

A woman strode down the sidewalk toward me, heels clacking as she walked. Cinnamon-colored pants. A bright white sleeveless top with a silky scarf trailing off her neck. Tired lines trailed down the side of her face, and she blinked bloodshot, bleary eyes.

"Nectarine and lemon?" I asked. She held up a hand to fend me off, but I held the mini cupcake toward her. "Seasonal, my good lady. Made with local tangerines from a farm outside town. You cannot miss the swap of the lemon and sweet tangerine. They really complete each other."

She hesitated, eyeing the hearty glob of frosting on top, and finally accepted. "Do you have coffee?"

"Tons inside. Free, too. Don't miss the scones. They're actually soft."

"Great."

She stepped inside. Out of the corner of my eye, I saw a group of men headed toward the store, at least nine strong. By the time I spun around to fully face them, they were only a few steps away.

William smiled from the middle of the pack. "Hey Rachelle!"

"Hey!" I cried. "You came!"

"Of course. I just had to borrow a few things. I brought a bunch of hungry college boys."

"Perfect."

"Don't worry," a blond quipped with a wry smile. "More are coming later."

"Plenty more," said another. William shot them a quelling look, then turned back to me.

"These are just the frontrunners to take to the streets and get word going. Hey guys, this is my friend, Rachelle."

"Hi Rachelle," they chimed in unison.

A warm little thrill darted through me. Friend, eh? That had never happened before. I smiled. All of their eyes gleamed with hunger. William was older than all of them by several years, but that didn't matter. Bodies were bodies.

"You ready to sell yummy cupcakes and other delights in exchange for free food?" I asked.

"Oh yeah."

"Give us the goods."

"I need sugar!"

Their responses made me grin. "Sweet. Your job is to eat a few samples and adore them. Then take them to the people out here and get them to come in."

One of them reached for a Coke cupcake. "You got it, sister."

"Anything for free sugar," another said.

A third arm grabbed for one. "Is that a Sprite cupcake? *What?*"

"OMG!" A blond with muddy hazel eyes yelled, frosting smeared on his lips. "This is the best cupcake I've ever eaten in my life!"

A pigeon fluttered away from the eaves with a squawk. Two people on the other side of the street jumped. I laughed. William grabbed the pan from me and shoved it toward one of his friends.

"Georgio, turn on that Italian charm. Start giving away samples.

Brent, JC, grab pans inside and load up. Charlie, Shane, you're in charge of the cookie bar. Start giving out samples and bags while I set up."

While his friends barreled into the store—pretending to fight over who got the next free sample—the two teenage boys slipped out of the bakery with two cupcakes each. William turned back to the road, shaded his hand over his eyes, and peered up the street.

"Wow," I said. "Nine people? This is awesome, William. That'll make all the difference in the world."

"It's nothing."

"Actually, it's . . ."

"No, I mean it's nothing compared to what's coming."

My brow furrowed.

"What do you mean?"

He grinned, put a hand on my shoulder, and spun me to face the other direction. Down the road, a swelling crowd was creeping this way. Two of the other guys who had originally come with him appeared from the back of the store, carrying an amp and a guitar case.

"What's going on?" I asked.

"Nothing." He shrugged, lips twitching. Then he pushed up his long sleeves, revealing two tattooed arms. "Just a little mini concert to get some attention."

A slow grin spread across my face. "Your band is coming?"

"No. Just me. Thought this was the perfect day to rekindle my relationship with music." He nodded to the people who had started to surge down the road. "When I left the band, a faction of people split off and followed me. I played live gigs for them for a while once I made it out of the hospital."

My jaw dropped. "Is that . . ."

He grinned. "Yep. That's them."

Spending all afternoon behind the counter left me feeling sticky, like I'd been coated in a layer of honey and double dipped in frosting. William and his friends sent so many people into the Frosting Cottage that the air conditioning couldn't keep up. A hot shower—and a long drink of cool water—sounded just right.

"Lock 'em," Sophia said with a weary wave at the door. "We're out of everything anyway."

Crumbs littered the glass display case and tables. A few cupcakes remained—mostly the healthy black-bean chocolate concoction—but all the cookies were gone. The five types of lemonade were drained. Cupcake liners littered the floor.

Weary to the bone, I shut the door, locked it, and flipped the sign. Sophia grabbed a broom, then sank back into a chair. William stretched his legs out in front of him, eyes bright. His guitar sat behind him, propped against the wall.

"Well," Sophia said, hands clasped in front of her. "That went beautifully, William. I didn't know you could take requests or sing folk music. I shouldn't have assumed your talents were limited to rock."

He spread his hands. "I aim to serve."

"How did that feel?" I asked with a grin. "Performing again?"

A sly smile slid across his face. "Amazing."

Sophia giggled, appearing half drunk. "I can't believe we got in trouble because the crowd blocked traffic."

"Then *more* people came," I said.

"Not our fault. I was just singing with a guitar," William said, eyes closed. Sweat saturated his shirt and face. No doubt I looked as ragged and worn as they did. For several minutes, we sat in the silence.

The soda cupcakes sold out within two hours of William starting to serenade the crowd. His voice was sweet and flowing, a little bit thick at times. Just the right mix of refinement and passion. Several customers had already put in orders for a dozen cupcakes tomorrow afternoon. I'd have to come back by six in the morning to get them all done in time.

What a wonderful problem.

"Well," Sophia said, slapping the arms of her chair. "I owe you two big time. Not only do we have orders for more soda cupcakes, but I scheduled five bridal consultations and three catering consultations. That alone is going to see us through July and into August. I would call this a success."

"We have a lot of baking to do," I said.

She grinned, eyes illuminated. "I know! Good thing William's gotten us a ten percent discount on delivery, huh? Thanks, kiddo, for all you did today. I owe you."

"Never," he murmured.

She whacked him in the leg. He waved her off with a tired grin, eyes still closed, his foot bobbing to the music. I pushed up and grabbed my crutch. My ankle throbbed but not as badly as I'd expected. When I grabbed the broom to start sweeping, Sophia snatched it back and batted me away.

"Go on, Rachelle. Go home."

"But—"

"I'll get this. It's pathetic watching you try to navigate a crutch and a broom." Her eyes twinkled. "Besides, I need to stay and frost those cakes, anyway. Couldn't do it with so many people coming in and out."

"You're going to be here forever tonight."

"Yeah." She shrugged. "But I love it. I'll be fine. I'll just sleep on my couch in the office again. There's a shower in the back bathroom, anyway, and the A/C works better here. Besides, William is going to go get dinner for me and keep me company, isn't he?"

He lifted a hand. "Chinese, for sure."

"Not to mention the fact that I need you back here by six in the morning to get those orders filled for the afternoon." She snatched the tip jar off the counter and shoved it toward me. "And don't forget this. You earned it. I'll see you tomorrow morning, bright and early. I'll provide the coffee, like always."

I set the jar on William's lap as I moved past him.

"Take it for your college fund. *You* earned it today, my friend."

Sophia shoved my backpack into my chest. With a delicious thrill, I remembered that I had driven to work that morning. Yet another thing that went well today.

"Oh, I saved you a couple of the soda cupcakes to take home to your mom," Sophia said. "They're boxed up and in your bag. Sprite, Coke, Pepsi, and Fanta. Let me know what she thinks of them."

"Ah. Thanks."

"Go home. I'll see you tomorrow. Cannot wait!" Sophia fluttered around, hands clapping, whirling in circles that made William smile like a drugged man. "Can't *believe* how many sales we had today!"

After sliding my backpack on, grabbing a cold water bottle from the fridge, and snatching a small quiche from the display case, I dug my keys out of my pocket with a yawn.

"See ya," I called, waving. "Thanks again."

Heat blasted my face when I slid into my car and set my bag on the opposite seat. My phone rang as I tore into the quiche with a savage bite.

Lexie.

I quickly swallowed the food and answered it.

"Hey, Lex!"

"How did it go?" she asked. "I'm dying here. Did the Coke cupcakes sell out? Those are my favorite. Although I still think you should consider a mint Oreo variation. Or a birthday cake Oreo cupcake! They have those now, you know. I'm convinced Nabisco is out to see me gain eighty pounds."

The happy chirp of her voice relaxed me. I turned the engine on and blasted the A/C. It hit my face with hot moisture at first, then slowly cooled. I took a bite of quiche.

"A raving success. Mostly thanks to William. And his friends."

"William?"

"Oh, a friend I made. Long story."

"I won't forget him, but tell me everything else first. Did you save The Frosting Cottage? Was everyone super excited about your random ideas? Did they sell out? What happened?"

I combed through the details of the day, right down to how deeply weary I was, and polished off the quiche. The car cooled down, and my leg stopped throbbing. Having food in my belly settled my ravenous hunger pangs.

"Bitsy and Mira came in the afternoon after the girls got out of school, so it was fun to see them there."

"Did Bitsy eat something with sugar?"

"Yes! Well, sort of. She bought the healthy cupcake we were attempting that failed miserably. She even bought a cupcake each for her girls."

Lexie gasped. "Miracle!"

"She broke her recent no-sugar streak and tried the taste-tester Pepsi cupcake on Mira's pleading."

Lexie laughed. "Of course."

"Anyway, it was really fun to see them at the store. I wish you could have been there to see William sing Lana's favorite song. Bitsy was mortified when Lana requested it, but William just laughed."

"The theme song from Teenage Mutant Ninja Turtles?"

"Yep. How amazing is that? He just played it after she asked. He's really talented. I mean . . . blew me away. People just shouted songs from the crowd, and he'd play them on his guitar and sang beautifully. Either he knows way too much music, or he's one of those gifted people who can figure it out as he goes."

Her tone deepened. "You're talking about him quite a bit. Am I sensing something? A little . . . *crush* perhaps?"

I scoffed. "Hardly. I just . . ."

The words faded.

She giggled. "Oh, Rachelle. I know everything about you, my friend, and you are crushing bad."

"He's just a friend."

"Fine. But you can still crush on a friend. Also, he sounds awesome."

A man of many facets, that was William. Awesome was certainly one of them. His relationship with Sophia still awed me a little. The two of them were best friends, despite their past.

"I'm not doing the dating thing right now," I said, fidgeting. "You know that."

"I didn't say you had to date him. I'm just pointing out what I see. That's it."

I pressed my lips together. I'd never had a man as a friend. They'd all been dates. Lovers. One night stands. The idea of broaching into friend territory first was infinitely overwhelming, new, and terrifying.

But pretty wonderful.

"Give me some time to think about this one," I said. "In the meantime, I need to go home, and shower, and crash. I have to be at the bakery in the morning at six. We have a ton of orders to fill and don't want to make anyone wait. Not to mention restocking the store as people come back."

"A beautiful goal, as Bitsy would say. Hey, did you get any for your mom?"

I eyed my bag.

"Yeah. Sophia sent four."

"Good. You should tell her what's been going on."

"Ah . . . maybe."

"Rachelle . . ."

"You know we haven't been talking since I had that dream! It's just too weird. Not that we talked much before that, anyway. I can't get over how things really *are* between us."

"What do you mean?"

". . . I don't know. It's not easy to be around her. I just see . . ."

Someone who gave up on me.

"I know you can't get over what's happened between the two of you. Your mom has made some decidedly sucky decisions. That's why it's so important you at least try to talk to her. C'mon, it's food! You can bond over food with her anytime."

I fought off a rebuttal. It had been so easy to just avoid Mom and not think about how to broach the topic. Maybe never. Neither Mom nor I would want to discuss it, so what was the point?

The point is not running away, I thought. I couldn't avoid her forever. Not unless I wanted to become a shell of a person, the way she had.

"Fine." I let out a heavy breath. "I see your point. I'll try having another conversation with her, but it hasn't gone well in the recent past."

"I know, but you'll never regret trying, right? Just let me know how it goes."

"Of course."

"Drive home, be safe, get some water in you, and we'll chat later. Okay?"

"Yeah. Love you."

"Love you, too."

Only the blast of the A/C filled my car when I ended the call and set my phone aside with a sigh. The euphoria of the day had tapered into extreme fatigue, a pounding ankle, and a building sense of dread in my chest. It wasn't that Lexie was wrong.

It was that she was right. I needed to stop avoiding Mom.

I just didn't want to do it.

Into the Past

I don't want to do this, I thought as I stared at the back door. *I don't want to see Mom. I don't want to talk to her and be rejected again.*

She'd be in the house, absorbed in television and food. Crumbs would litter the kitchen counter. Or maybe it would be pristine and smell like Windex, a sure sign that she'd hidden a massive food binge and didn't want to leave any trace. We used to binge together, laughing at TV comedies, finding a restless kind of peace in the wild indulgence.

But I had to try this. I didn't know why, but I had to attempt to reach through to the mom who had to have been—or I hoped was—once there.

"I got this," I said, sucking in a deep breath through my nose. Hearing my own voice gave me strength. "I can do this."

With a sigh, I grabbed my bag, carefully swung it onto my shoulder, and slowly worked into the house with both crutches. Twilight fell behind me, welcomed by the chirp of crickets and the thick humidity that settled like a wet blanket.

Except for the television flickering in the background, only the kitchen lights illuminated the tired house. Remnants of kettle corn—she'd polished off three bags while watching the new *Thor* movie—littered the ground.

The shadows grew long and gray, highlighting spots of chipped paint and worn furniture. Envelopes and paper stacked high under the cupboard. Cups full of change. Piles of unfolded laundry. The clutter, in the dim light, seemed pervasive. Why did the darkness show more truth than the light?

My forehead furrowed. When was the last time the carpet had been vacuumed? I had a sinking suspicion it was right before I broke my ankle. I'd tried my best to keep up with what I could, but the long hours and annoying crutches prevented any in-depth cleaning.

Mom puttered around the kitchen, oblivious to my presence. The smell of burnt toast filled the air. I shut the back door behind me. A cup of coffee would put some power in my legs and voice.

"Hey, Mom."

At first, she didn't respond, just stared at a pan of browning sausage that filled the air with a sweet, reminiscent smell. Several cracked eggs rested near a bowl by a carton of milk, whipped to a light froth. Of course. Her favorite. Sausage omelets with mango salsa, Monterey Jack cheese, and hot sauce. A pile of buttered toast waited on the counter. She nibbled her way through food—three slices left, and who knows how many already gone—whenever she cooked.

"Have a good day?" I asked, infusing strength in my voice. She jerked up, startled, and blinked.

"Oh," she said. "Hi."

"Would you like some coffee?" I asked, setting my bag aside. "I think I need a small cup just to get me through a shower."

"Sure."

For a long stretch of time, the only sound that filled the air was the whir of the coffee machine. I shouldn't drink coffee right now. Not when I just wanted to crash before an early morning. But I couldn't stop my hands from doing *something*, so I kept going through the motions.

"Busy day?" I asked.

"Not really."

"Good."

But is that a good thing? came the thought. Another silence. Mom stirred the sausage. I contemplated the box of goodies sitting in my bag. I could throw the cupcakes away and ditch this attempt. She'd never know. But something in the slope of her shoulders and the way her lips tugged down prevented me. I couldn't stop seeing her as a young woman, lost, with a husband she felt was trying to control her and a daughter to take care of.

"The bakery I worked at had a big sale today," I said. "We sold out of almost all the cupcakes and other goods."

"That's nice."

I cleared my throat. "Sophia, the owner, sent a few cupcakes home for you if you want to try them."

Her head perked up. "That was nice of her," she said, infused with new energy. "What flavors?"

My heart took a dive. *Why won't you see me? Why do you only see food?* I swallowed and reached for the bag, extracting a white box from it. When I pushed it toward her, her eyes expanded.

"Soda flavors," I said. "Coke. Pepsi. Fanta. Sprite. You like Sprite, don't you? Sophia and I came up with the recipes over the past couple of weeks."

Mom's eyes gleamed as I opened the box, revealing the delicious pastries inside, but she schooled the expression into one of casual indifference. She looked away but peered at them from the corner of her eye.

"Sounds yummy."

I reached in and pulled out the Sprite cupcake, drizzled with yellow-and-green sprinkles on top of a pillowy white frosting. "Do you want to try it? Maybe we could cut it in half and split it? I only tried a small sample."

"No."

Her quick reply, almost a snap, startled me. I blinked.

"Oh."

"I just . . . I'm not hungry right now."

She turned back to her sausage. The cloying scent of burnt meat filled the air as she whipped it around the greasy pan. Then she dumped a bowl of whipped eggs into the mess. They sizzled and jumped around on the hot skillet, filling the gaps between the sausage.

"Oh. Right. Okay." I set the cupcake back inside. "It was really fun, actually. I made and frosted these cupcakes."

"That's nice."

See me! I wanted to scream. *See anything but your food!*

With a deep breath, I silenced the little girl screaming inside of me. "Thanks. I've really enjoyed working there."

"Good."

Another pause. Mom stirred the eggs and sausage with almost frantic flicks of her wrists, her eyes darting to the box every so often. I took it to the fridge and set it inside, cognizant that she was discreetly monitoring my every move. Why wouldn't she eat the cupcake? She wouldn't even touch it. Acknowledge it.

Desperation fueled my next breath. The words tumbled out of my mouth before I could stop them.

"Mom, is there a reason you won't try the cupcake?"

"I'm on a diet."

My brow furrowed. "Really?"

She scraped at the pan with renewed frenzy. "Yes."

"Then I'll just throw them out."

"*No!*"

Rage bubbled under my skin. So it was me. It was *me* she didn't want to eat the cupcakes with. She wanted the cupcake, just not with me. I turned away, nostrils flaring. Tears pricked at my eyes. This wasn't even a new feeling of pain. I realized with a wash of bitterness that I'd felt this rejection before. All the dance recitals she missed. My high school graduation. Every event a parent could possibly be expected to attend—and she never did.

"Why don't we ever talk about my grandparents. Your . . . parents?" I asked, whipping back around to face her. "Why? Why don't we talk about them? Is it because Grandpa was controlling? Did he do something awful to you?"

She froze in the middle of shutting off the stovetop. "My parents?" she whispered. All the color drained from her face.

"What did they do that was so awful?"

Her shoulders slumped. She swallowed heavily. The long folds of her robe—her mussed, greasy hair puffed out on one side—meant she hadn't changed since yesterday. Had she even gone to bed last night? The low drone of Matlock played like a dull, vapid ghost in the background. Maybe she hadn't gone to bed. There had been many times I'd woken up to go to the bathroom and found her there, sleeping on the couch.

She pressed her lips together. "There's nothing to say." She lifted the pan with a grimace—she'd been standing too long—and dumped the eggs onto a waiting plate. The food filled it entirely, some spilling off the sides.

"Nothing at all?" I pressed.

"No."

"Are they still alive?"

She still didn't face me, the greasy spatula in her hand as she dumped mango salsa onto the fluffy eggs. "No."

"Really?"

"Yeah."

I leaned against the counter, attempting an unaffected response. But I couldn't hide the pain in my voice. "Can you tell me more about them? Give me something about my family that I can understand?"

"Why?" she muttered.

If the tension in the room grew any tighter, the air would shatter. Coffee ran into my favorite mug in a stream from the coffeemaker. I ignored it.

"They're my family, too, aren't they?"

"They shouldn't be anyone's family."

"Why not?"

She shook her head in a determined back-and-forth.

"What happened? Why won't you ever talk about them?"

"Leave it alone!" she snapped. The smell of burnt sausage filled the air. The toaster popped. On autopilot, she buttered two pieces of bread and tore into both with a savage bite. She dropped them on top of the eggs.

Was her inability to look in my eyes new? Did she never look *at* me? I could see myself at sixteen, silently begging her to catch me while I snuck boys into my room. *See me,* I could imagine myself saying. *Please see me.*

For a moment, I was stuck in a memory. Teenage Rachelle trying to talk to Mom while she fixed dinner. Screaming. Crying. Mom's stony, rigid face. I jerked out of it with a shudder.

Pockets of pain.

How could I say what I felt without giving her a heart attack? Would Mom panic? Would she scream? No, Mom didn't scream. She just retreated. Fell back into that shell where she saw nothing, not even me.

"I started therapy, Mom."

The sentence fell out of my mouth like gunfire. Fast. Heavy. A weighty staccato. Mom blinked. Her forehead creased into deep grooves that reminded me of garden furrows.

"Why?"

"Because I'm messed up. I need help. Sometimes I feel like I'm out of control and . . ."

She stared at her plate.

"Okay."

My heart tingled like a hot breath of fire. "I . . . I just wanted you to know. I didn't know if you'd care or . . ."

"I hope it works."

She grabbed her plate, turned, and moved toward the couch without a word. The fire built in my chest, dancing with long tongues of rage. I followed just behind her, hobbling with only one crutch.

"Don't you see?" I cried, tears thick in my voice. "I'm messed up! I need help. I've been crying out for help since I was a little girl, and you didn't do anything. Just like now. You're not saying anything!"

The words rolled out like thunder. She stopped only a few steps away, her wide robe swaying with every movement. Her nostrils flared. I held my breath. Would she *actually* say something? Would she be angry, or frustrated, or at least feel betrayed? Yelling would be far preferable to this toneless silence.

She started walking again with a clenched jaw. Then it all slipped away when she grabbed the remote and fell behind her glass mask like a light switch. On. Off.

Desperation surged through me. I stormed after her.

"Mom!"

"What?"

"Say something! Please. I beg you."

"Good luck."

"Don't you care? Don't you care that I hated myself my whole life? That I tried hard to be anyone *but* me? All the costumes. The outlandish attitude. The sheer amount of food?"

She barreled now, moving fast. "I'm not talking about this."

"But *I* want to."

"No!"

She sank into the couch and held the plate up to her chin, obscuring my view of her face. She jabbed angrily at the remote.

"*Mom!*"

"Stop it, Rachelle!" she barked. When she turned to me, terror filled her eyes. "There's no reason to visit the past. No reason to get into this. I won't do it."

"It makes the present better!"

"The present couldn't get any worse!"

Her voice had turned shrill. A piece of toast fell off the plate. She let out a riotous shriek, snatching it as it dropped. She turned back to the remote and flipped through channels at a frenetic speed. I strode across the room, reached for the plug, and yanked it from the wall. The TV faded to a gray screen, then black. A strange silence followed. When had I last heard nothing in this house?

Maybe never.

Her breathing grew heavier until it was almost a pant.

"I need your help," I whispered. "I can't move past this on my own. I can't learn to love myself if I don't have the truth. If I don't know what happened. Where I came from. Why you . . ."

Why you don't see me.

Her voice was gravelly when she said, "Plug it back in."

"Did you hear me? Can you just *see* me instead of the TV for once?"

"Plug. It. Back. In."

"Mom . . . please."

The seething, low rage in her voice frightened me. "Go away," she growled. "Leave me in what little peace I can find."

I paused, feeling my heart shrink, crinkling like wax paper.

When I didn't move, her face screwed up in wrinkled concentration. She set aside her plate and fork. With a grunt, she pushed up off the couch. The ratty fabric of her robe hung around her as she waddled toward me. Her bent body seemed to have taken the shape of the couch. I swallowed, tears in my eyes, as she ripped the cord from my hand and plugged the TV back in, nearly falling down in the attempt. A blast of noise filled the room.

Mom worked her way back to the couch, breathless.

Tears filled my eyes. I stepped back, Bitsy's voice whirling through my mind. *You're learning how to live as you. That's worth all the pain. Trust me, Rachelle. You're doing the right thing, no matter how much you question it.*

"There are reasons to go into the past," I whispered. "I'm tired of hating myself. I wish you were, too."

I retreated to my bedroom and slammed my door. Then I dropped to my bed, stuffed earplugs in my ears, and covered my head with a pillow until I couldn't hear anything but the sound of my own breathing.

Murky dreams and restless sleep consumed me that night.

I spun in and out of wild memories. Mom and I in the kitchen together, eating everything we could fit into our mouths. Then Dad stepped into the picture in a red cloud, his voice booming. Mom shrank away like a minion obeying her taskmaster. I woke up in the middle of the night, shaking.

By the time the sun crept into the sky, I was wide awake, staring at the textured shadows on my ceiling. The sound of breakfast dishes clanking roused me from a stupor. The red numbers on my clock glowed a bright 5:15. Maybe Mom had been up all night after our argument.

I wondered if the cupcakes were still there.

At work, I didn't speak. I popped earbuds in and surrendered myself to the task. Cupcake after cupcake came out of the oven, following by swirling piles of frosting. Glitter. Sprinkles. Extracts. All the measurements put me into a lane, and I ran.

And ran.

I ran away from the simmering rage. The pain. The betrayal. The dark cloak of abandonment that rested heavy on my back. Until I arrived at Janine's that evening, I acted like it wasn't there. Like my heart didn't thud heavily every single second.

Margery greeted me with a smile. "Good to see you again, Rachelle."

"Hey, Margery." I paused in front of the desk. "I still haven't been billed. Is it . . ."

"All taken care of still." Her grin widened. "Don't even worry about it."

My brow wrinkled. Of course I worried about it. But I couldn't question her further because Janine beckoned for me. I hobbled into her office, sank into her couch, and stared at her.

"I will never talk to her again," I whispered.

Janine's eyes widened. "Well," she said. "There's a story waiting to be told. What happened?"

Relieved, I related the whole conversation in full. Fury kept my emotions in check—not a single tear threatened to escape. By the time I finished, Janine blinked.

"Certainly intense," she murmured.

"You're telling me."

Janine spread her hands. "I'm going to give you a little tough love here, Rachelle. You're changing your life, and your mom isn't. Welcome to being an adult. It's not your responsibility what other people do or say."

"If she tells me nothing, then there will always be unanswered questions. That's not fair!"

"What if your mom died right now?"

"Um . . ."

"Your ability to have peace has nothing to do with external factors. Happiness doesn't come from food, connection with your mom, running marathons, or losing weight. It comes from within you."

My eyes stung like a thousand needles pierced them. I longed to pace. Instead, I balled my hands into fists. Janine tilted her head to the side.

"What do you control, Rachelle?"

"Me," I mumbled.

"You *could* forgive her."

"I couldn't."

"Right now you're in pain. Of course it feels like it's too much, but forgiveness is the path out of this."

I reared back. "Whoa! Are you kidding? Forgiveness is the *last* thing on my mind."

"The power of compassion and forgiveness to bring you peace cannot be understated."

"She shut *me* out, remember? She ignored me. She values television more than her daughter. Don't you think she should be *asking* for it?"

"You don't have to wait for her."

"She's never going to ask."

"You're likely right. But not extending forgiveness is like drinking poison and hoping your mother feels the effects."

"I never said I wanted poison," I muttered.

"Holding onto this anger is like that. We need to dig into the source of your pain and root it out."

I looked away, arms folded across my chest. "I don't know how."

"You feel."

"Feel?"

"Yes. Whatever negative emotions you have, you feel them. Give them space and air. Sit with them for a minute. Then let them go. That's all emotions want. Acknowledgment. Isn't that all you wanted?"

I let those thoughts brew for a moment. They seeped through my mind like hot tea. What lingered beneath the surface was terrifying. There was anger and pain and betrayal. Darkness. Agony. Confusion. Uncertainty. I struggled for the right words as they crept closer to the surface.

"Those don't feel good."

"No." She laughed a little. "They don't. Of course, you could tuck them away, allow them to fester and sabotage your life the way they have been. The fallacy is that you think you need exercise or food or control to deal with your emotions. You don't. All you need to do is acknowledge, feel, let go, and forgive."

"But my way is so much easier!"

"Is it?"

Her direct challenge caught me by surprise. When I backtracked and thought of all the self-hatred, the days that I'd wanted to be someone else, the times that I'd feared I couldn't deal with life, I realized I was wrong. In the end, it wasn't easier to rely on food. Or even exercise. Years of Mom seeing only the television stood behind me. The weight of that lifetime would surely crush my heart. Tears filled my eyes.

"I'm not ready," I whispered.

"What will help you be?"

"I don't know. But I'm not now."

I picked up my crutch, stood, and fled the office with tears streaming down my face.

"Rachelle? Hello? Are you with us still?"

I jerked out of my thoughts to find Bitsy snapping her fingers in front of my face. Mira stared at me, her brow ruffled.

"You okay, honey?" she asked.

"Fine." I cleared my throat. "Sorry, did I miss something?"

"It's your turn," Lexie said from the computer. "We just finished reviewing our week."

"Oh. Sorry. I spaced out and missed it."

"I'm going to a family reunion with Bradley's extended family tonight," Lexie said. "Supposedly it's a huge family tradition. My mother-in-law has been baking pies for the last week to prepare for it and is super stressed out. They're expecting three hundred people, and all of them can't wait to meet the new bride." She fake gagged. "Yikes."

Megan held up a hand. "No more moose attacks."

Mira said, "I have a sewing convention in the morning. Leaving around four so I can get there in time. Can't wait!"

"And I'm taking the girls to visit my father in Chicago tonight," Bitsy said. "We'll only be gone for four days."

I sucked in a sharp breath and shook my head, freeing the thoughts that clung to me like heavy tentacles. "Okay," I said. "Sorry to force the recap. My turn? Uh . . . it was a . . . week."

The words nearly choked me. Megan frowned. Lexie bit her bottom lip. Only Bitsy raised an eyebrow, more curious than worried. I kept going, unable to bear their silent questioning.

"Ah, the sales are going great at the Frosting Cottage. I've been working twelve-hour days the past four days. Orders are pouring in, so that feels good. Tomorrow is a big day. Five consultations for Sophia, which means I have to help her with cakes and still keep up with the store supply. William is doing a gig I promised I'd go see tomorrow night. That's pretty much it."

"What about—" Lexie started, but I cut her off.

"No."

She nodded once. "Okay."

I opened my mouth, then closed it. When I looked away, I could feel all their eyes on me.

"I'm done," I said. "Nothing more to report."

"Great." Bitsy clapped once. "Sounds like everyone is busy this weekend, so we'll keep this meeting short. Make sure to eat intuitively while you're out, all of you. I sent an email to everyone with a new recipe. Try it out this week. Tell me what you think of the brown rice noodles. Interesting twist."

Unable to bear it, I stood up and left the room with one crutch. Outside, the air had cooled into a merely sweltering evening, but even the stuffy air felt better than Bitsy's small house. I stood on her porch and closed my eyes, getting lost in the chorus of crickets. Not even a minute later, the back door opened with a groan.

"Rachelle, honey?" Mira asked softly.

"Yeah."

"You all right?"

She came up next to me, standing so we stared out at Bitsy's darkening backyard. I could still smell hints of flour and sugar on my clothes.

"Just . . . a bit lost."

"Your mom loves you, you know." Mira put a hand on my shoulder. "I think she's showing it the best way she can."

The words stung. Maybe Mom did love me. Maybe she only loved television and food. In the end, it didn't change the past. And whatever rendition of love she operated on? I wanted nothing to do with it.

"I don't know if I believe that."

"Why not?"

"Her best?" I spat. "Really? Sitting on the couch, eating food, forgetting I existed. She hasn't even asked about my ankle in weeks. She forgot my birthday last year. Or maybe she just didn't want to deal with the fact that I had just lost forty pounds. She didn't even go to my high school graduation."

Mira opened her mouth to speak, but stopped. I waited, silently daring her to defend her again.

"Yeah," she whispered. "It's been really hard."

Tears filled my eyes. "I can't do it, Mira. I can't forgive her. What's worse is that I don't want to. I don't think she deserves it. That sort of charity? That sort of compassion? I never got that from her. Never!"

Mira blinked, her face devoid of judgment, expression, or emotion. Tears filled my eyes.

"She doesn't deserve it," I whispered. "I can't live like this anymore.

I've already decided that I'm going to move out as soon as I can. William has already told me about a few friends that have apartments."

"That may be for the best."

"It's the only way, Mira. I can't face her anymore."

"Can I give you a hug?"

Mira held out her arms, her eyes sparkling. The tears welling in my eyes dropped down my cheeks. I fell into her embrace for several long minutes.

"You going to be okay?" she asked, pulling away to look right in my eyes.

"Yeah."

She put a hand on my back. "Whatever happens, just give it time? Time really does heal all wounds. And remember we love you. More than you could ever know is possible."

Hope

I woke up the next morning feeling as if I hadn't slept.

My eyes were like sandpaper, my legs heavy. Several minutes passed before I could collect my scattered thoughts and roll out of bed. As always, the television droned in the background when I made my way to the bathroom, using the wall as a support instead of my crutches. My first appointment with the physical therapist was next week, but Dr. Martinez had advanced me to partial weight bearing. The freedom, on occasion, made me giddy.

Still, I cursed those crutches.

By the time I splashed cold water on my face, brushed my teeth, and put my hair into a French braid, my mind seemed to have caught up with my body. I stared into the mirror, able to easily conjure up five nice things about myself. The momentum stopped there.

I am not defined by my roles, I thought. *But . . . I don't know what I am defined by.*

No matter how hard I tried, I couldn't bring up a forgiving thought about Mom. Neither of us had moved toward each other. Neither of us had made any attempt at reconciliation.

It felt too raw.

With a hiss, I stepped out of the bathroom, surprised to see Mom on the couch. She'd been in her bedroom every minute I'd been home, and I'd wondered if she listened for my return or just stayed locked up. But now she sat on the edge of the couch, a hand on her left shoulder. I paused. Was it the morning light, or did something seem . . . off?

I opened my mouth to ask, then stopped. No. Now I was just imagining things.

After sliding into a pair of jeans, a t-shirt, and my new ankle brace, I shoved my feet into flip flops and stepped back out of my room. Mom attempted to stand but fell back with a gasp. I paused.

"Mom?"

She put a hand to her chest.

"Rachelle."

I hopped toward her. Beads of sweat popped up along her pale face. She blinked as if dazed. Her breathing came fast and shallow.

"Mom? You don't sound too good."

"Chelle. Get . . ."

"Mom?" I crouched next to her. "What's going on?"

"Call . . . call 911."

"What's wrong?"

Her body seemed to give out from beneath her. She fell back against the couch with a cry. "Can't . . . can't breathe!"

All the blood drained from my face as I ripped my phone out of my pocket and dialed 911. In a shaky voice, I said, "Send an ambulance! I-I think my mom is having a heart attack."

Hours later, a female doctor in a crisp white coat and scrub pants stood next to the gurney as I slid inside Mom's room in the ICU. The nurse assistant who'd escorted me from the waiting room, where I'd been since Mom left the ER and went into surgery, slipped away. The doctor regarded me with warm eyes and extended a hand. I accepted, then glanced at the bed, where Mom lay in a lump.

"You must be Rachelle, Melissa's daughter?"

"Yes."

"I'm Dr. James, a bariatric specialist. I'm working with your mother's cardiologist, Dr. Wu, to get both of you through this the best we possibly can."

She had a firm handshake and bright green eyes. When she looked at the bed, hesitation flitted across her face.

"I'm sorry," I murmured. "It's been a long day. What's a bariatric doctor again?"

"I specialize in patients who are morbidly obese."

"Right. Thanks."

A weight doctor, I thought. *It's finally come to this.* How strange that a doctor who specialized in obesity should be so thin.

"It must not be looking good," I whispered, my voice shaky.

Dr. James frowned. "No. It's not. To be honest, we were lucky to get her here at all."

My gaze trailed over to the bed, even though I wanted nothing less than to see her there. Her pale face seemed anemic beneath the glaring lights. I hardly recognized her, she was so pale, lost in the white sheets and mess of tubes in the terrifying room. White, green, and blue lines oscillated in waves on a machine next to her bed. A nurse in pale blue scrubs bustled around her, adjusting monitors and IV machines and scrawling out numbers on a paper towel.

I recalled the flashing lights outside our house. The puzzled expressions of the paramedics as they attempted to get Mom onto the gurney but were unable to move her. The glazed, pained expression in Mom's pale face, as if she were slipping away moment by moment. Her breath had fogged up the mask they put over her mouth. Once we'd made it to the hospital, everything had moved so fast that I'd just stood back, waiting for someone to tell me what was happening. The whole thing felt frightening and foreign, like it was happening to someone else.

"Was it just her heart, then? I-I'm still not sure what happened."

"No," Dr. James said. "Things aren't looking very good for several systems in her body, but it was her heart that caused this. Her heart's weak for many reasons, mostly because of her weight."

I nodded. Her words seemed to flow in and out of my mind. My brow furrowed.

"Is . . . is she going to be all right?"

Dr. James hesitated, as if holding back an instinctual nod. She glanced at Mom in what seemed to be an instantaneous assessment. For several moments, neither of us spoke. The weight in my chest grew.

"It's very difficult to say right now," she murmured. "Your mother has suffered a massive heart attack. They put in a stent to open the blood flow back up, but we found that she needs far more intervention than that."

"Like what?"

"Open heart surgery. We need to replace four blood vessels currently feeding her heart with new ones. In other words, a quadruple bypass. Without it, she may not survive."

The words fell like bombs. *Quadruple bypass. Open heart surgery. May not survive.*

"Can she even survive the surgery?" I asked in a hoarse voice.

"That's one of the questions Dr. Wu is worried about and why I'm here. Our first problem is that our OR table doesn't support someone of her weight. Her lungs are another issue."

"What's the weight limit?"

"Five hundred pounds. WestEnd has been working on getting newer beds for a while now, but they're very expensive."

"She's more than five hundred pounds?"

Dr. James nodded. "We're trying to find a hospital we can transport her to that has newer operating tables and can accommodate someone of her size. For now, she's mostly stable while sedated, so we plan to keep her that way until her surgery. Hopefully by the morning. Unfortunately, we also found several lung issues related to her obesity that need to be dealt with right away."

"Lung issues?"

"Something called Pickwickian Syndrome."

"I-I've never heard of that."

Dr. James folded her arms in front of her. "She doesn't breathe deeply enough because of her weight, which alters the levels of oxygen and carbon dioxide in her blood. Over time, that can be detrimental to her heart. I believe it predisposed her to the heart attack. Now that she's here, I want to look into her liver as well."

"I see," I murmured.

Like a landslide, everything was falling apart. Tears welled in my eyes, but I blinked them back. Dr. James gestured to the machines that swooped down toward Mom's arm, where an IV had been taped.

"We'll monitor her closely. It would be misleading for me to say that your mother will simply recover from this. Perhaps she will. But it's more likely that some time will pass—not to mention a lot of rehabilitation—before she's back to a functional state."

If she survives the surgery, I thought.

The air in the room seemed to grow heavy in the long silence that followed. Dr. James put a calm, affectionate hand on my shoulder. "We're going to take good care of her, Rachelle. Please let me know if you have any questions. I'm going to go look at a few of her lab results and talk to Dr. Wu. I'm sure he'll be in to talk to you this evening."

"I'll let you know. Thanks, Dr. James."

All her words ran through my head like a ticker tape as her hand fell away. *Pickwickian Syndrome. Therapy. Rehabilitation. Functional state.*

"I'm going to step into the hallway and confer with the team in charge of caring for her. As soon as I have any information, I'll make sure you're told."

"Thank you. That would be very helpful."

The nurse was still moving around the room, making notations, studying screens. I wondered if she knew Megan. When slim Dr. James stepped into the hallway, I sank to a chair against the far wall, my knees weak. Part of me could hardly believe it was Mom who lay in that bed. The speed at which it had happened stunned me. At the same time, the inevitability of it made me wonder if I hadn't been waiting for this day all along. What other end would she meet after such a life?

Another gentle touch rested on my arm. The nurse crouched next to me. "You all right?" she asked.

"Yeah . . . I'm fine."

"My name is Dana. If you need anything, I'll be here until seven tonight."

I glanced at the clock. Just past noon. Dana reached over to Mom's bed and pulled a contraption off it.

"Just hit the call light and let me know if you need something. Don't worry, I'll be in and out a lot today. Right now, assuming we can get the bed across town, we're hoping for surgery around six in the morning. I'll keep you updated as more details come in, all right?"

I nodded, even though none of it really made sense.

Dana glanced around. "Is there someone we can call? Any family members you want here so you're not alone?"

Bitsy was gone to see her father. Lexie to the big family reunion—and at least ten hours away, at that. Mira had left for her sewing convention. I'd texted Sophia on the way to the hospital to let her know I wouldn't be in because Mom was being rushed over. The thought of calling Janine ran through my head, but I stuffed it away. Not only had I left without explanation last time, but she couldn't do anything and I didn't want to face my emotions right now. No one could do anything. Thanks to Mom's reclusive lifestyle, there was no one left in our life.

Just as I opened my mouth to say *no*, my phone rang. I glanced down.

Megan.

"Yeah," I whispered, tears filling my eyes. "I do have family. She's calling me right now."

Ten minutes later, I stood at Mom's bedside, repeating all the stats and numbers Megan had asked me for.

"What does the monitor on the left say?" she asked. "The one with the green line?"

"The heart rate?"

"Yeah."

"126."

"High. How about the blue one?"

"97."

"Good. You said Dana is your nurse?"

"Yeah."

"Excellent. She's one of my best friends and my old workout buddy. If you're comfortable with it, you can add me to your approved list and give me a four-digit code. Then I can call and get updates and ask all the right questions."

I closed my eyes with a relieved exhale. Just knowing I wouldn't be alone eased some of the ache in my chest. Megan had worked in this very unit. She knew these terms. These patients. These people. She'd be honest with me. She'd dumb things down for me.

She'd be by my side.

"That would be amazing. Thanks, Megan."

"Just let Dana know. I'll call her at the desk once you tell her."

"Of course. As soon as we hang up."

The confidence in her tone, although it meant nothing regarding

Mom's situation, calmed me. Megan had a way of taking charge. I needed that.

"Megan, how did you know I was here?"

"Mira texted me."

"What? How did she know?"

"She said Sophia called her."

"Oh." I drew in a deep breath, then shook my head at the strange stepladder of conversations. I thought about calling Lexie—if Megan knew then surely everyone knew—but held off. Likely she wouldn't be paying attention to her phone while swamped with Bradley's family, and I didn't want to distract her with worry. "Thanks for calling."

"Are you kidding?" Megan cried. "Of course I'm here for you. Look, Chelle. There are a few good things here. Dr. Wu is the best cardiologist in the hospital, and Dr. James is a very thorough physician who can make things happen. That's huge."

"Good."

She drew in a deep breath and let it back out, the sigh audible even over the phone. In the background, a male voice spoke quietly.

"But still . . ." she said. "This is going to be tough."

"Can you tell me she's going to be okay?"

My knuckles ached from how tight I clutched the phone. I moved it to the other ear and leaned back against the counter. Mom lay there, inert, her forehead wrinkled slightly as if in a perpetual grimace. Of course Megan couldn't tell me that. But still . . . something deep inside me wanted to hear it, a desire that warred with the bubbling rage that simmered beneath the fear.

"No," Megan said. "No promises. I'm sorry. Sounds like she's stable right now, from what you've told me, which is good. Her numbers are fairly strong, and Dana will take good care of her."

My shoulders slumped. "I know."

"If they can get her a table outside of WestEnd Hospital, Dr. Wu is the surgeon with the best chance of getting her through. If he can operate over there, which is another question I'll ask Dana."

"Okay."

"But I'm more worried about *you* than her."

I shoved a hand through my hair.

"I'm fine."

"You're not."

My nostrils flared, but I let the rush of anger go. She was right. "No," I whispered. "I'm not."

"You need to take care of yourself first. Have you had anything to eat?"

"I'm not hungry."

"Eat something small anyway. There's going to be a lot of people coming in and out. Protein bar, or something. You'll need to keep up your energy. Okay?"

"Yeah."

Her voice softened. "Seriously, Rachelle. How *are* you?"

"I yelled at her."

"What?"

"My mom. I yelled at her a couple of days ago and haven't spoken with her since. We got in a fight, and it was really ugly. Now she could die."

Megan sucked in a sharp breath. "Yikes. What was the fight about?"

Explaining the fight was different now because I felt no rage. Just hot, heady shame. Impossible to fight. Tenacious and sticky and relentlessly dark. Somewhere, in the midst of all this, came currents of fear and guilt and terror. The image of little Rachelle as she lost her dad slipped through my mind constantly.

"What do I do, Megan?" I whispered. Tears filled my eyes again. "There's nothing I can do to help her here. I'm so . . . helpless. She could die today or tonight or during the surgery or after the surgery. I'd never have a chance to apologize."

"You wait and hold onto hope. Don't give it up yet, okay? Miracles happen all the time. Just hold on. Your mom may not make it, but your family is still with you. If it gets ugly, I will fly out first thing in the morning. My mom can cover for me at Adventura. Bitsy, Lexie, and Mira will be at your side as soon as they can, I'm sure. Rachelle, whatever happens, we got you."

"I know," I whispered. "Thank you."

"You can get through this, Rachelle. You're steel, girl. Solid, steel girl power."

Compassion

Minutes ticked by, and nothing changed. No definitive news. The other OR was shuffling their schedule, trying to deal with their own onslaught of emergency surgeries. Things were moving behind the scenes. Meanwhile, Mom lay in a heap on the bed, breathing through a tube, oblivious to everyone fighting for her life.

The day passed.

Night fell. The hospital dimmed the hallway lights. Carts rattled past. Megan texted me whenever she had updates to make sure I understood what was going on. I attempted to get dinner but only picked at a grilled chicken Caesar salad before setting it aside. A new nurse rotated in—a broad-shouldered man named Darius with dreadlocks and a quick grin. I tried to remember his name but constantly forgot it and had to consult the whiteboard.

I lay on my back on a small couch at the far edge of the room, my ankles propped on the end. My phone glowed softly on the floor, plugged into the wall. I fidgeted, feeling the urge to text Lexie, but held back. Why interrupt her important weekend? There was nothing she could do here.

Still, I longed for her stable presence.

I continued to stare at the ceiling. My mind raced, overcome by a barrage of emotions, unable to contain or understand them. Instead, I let them slide by, viewing them as an outsider would a movie. Out of the corner of my eye, I caught a glimpse of Mom's lumpy form. I looked back at the ceiling, my nostrils flared.

The clock ticked.

More time passed.

9:12.

10:46.

11:34.

If I looked over, I knew what I'd see, because I'd seen it all day. Mom's limp hair, streaked with gray. Pale skin—the testament to her sheltered life that rarely, if ever, had sunlight. No fresh air. No real freedom. No interaction with people outside television characters. She lived in a bubble and never left. Never felt the wind on her face. Never stepped into a store and smelled fresh vegetables. Never ate at a restaurant and experienced new tastes on her tongue.

Tears filled my eyes. Was that really living? What had she truly loved? Could she finish out this life saying she'd really lived and loved and learned? No. Because . . . who had loved her? Maybe it all started in her mysterious past, with a father that hid food from her and a mother that . . . who knew what. *This,* I thought, *is why Mira and Bitsy were able to have compassion for her.*

Did Dad love her? Maybe, but it didn't sound like a functional love. Me? In a strange, disjointed kind of way. Even I enabled her, and the thought made me sick. I still lived at home. Cleaned. Shopped. Allowed her to wallow in her self-hatred without trying to help her.

Who had been Mom's Lexie? Her Bitsy? No one.

There were so many shadows in her murky world. So many unknowns. So much she hid from in a prison without bars. A tear trickled into my hairline. "Oh, Mom," I whispered. "There's so much more than this small, distracted world you've created for yourself."

Now it could be too late. For her.

Not for me.

Maybe that's what Janine meant by finding peace through forgiveness.

I rolled off the couch and pattered to her bedside in a scratchy pair of no-slip hospital socks Dana had given me before she left. Mom looked worse in the dim lights. Despite her size, she seemed small. Swallowed by something that wasn't actually her. Lost in a maze of fears. I placed one hand on the railing and stared down at her.

"Why?" I heard myself ask. "Why did you lock yourself away?"

There was no response. Something tingled deep in my chest.

"Why did you give up?" I whispered. "Why did you forget that I was there? You missed all my recitals. You never went to my sixth-grade choir concert. As soon as I liked something, you didn't, like a switch had turned off. If I didn't love food and television and hiding . . . it's like you didn't love *me*."

Surely Janine had it wrong. Pain this deep could never go away. A cry tore out of my throat. I bent over the hospital bed and let my sobs go, my shoulders shaking as I leaned over her bedside.

Memories flew by in a blur, as if little, aching Rachelle had taken over my mind. Standing on the dance stage and staring at an empty seat in the crowd—imagining that should have been my mom's spot. Scoring a home run with no parent to cheer for me. Playing dolls for hours by myself in my bedroom while Mom watched TV.

"I was alone!" I cried. "You let me be alone. When I needed you, you weren't there. You weren't! You were lost in television and food and whatever fears you allowed to control you. I needed you! And I can't just forget that. I can't just . . . I can't just forgive you for not being there. Because you could have been."

A shuffle from the hallway caught my attention. I clamped my lips together and lowered my voice to a whisper. The noise passed. I wiped the tears off my cheeks.

"And now you could die. I'll be an orphan with a legacy of pain and regret and issues that have never been dealt with. How dare you? How *dare* you!"

A long silence passed. Was this really the right thing to do? To feel my anger, to tell her of all my years of pain on her deathbed? Could she even hear? If she could hear, this could be the last thing I said to her. Was it any better than when we argued?

Could I really let the truth be the last thing I ever told her?

A light knock sounded on the door. "Sorry to interrupt," Darius said. "I have some news."

My head jerked up, and I found him standing in the doorway. I wiped self-consciously at my face.

"Oh, you're fine." I sniffled, turning away. "Do what you need to do."

He advanced into the room a few steps.

"I just received word from the OR at East View, and they're ready for your mom. Dr. Wu has surgical privileges over there, so he's going to meet you. They have a slot for her in three hours. If we get her into the ambulance now, we can transport her in time for the slot. I need to prep a few things first."

My heart nearly seized. I whirled back around.

"Now?"

"Now."

Darius nodded once and turned without another word, leaving me scrambling mentally. Now? Mom couldn't go now! I wasn't . . . I wasn't ready! This was the moment that would decide the rest of both our lives. *I might never see her again.*

"No!" I whispered. "Not yet."

Of course she'd get a slot *now*! Just when I'd found the courage to speak the truth. My anger broiled hot, gelling into a slow-burning rage that I knew could burn forever.

Could.

Beneath the bubbling magma lingered a familiar, frightened little girl. Little Rachelle stared at me with her wide eyes from the back porch. Weren't we the same? Wasn't I really her, only deeper in denial and twice as frightened? In the end, I was nothing more than a girl who wanted her mom. Which meant I still loved her.

Which meant I wanted more for her than this hell.

I clung to the side rail.

"Mom, please," I whispered. "Please make it through the surgery. Be strong. Just . . . come back. I know we can work this out. We can. If you just live through this, then you can actually *live*. Do you see?"

Mom's life scrolled through my mind again. A questionable childhood. A marriage that ended in abandonment. A rebellious, wild teenage daughter. Life behind a screen of fear. A path that led to dead ends in darkness.

There was no Lexie. No bakery. No accomplishments. No friends. No real love. No confidence. No happiness. The soul-sucking darkness of her self-inflicted bubble overwhelmed me. Mira had been right when she said that Mom was doing the best she could. Maybe she was. Maybe this was all she could do. Mom had never lived or really loved.

That was something to mourn.

Two nurses walked by, talking quietly. One of them stepped into Mom's room and began messing with the cords. I stepped back and texted Megan in a panic. More nurses swarmed the room.

She's going in now.

Megan replied almost immediately.

That's good, Rachelle. Sooner is better.

I'm scared.

That's okay. They're going to take really good care of her. I know all of them. They're the best at what they do. I've already talked to Darius tonight. She's in the best possible place for success.

The nurses were talking fast. Darius came over and said a few words to me. In my frantic haze, I caught only *surgery* and *transfer to East* and *good hands*. One of the orderlies flipped the brakes off the bed.

No, I thought. *No!*

"All right," a man in a blue suit and cap said. He twirled a finger in the air. "Let's get rolling."

My entire body froze. Mom was leaving. I might never see her alive again. Odds were against her survival. This was my chance to find peace. This was my chance to forgive. The bed lurched forward.

"Wait!" I cried.

They paused. I rushed to her side with a sob, reached down, and clasped Mom's inert hand in mine.

"It's all in the past now," I said. "I forgive everything. I'll be waiting when you get back."

There was no flood of warmth, no sudden burst of light in the clouds. Pain and confusion still roiled in the background, but I didn't feel the same fear. Instead, I comprehended the place of darkness where Mom lived. A vein of something—Janine would call it compassion—ran deep through my heart, fracturing my own bitterness.

Mom had raised me. Loved me, in her strange, distant, never-leave-the-house kind of way. The fact that I still lived and breathed meant she loved me enough to do *something* to keep me alive. She had fought for me once. And she stayed when Dad didn't.

That counted.

She might never have known life or friendship or allowed herself to have a true family, but I did. Despite her struggles, I could still be happy. Lexie and Bitsy and Mira and Megan loved me.

My happiness wasn't Mom's responsibility. She'd done the best she could. For me, that was enough.

"Bye," I whispered. "I love you."

They wheeled her out of the room in a rush, calling to each other, haphazardly coordinating IV poles and corners and transport machines. I watched them go, a strange feeling of terror and strength inside me all at the same time. *Steel core,* I thought. *Wicked smart. I can do this.* The room seemed too big and too small all at once.

In the aftermath of everyone leaving so fast, a familiar head of blonde hair filled the doorway. A sob tore out of my throat.

"Lexie!"

"Oh, Chelle," she murmured, tears welling in her eyes. "I came as soon as I got the text from Mira. I'm so sorry."

Her clothes were wrinkled, her eyes bleary, her hands jumping around like she'd consumed a ton of caffeine to stay awake. I choked up. She rushed into the room and wrapped me in her arms.

"I'm so sorry, Rachelle," she whispered. I clung to her, sobbing.

"Me too," I whispered. "Me too."

Lexie drove me to the other hospital, shoving yogurt drinks and granola bars my way. Once there, we shuffled into the ICU waiting room, checked in with someone at the main desk, and collapsed on a couch, pressed close to each others' sides. The night climbed toward morning while we talked quietly. She kept her arm firmly around me while we reminisced, sometimes laughing. Sometimes crying. She helped me see that there had been good times with Mom.

Those counted too.

I fell asleep on her shoulder around five, then woke up to her nudging me in the ribs around nine-thirty.

"Rachelle," Lexie said. "Wake up."

A female nurse stood in the room, wearing bright green scrubs and a tight hat over a head of red hair. Sunshine streamed through the windows, illuminating dust motes in the air. I pushed upright, half awake.

"Is everything all right?" I asked, rubbing my eyes.

The nurse nodded with a vague smile. "You're Rachelle Martin?"

"Yes."

"The OR just called. Your mother made it through the surgery. There have been a few complications, but she's recovering in post-op. The plan is to have her come to the ICU immediately after she stabilizes. You should be able to see her after they get her settled. Maybe two or three hours."

The words hit me like a gut punch. I grabbed Lexie's hand.

"She's alive?" I whispered.

The nurse smiled. "She's alive."

"Rachelle?"

I jerked out of my thoughts several days later. Two people stood in the doorway of Mom's ICU room with two beautiful bouquets of flowers in their arms. I straightened up.

"William? Sophia?"

William smiled. "Hey. Thought we'd come check and see how you were doing."

Sophia stepped toward me. "These are for your mom," she said, holding up a vase of pink roses and sprigs of baby's-breath. "I hope she gets to see them soon."

Once Sophia set the flowers aside, she reached for me, arms outstretched, and wrapped me in a warm hug. William set another vase of flowers and a box aside.

"We brought you some goodies." Sophia squeezed me tight. I fell into her warm embrace with relief and gratitude. "I thought a little sugar couldn't hurt at a time like this."

"Thanks so much."

Balloons already festooned the room thanks to Mira and Bitsy and Megan. Lexie hadn't budged from my side until this morning, when she'd left to go back to her in-laws'. Homemade food from Bitsy was tucked into an organized plastic box on the shelf, complete with utensils and a Nalgene of cold water. She brought me a new dinner every night—and promptly organized all the nurses' supplies and cleaned up the room with an antibacterial wipe. The TV droned in the background, muffling the *tick* of the machines. I reached out and turned it off.

"Fruit tarts," William said, tapping the top of the white box with a wink as Sophia pulled away. "Because I know they're secretly your favorite, too. And these flowers are for you."

I laughed and accepted a bouquet of white lilies, then hugged him. Despite his lithe figure, he had strong arms and held me in a tight hug for several long seconds. I breathed it in, relishing the sweet tinge of friendship in an otherwise dismal day. *I am loved. My happiness really isn't conditional on Mom's actions.*

Sophia glanced at Mom as I pulled away from William, wiping a discreet tear from my eye. Her brow furrowed.

"Mira has been keeping us updated," she said. "Sounds like it's been pretty scary for a while."

"Yeah. She had complications post-op that made things tense for a few days, but she's doing better now. Her chances of making it through were never great, anyway, so this is pretty miraculous. And Sophia, I'm so—"

"Don't you dare apologize!" Sophia held up a hand. "William has been filling in for you. Mira, too. He claimed you'd already started training him a few weeks ago. I turned down a few cakes, but it's been a great break. And we've had so many soda cupcake orders that they've more than made up for the cakes."

I laughed. "Good. I'm glad it's worked out okay. Thanks for being so understanding. Once Mom is awake and stable, I'll be fine to come back."

"We may not even need you again. Turns out I'm not too bad at piping frosting," William said with a smug grin.

Sophia laughed. "Don't listen to him! We desperately need you. You're in our small bakery family now. But the store is fine. Don't worry about us. We're more worried about your mom. Is there improvement?"

A flare of warmth bloomed in my chest.

"Yes." I folded my arms over my middle. "At least a little. They're hoping to take the breathing tube out tomorrow if she can maintain without it for an hour. No signs of infection, which is really good."

I braced myself, but there was no judgment in their eyes. No disgust when they saw Mom on the bed, covered with a light sheet, kept alive by beeps and whirs and machines. Her body filled the specialty bed, but they didn't seem to care.

"Can we do anything to help you?" William asked.

"This is wonderful."

"It just so happens that we know the ICU life very well," Sophia said with a wink and a nudge at William. "So don't be afraid to tell us if you need a night off or someone to scream at. We get it."

A sheepish expression filled his face, but I saw no shame in it. Perhaps William had continued to confront his own demons, the way I did. I smiled at both of them.

"Thanks."

"We'll head out," Sophia said. "We need to get the store opened. But text us both and keep us updated?"

"Of course."

"You'll need a break soon," William said, touching my shoulder with a gentle hand. "Depending on how things go, I'll pick you up for lunch tomorrow, all right? I'm serious. You need to get out of here."

"Sounds good to me," I said, almost *too* quickly. He just grinned.

With another round of farewells, they left. Just as I sank back into the chair, suffused with a giddy afterglow at the thought of going to lunch with my *friend*, my phone chimed. I glanced down at a text from a familiar number. My heart nearly stopped.

Chris.

> *Hey. Just heard about your mom from Bradley. Hope things are going okay.*

A long pause followed. I blinked, staring at the screen. So much of my angst around losing Chris came from the fear that I'd messed up my only chance at happiness. That I'd proven my true self in that drunk escapade.

But that girl wasn't Rachelle.

Just as I wasn't the girl with crutches. Or the cupcake designer or the best friend or the rebellious daughter. I was *all* of those things. I was a lump of insecurities and memories and strength and intelligence and a willingness to fight hard when the cards were down. I wasn't a single role. I was *many* roles. None of them, alone, defined me. I could be marathoner, daughter, cupcake-baker, and more.

I was Rachelle.

No role, no symbol, no person could change that. My identity didn't hinge on Chris, a marathon, or even a functional parent. It just hinged on me. For the first time, I could look back on that embarrassing night with Chris with gratitude that it had happened. Without it, I would never have come this far.

With a deep breath, I wrote back.

> *Thanks for the message and thinking of me. And thanks for being a good friend to me when I had that difficult time that one night. I needed that, and you were there. I'm grateful.*

I sent the text without caring whether he'd respond or what he'd say. Chris was a closed chapter in my life. One I could now move forward from.

No matter what he said, it simply didn't matter anymore.

The Right Thing

"Mom? Can you hear me?"

Mom's groggy, swollen eyes opened into mere slits, then closed again. Her breath was ragged and a little weak. They'd taken the breathing tube out of her mouth. Without it, she seemed less frail. I brushed a lock of hair out of her face. Her eyes fluttered open again halfheartedly.

"Hey," I said with a smile. "It's just me."

She blinked several times. Her eyes darted around the room. When she tried to speak, nothing came out. Her nurse, Jessica, stood on the other side of the bed. She held out a styrofoam cup with a straw and a little ice water.

"Here, Melissa," she said. "Take one small swallow. It'll help your throat, which will be sore from the tube."

Mom attempted it, then managed to whisper, "Where am I?"

"At the hospital," I said. "Do you remember the ambulance coming?"

She nodded.

"After we arrived in the ER and they put a stent in your heart, you went to the ICU, then transferred here for a quadruple bypass surgery. You've been sedated for several days while you recover."

Her eyes appeared sluggish, as if her thoughts were thick and slow. I doubted she'd remember the conversation with all the sedatives in her body, but it was good to see her responding to *something*.

"So . . . tired," she murmured, her eyes dragging open slowly. "Pain."

"I know, Mom. Go back to sleep. I'll be here all day. Jessica can get you some more pain meds, all right?"

With great effort, she looked at me again. Tears filled her eyes. "So sorry," she whispered. Her lower lip trembled. I shook my head.

"No, Mom. Don't apologize now. All is forgiven. Everything is fine. We've both made mistakes and both have a lot of change ahead of us. You're strong. You pulled through. Now we'll get you through the rest and move forward from there, okay? For now, you just heal."

She turned her head toward me and nodded a little. Her eyes fluttered closed, back into sleep, and her face relaxed. I let out a long breath and pressed my forehead to hers.

"We'll get through it together."

Janine wore a plum outfit the next time I saw her, with a pencil skirt that stopped just at the knees. When she crossed her ankles in her tan pumps, something in her put-togetherness comforted me, like there *was* something stable in this shifting reality we called life.

"I'm very proud of your effort with your mom." Janine gave me a warm smile. "That was a difficult situation you were in."

"Thanks."

"How do you feel now?"

"Lighter."

"Good."

"More available in my own head. For now, anyway."

"I feel I must warn you that forgiveness isn't always one and done. As you and your mom rebuild or start fresh, you'll both continue to make mistakes. And you'll have to work on forgiving those as well."

"I can do that."

She gave a satisfied nod. "Good. Welcome to adulthood, where no one is perfect and all of us need compassion."

I swallowed, thinking about the new landscape ahead. Living in the trailer without Mom for the past several weeks had been surreal and quiet. Even though Mom never said much, she had a far greater presence than I'd ever realized.

"You know what surprised me the most?" I asked. "Understanding things from her point of view."

"There's an expectation that parents must be perfect, but that certainly isn't truth. No one is infallible. To expect that would be to set everyone up for failure. Do you still plan on moving out?"

"Yeah. But not because I'm angry at her. Because it's the right thing to do. When it comes to my mom, I'm part of the problem. But . . . I'm scared to leave."

"Living with your mom has enabled her to be reclusive. If she has to get out for food, maybe that could change her own paths. Maybe not, but at least she has more opportunity."

I met Janine's eyes, understanding from her suddenly soft tone that she was trying to break something to me gently. I *had* enabled my mom's reclusiveness all these years. Shopping for her. Running the errands. Filling the car with gas. Even cleaning the house. It left a heavy, ugly feeling inside me, like a cloud about to burst. There was still so much more to do.

"I'm not done yet here, am I?" I asked.

Janine held out her hands a little, in an open gesture.

"You control your own path, Rachelle. But if I were to weigh in with my professional opinion, I would say, no. You aren't. We've made excellent progress, and I'm very happy about your work. But I believe there are areas we haven't explored yet that need a little more light."

Mulling that over brought me a modicum of relief. I could *feel* I wasn't done yet. Knowing I could come back to Janine every week to chip away at the glacial ice blocks still locked around my heart made me less afraid.

"Thanks," I said with a smile.

She sat a little straighter. "It's my pleasure, Rachelle. Truly."

The acute care rehabilitation center smelled like alcohol when I stepped inside.

Two nurses waved at me from behind a medication cart as I slid past them and down Hall C. Mom's room sat near a fake bouquet of flowers and a window. I slid inside, sandwich bag rustling in my left hand, a bottle of water in my right.

Mom sat in a wide chair in the middle of the room. Oxygen tubing still stretched across her face, but her hair appeared recently brushed and lay on her shoulders in damp strands. Her room felt crisp with air conditioning and a light floral scent, belying the sultry August heat outside.

"Hey, Mom." I closed the door with my hips. "Today going all right?"

"Hi."

I set the bag on a table and pulled two sandwiches out. She grabbed her remote and muted the TV. I set a six-inch sandwich in front of her, then grabbed mine.

"Turkey," I said. "No mayo. Whole wheat. Lots of veggies. Extra mustard in the packets. Your favorite water bottle here." I dug into my pockets and pulled out a few sugar-free flavoring packets. "And there was one black cherry left. I'll go grab some more later today."

The oxygen hissed as she pulled another breath in.

"Thanks."

Although pale, she seemed brighter than she had in years. The oxygen and CPAP machine had been helping her sleep at night. Thanks to the portion-controlled food—and the lack of constant snacking—she'd dropped twenty pounds since leaving the hospital three weeks before. Although her chest pained her and she acted terribly shy around most of the staff, I imagined being around people again had helped. Her anxiety attacks about not being home had decreased, though I still saw wildness in her eyes every now and then.

Mom unwrapped her sandwich. I sat down across from her. "I walked to the end of the hall today," she said.

"Nice. That's ten feet farther than yesterday." The wrap around my sandwich crinkled when I peeled it back. "Plan on going farther tomorrow?"

She nodded.

"How does it feel?"

She paused, lip jutted out in thought. "Painful on my knees, but . . . not so bad."

"Good."

For several minutes, we ate in cordial silence. Mom had been unusually quiet, staring out the window instead of at the TV—which still rang in the background. Sometimes I felt moments of total clarity about our relationship, and other times a sense of uncertainty. Could we really rebuild? Would things actually move forward, or would she disappear again into food and television as soon as she returned home?

I didn't know. Her choices were her own.

"Any news from Doctor Wu?" I asked, leaning back in the chair.

"Still no infection, which is good. Pain control is better. The swelling in my legs is going down. If things continue this way, I'll be home within weeks. Hopefully by the end of the month."

"Excellent."

She paused, the sandwich halfway to her mouth. Then she set it down and looked at me—or close enough, anyway. She never made eye contact.

"You're going to move out, aren't you?" she asked.

I sighed. "I've been thinking about it. I think it's time, once you're safe enough on your own."

Without me to clean the house and run all the errands, she'd be forced to maintain some semblance of life and activity. Sophia also owned the studio apartment above the Frosting Cottage. She was going to let me rent. A long silence swelled between us. She picked her sandwich back up.

"I understand."

"But I'm going to wait until I know you're back on your feet and in a good place."

She nodded once. "Thanks."

Her lack of protest was as good of an acceptance as I'd get. In some ways, I could almost consider it an apology. Mom had never balked at the idea of me moving away because it had never been brought up, as if we both lived under the assumption that I'd stay there forever. Maybe I would have.

"Mom?"

She turned my way. "Hmm?"

"I'm glad you're doing okay."

She paused, blinked, and managed a faltering smile. "Me too." Her eyes flickered to the clock hanging above her door. "How much longer?"

"Ten minutes."

"She's nice?"

"Annoyingly so."

She chewed on her bottom lip and played with a piece of lettuce that stuck out the side of the sandwich. I set mine aside, leaned forward, and covered her hand with mine.

"Mom? Janine's great. There's no reason to be afraid. It's really nice having someone to talk to judgment-free."

Mom hesitated, then nodded. She turned back to her sandwich to finish it off. I sank back into the chair with a little sigh.

No gauge existed of how Mom would truly react to anything when she moved back or I moved out or when Janine dove deeper into her issues. Mom's illness was more than just television and eating. It was retreat. Terror. Abandonment.

Even more questions floated around us about what would happen after the acute care center stay was done. How would we pay the medical bills? Would she be able to get herself to appointments? There were a lot of things to figure out.

But at least my happiness wasn't one of them.

"It's so . . . weird."

Bitsy and I stood in the kitchen, glancing over the house. Without Mom's potato chips rustling or TV blaring, everything seemed too quiet. Strangely silent in a way that strangled any sense of *home* out of the place.

"It's . . . tired," Bitsy said, running a finger over a stack of unread newspapers still in their plastic wrapping. Beneath it, a cardboard box filled with cans of corn pressed into the carpet. It had been there awhile, if I remembered right.

"I guess you're right. Now is a good time to start over."

She nodded. Now that Mom wasn't occupying the room, I gazed on everything with a more critical eye. Thick layers of dust on the mantle. Matted carpet. Crumbs on the couch, which showed wear on only two cushions. Bitsy squinted, peering at the window. Her nose twitched. "How long since this place has had a good scrubbing?"

"Well, before I broke my ankle. The chaos must be killing you."

"I'm feeling twitchy."

I glanced at the piles of junk mail Mom hadn't thrown away. Coupons littered the counter. A paper cup filled with old pencils teetered on the edge of the counter. The dusky air seemed to settle into my skin. My arms itched.

Bitsy shoved her sleeves higher on her arms. She nodded toward the windows. "Well," she said. "Let's get to work, then. Open those windows up. Let's move the TV into the garage so we can have the carpets cleaned. We're going to revolutionize this hovel."

For the next two hours, I obeyed Bitsy's commands like a soldier. She rooted around beneath the sink, extracting cleaning supplies, sponges, paper towels, and old vacuum filter bags. What she couldn't find, she provided from the back of her car, where she kept the cleaning supplies for her maid business. While I threw open windows and doors and vacuumed blinds, she sorted through the food in the pantry and fridge, throwing out anything expired—and a few of Mom's unhealthier stashes, like entire bags of jelly beans and licorice.

She fired up the vacuum and attacked the moldy candies hidden beneath the couch. Deep indents in the carpet proved that the furniture hadn't been moved in years. I pitched old kleenex and candy wrappers into the garbage. Bitsy dusted every surface. Then I washed countless dishes, and together we scrubbed all the kitchen cupboards. Putting a fresh face on everything made it seem as if I could rub out the past and start anew.

The trailer, though still shabby, smelled like pine instead of mildew. Hot, fresh air drifted through the room, washing the old, damp smell from every corner. I'd rearranged the front room, removed the TV, and put a picture of Mom and me on the mantle. One quick call and the carpets would be cleaned the next day. Mom would freak out when she came back, even though we hadn't touched her room.

But maybe she wouldn't. I never thought she'd talk to Janine either.

The chime of a text message caught my attention. I pulled my phone out of my back pocket.

Hey, you up for watching me do a gig tonight? William asked.

I grinned, then wrote back. *Definitely.*

> *Sweet. I'll pick you up at six. Let's do dinner before.*

"C'mon," Bitsy said, hauling the last of nine black garbage bags to the front door. "Let's take all this out to the garbage and go for a short walk. It's about time you start working that ankle again. Can't believe your physical therapist approved you for full weight bearing."

"It's wonderful, isn't it?"

"Your marathon would have been today."

"I know."

"How are you feeling about that?"

I grinned. "Marathons can come later. This feels better."

I wrapped an arm around her shoulder, even though both of us were covered with dirt and grime. Looking on the fresh rooms eased some of the discomfort I felt knowing I'd soon start packing to move out. At least I could leave Mom in a good space and let her decide if she would maintain it.

"It was you who paid my counseling bills, wasn't it?" I asked, struck by a sudden thought.

She cast me a sidelong glance. "I never said that."

"I figured it out."

"Not just me," she said. "All of the Health and Happiness Society pitched in. For Lexie and Megan, they felt like it was one of the only ways they could support you from far away. For me and Mira? We just love you."

I tightened my hold on her.

"Thanks."

She squeezed me close. "Anytime. The Health and Happiness Society sticks together. Dirty houses and all."

Acknowledgments

You'll Never Know was like birth.

Months in the making. Lots of thought, planning, ideas, and stalling.

LOTS of stalling.

Then it hit me all at once, and I knew I had to stop putting off my own demons and get Rachelle's story into the world. Within months, this book rushed into the world, ready to go. It's like she finally knew what she wanted to say. Or, perhaps, what I felt needed to be said.

For this book, I have to thank my excellent team of beta readers that had my back—and made this book as sculpted and beautiful as it is. Jennifer J, Kristen P, the *other* Kristen P, Darcee, Karli, Ta-rah—who is my Lexie—and Kelsey K.

My production team always amazes me, so thanks to Kella, Jenny, Catherine, and Carissa for your help and endless patience. I adore all of you.

Jennifer, Ginger, and Nancy—you'll never know what you've given me. Thanks for being my Janine.

LM and BG—you are my world.

Most of all, thanks to Husband, who saw in me (and my books) what I never saw in myself.

About the Author

Katie Cross grew up in the mountains of Idaho, where she still loves to play when she gets the chance.

If she's not writing, you can find her traveling, working as a nurse, trail running with her husband and two dogs, or curled up with a book and a cup of chai.

To learn more about Katie, visit katiecrosschicklit.com.

Bitsy Begins Again.

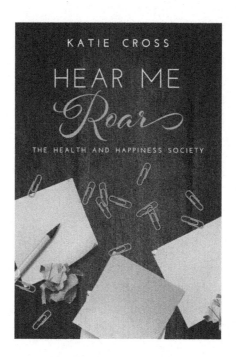

Made in the USA
Monee, IL
10 June 2020